In the faint light I saw Darci's eyes narrow with stubbornness.

"I'm not going without you. We don't even know how many people are in the house."

"I think two. We heard one come through the back porch, and one came in the kitchen window."

A loud crash from the living room below made us both jump.

I gave her a small shove towards the window. "We don't have time to argue. Get out that window and go for help."

With a sign of resignation, she hurried to the window and slowly slid it open. Flipping the strap of her purse over her head and across her chest, she threw a leg over the sill. With one last look, she disappeared into the night.

I was alone—alone in the house with two killers.

The Ophelia and Abby Mysteries
by Shirley Damsgaard

WITCH HUNT
THE TROUBLE WITH WITCHES
CHARMED TO DEATH
WITCH WAY TO MURDER

SHIRLEY
DAMSGAARD

WITCH HUNT

AN OPHELIA AND ABBY MYSTERY

AVON BOOKS
An Imprint of HarperCollinsPublishers

This is a work of fiction. Names, characters, places, and incidents are products of the author's imagination or are used fictitiously and are not to be construed as real. Any resemblance to actual events, locales, organizations, or persons, living or dead, is entirely coincidental.

AVON BOOKS
An Imprint of HarperCollins*Publishers*
10 East 53rd Street
New York, New York 10022-5299

Copyright © 2007 by Shirley Damsgaard
ISBN: 978–0–06–114711–1
ISBN–10: 0–06–114711–7
www.avonmystery.com

First Avon Books paperback printing: June 2007

Avon Trademark Reg. U.S. Pat. Off. and in Other Countries,
Marca Registrada, Hecho en U.S.A.
HarperCollins® is a trademark of HarperCollins Publishers.

Printed in the U.S.A.

10 9 8 7 6 5 4 3 2 1

To three strong women—my BFF's, Cheryl Powell, June Russell, and Cindy Vokes. You've laughed with me, cried with me, and been the voice of reason when I needed it. I couldn't have made it through the last five years without you.

It's your friendship that has inspired the one between Ophelia and Darci. (You've also inspired a few other things, too, but we won't go there!)

Acknowledgments

A novel isn't created in a vacuum. It takes a lot of help and inspiration from a lot of people to put Ophelia and Abby's adventures on the bookshelves, and I'd like to thank the following:

The staff at Avon—the copyeditors, proofreaders, sales reps, cover artists, my publicist, Danielle, and especially my wonderful editor, Sarah Durand. It truly is a joy working with you on this series! (And a special thanks, Sarah, for always answering my gazillion emails!)

Stacey Glick of Dystel and Goderich Literary Management. No matter what else is going on in your busy life, you've always been there to offer your support and guidance. You're terrific, Stacey!

My writing buddy and dear friend, Joanna Campbell Slan. You spotted the holes in the plot, caught the missed commas, brainstormed with me, and were my rock when the boogey man of self-doubt tormented me. I've learned from you, Joanna, and our friendship means more than I can say! And until I can think of something more creative, "thank you" will have to do.

Paul Steinbach of the Iowa State Medical Examiners Office, for continuing to feed me ideas on how to do my characters in. Honestly Paul, truth *is* stranger than fiction.

Doug Helvie, Rune master, for his insight into the runes and their meanings. Thanks for the tips on Ophelia's rune readings and allowing me to pick your brain long distance.

Doug's lovely wife, Anna, a guide with New Bern Haunted History Tour in New Bern, North Carolina. Thanks, Anna, for the suggestions on hauntings. I used all of them!

Mark Shepard for his years of experience in law enforcement, which helped with my inspiration for this book.

The booksellers who continue to promote Ophelia and Abby to their customers!

My family and friends. I know it's not always easy being around a writer—I tend to whine a bit—but I'm thankul you love me anyway.

And as always, the readers. It's your interest that keeps the series and me going. And one of these days, I promise, I will get that newsletter sent out!

WITCH HUNT

Prologue

Blood dripped from Darci's elbow, leaving bright red polka dots across the bathroom floor. A trail of crimson dots that would lead right to us.

I turned the flimsy lock on the bathroom door and then hobbled over to the chair sitting in the corner, next to the tub. Dragging it to the door, I shoved it beneath the doorknob. One good kick from the other side would no doubt bust the door open and send the chair airborne, but at least it might slow the intruders down long enough for us to escape out the bathroom window.

I looked down at the cast on my leg. Who was I kidding? I wasn't going anywhere. Noticing Darci's purse still hooked over her shoulder, I pointed at the bag.

"Your cell phone," I said in a hushed voice.

With a look of excitement, she tore it open and pulled out the phone. Her face fell. "The battery's dead."

"Can you climb out the window?"

She looked at the gash on her arm caused by a flying shard of glass hitting her when the mirror shattered. "Yeah, I think so. The bleeding's stopped," she whispered while dabbing the cut with a washcloth. "But you can't get out the window with your broken foot." Her voice rose in desperation. "I can't leave you here."

Limping over to where Darci stood, I gripped her other arm. "You have to," I said in a hushed tone. "Climb out the window, onto the porch roof. From there, it's an easy drop to the ground."

In the faint light I saw her eyes narrow with stubbornness.

"I'm not going without you. We don't even know how many people are in the house."

"I think two. We heard one come through the back porch, and one came in the kitchen window."

A loud crash from the living room below made us both jump.

I gave her a small shove toward the window. "We don't have time to argue. Get out that window and go for help."

With a sigh of resignation, she hurried to the window and slowly slid it open. Flipping the strap of her purse over her head and across her chest, she threw a leg over the sill. With one last look, she disappeared into the night.

I was alone—alone in the house with two killers.

One

The honeymoon was over. The sweet, quiet thirteen-year-old girl from last August had now, in May, morphed into a drama queen. In the evening, my phone rang constantly with calls from her friend, Nell, whom she'd spent the entire day with at school. One would think they'd talked over everything there, but evidently they still had important issues to discuss. Every weekend there was some event that required her attendance. And if she didn't go, she said she'd die. For a thirty-something librarian who had lived a peaceful life, becoming a foster mother was a change that had left me reeling. I was in over my head.

My beloved grandmother sat at her kitchen table and listened to my tale of woe with a small smile playing at the corner of her mouth. Her green eyes held a distinct twinkle.

"You think this is funny, don't you?" I said, leaning up against the counter in Abby's kitchen.

Her smile widened while she tucked a stray strand of silver hair back into the heavy braid coiled at the top of her head. In her seventies, her face bore the traces of the lovely young woman my grandfather had brought to Iowa all those years ago. And when she smiled, that young woman seemed to peek out.

"Yes, I do. I can recall similar conversations I had with your mother when you were a teenager," she said in a voice still rich with the tempo of the Appalachian Mountains where she'd spent her girlhood.

I frowned. "Wait a second. I never spent hours on the phone every night after school. And most of my weekends were at the library, not running around some mall."

"That's right." She nodded. "You did spend most weekends studying, but I do recall one weekend at Halloween—"

"Hey, that wasn't my idea. Linda had a crush on the dean's son. She wanted to get his attention."

Abby's laugh rang out. "Well, you succeeded. You not only got the son's attention, but the dean's and the campus police."

I lowered my eyes and traced the toe of my shoe across the wooden floor of Abby's rustic kitchen. The smell of wood smoke from her cook stove mingled with the scent of the dried herbs hanging from the open beams, as I remembered all too well the incident Abby was referring to. My girlfriend, Linda, thought she was madly in love with the dean's son, but he wouldn't give her the time of day, so one Halloween we decided to change all that and decorate every bush and tree in his yard with toilet paper. The pristine white streamers looked lovely waving in the moonlight, or at least we thought so until the campus police rolled up the driveway and busted us. Not a good situation to be in when both your parents are professors and the dean is your mother's boss.

I think I got grounded for a month over that little escapade.

Abby's voice jarred me out of my trip down memory lane. "And then there was the time you and Linda—"

"Okay, okay," I grumbled. "I get it. I put my mother through my share of drama, too."

She walked over to me and placed her hands on my shoulders. "It's going to be all right, Ophelia. Kids don't come with instruction manuals. All you can do is love them."

A frown puckered my forehead. "I do love Tink. She's had a tough life for someone so young. Losing her mother at such a young age, then being forced to live with her psycho aunt for all those years."

A shudder ran through me as I thought of Juliet Finch, Tink's aunt and former guardian. When we'd met the Finches last summer, Juliet had been trying to use Tink's talent as a medium for her own purposes. She tried to keep the kid drugged, and Tink's only ally had been a Native American shaman, Walks Quietly. Juliet's plan backfired and landed her in a state mental hospital in Minnesota. Her husband, Jason, had been more concerned about Juliet than Tink, and I knew we could give Tink the love and support she deserved. Jason willingly signed Tink's custody over to me, and we'd brought her back to Iowa.

Abby picked up on my thoughts—a side effect of having a psychic grandmother. Her hands tightened on my shoulders in a comforting squeeze. "Don't worry about Juliet."

A sigh slipped out and I stepped away from her hand. "But what if she wants Tink back someday?"

Abby crossed her arms over her worn flannel work shirt and gave me a hard stare. "Quit borrowing trouble," she said in a stern voice. "Jason Finch signed legal custody over to you—"

"Yeah," I interrupted, "but Jason adores his wife and will do whatever Juliet wants. If she's ever released and decides she wants Tink back, Jason would move heaven and earth to give her what she wants."

"Nonsense," she said, with a toss of her head. "The Finches can't give Tink a stable home."

"But Juliet is her only living relative," I argued.

She gave my shoulder a little shake. "You worry too much."

Chewing on my bottom lip, I shrugged. "I don't know, Abby, lately I can't shake the feeling something's up."

"Ophelia," she said, her voice full of exasperation, "stop it. We may be psychic, but it doesn't mean we 'see' everything. The future will unfold as it should. And whatever happens, we'll do our best to make sure Tink's best interests are protected."

"What about now? Am I doing what's in Tink's best interests?"

Abby gave me a questioning look. "What do you mean?"

"Am I giving her what she needs?"

"Do you mean her training?"

"Yes." I paced across the kitchen floor. "She's working in your greenhouse after school, and I know you've been coaching her. Is she gaining more control?"

"Hmm," Abby pursed her lips and stared off into space. Nodding once, she looked back at me. "Yes, she is. Tink is a thirteen-year-old girl, so there are all those hormones beginning to bounce around. And she wants desperately to fit in with her new friends." She paused. "But her focus and control is really amazing for someone so young."

I stopped and narrowed my eyes at Abby. "Are you sure?"

"Of course I'm sure." A quick smile darted across Abby's face. "After all, she hasn't *said* anything about seeing any ghosts."

I stopped my pacing. "Ghosts? Tink has been talking about ghosts?"

"No, she hasn't been talking about ghosts—I'm teasing you. But remember, Tink is a medium, dear. Lost souls will always be drawn to her."

"Like Great-Aunt Mary?" I didn't like where this conversation was leading.

Abby gave a small nod. "Yes."

"Peachy," I grumbled, remembering Abby's stories about growing up with a medium living in the same home. "And this focus and control she's learning is going to prevent those 'lost' from being drawn straight to my house?"

"Yes," Abby replied with confidence.

I scrubbed my face with my hands. Abby had always been more comfortable with our family's heritage of folk magick, healing, and various psychic talents. I'd struggled most of my life trying to accept mine. Would Tink grow into her talents? Or would she spend her life hiding her gifts from everyone, including herself?

The ringing of my cell phone broke the silence and startled me out of my thoughts. Crossing quickly to the kitchen table, I picked it up and answered.

"Can you come get me right now?" asked Tink in a quiet voice.

Caught off guard by the suddenness of her request, I stumbled over my words. "Yeah, ah, sure." I looked at my watch. Nine o'clock in the morning. Usually at a slumber party, the girls stayed up half the night and then slept away most of the morning. Why was Tink up so early?

But before I could ask, the line went dead. Puzzled, I flipped my phone shut and looked at Abby.

"Tink wants me to pick her up now."

"That's right. She spent the night at Nell's, didn't she?"

I dropped my phone in my purse. "Yeah. A slumber party. Big deal, too. The three M's were going to be there."

"The three M's?" Abby asked, her voice perplexed.

I nodded. "Mandy Simpson, Mindy Jones, and Melinda Polaski. They're in the 'in' crowd," I said, making quotation marks with my fingers. "I was surprised Nell invited them. She never seemed to care much about that kind of thing before, but . . ." I shrugged. "Who knows with teenagers, right?"

Abby gave me a gentle smile and stood. "Ophelia, quit worrying. You're doing fine as a mother."

Arching an eyebrow, I looked at her skeptically.

She laughed. "You are. Remember, all you can do is love them."

Ten minutes later I was turning the corner into the new development where Nell's family lived. Both sides of the street were lined with the same kind of modest ranch-style houses. The only house that had any distinction was Nell's. Her mother had a fondness for yard ornaments, and their lawn was littered with a bird bath, pink flamingos, a black and white hen with bright yellow chicks in a row behind, and various other animals whose likenesses had been forever preserved in hard plastic or concrete.

Before I even stopped the car, Tink came scurrying out the front door, with her sleeping bag and pillow tucked under one arm and her backpack slung over one thin shoulder. After shoving her stuff in the backseat, she slid in next to me. The bill of the baseball cap covering her pale blond hair was pulled low on her forehead, shading her violet eyes.

"You're late," she said, slumping down in the seat.

I gave her a sideways glance while I backed the car slowly out of the driveway. "Good morning to you, too."

She sunk a little lower in the seat. "'Morning," she replied without turning her head.

"Did you have a good time?"

Tink hunched her shoulders. "It was okay."

Her attitude surprised me. She and Nell had spent hours on the phone planning this slumber party, and Tink had been so excited about it. And the three M's attendance was considered quite a coup.

The three M's—Mindy, Mandy, and Melinda—the undisputed leaders of Tink and Nell's class. I'd learned all about them courtesy of my assistant, Darci. When Tink had come home with me to Summerset, Darci took Tink under her wing and played the role of unofficial aunt. She'd decided it was necessary to find out all she could about every kid in Tink's class. Darci had a great source—her friend Georgia, the biggest gossip in town. Georgia knew everything. I swear, she could scent out a story or a rumor like a bloodhound. And what she didn't find out on her own, she managed to worm out of her boyfriend, Alan, a deputy with the sheriff's office.

But even without Darci's help I would have figured out the dynamics after one look at the three M's. They were all blond, all petite, and all terminally perky. They went around looking like someone had taken a cookie cutter and cut them out of the same piece of dough. They dressed alike and talked alike, but Mandy and Mindy didn't make a move without Melinda. I'd had girls like that in my life, too, when I was a kid. They could either make your junior high days easy or a living hell.

Had Tink felt a few flames at the slumber party?

"Did you do anything crazy?" I asked, keeping my eyes on the road ahead and my tone nonchalant. "Put anyone's underwear in the freezer? Torment the first person who fell asleep?"

Tink gave a heavy sigh. "That stuff's stupid."

"Okay, then what did you do?"

"The usual."

I tried again to get her talking. "Things have obviously changed since I was thirteen, so what's usual these days?"

Tink shifted in her seat and turned her head toward the window. "Look, I'm tired and I don't want to talk right now."

The rest of the short drive home was silent. How do you force a reluctant thirteen-year-old to talk? The answer—you don't. I would just have to wait until Tink was ready to open up.

My Victorian cottage sat on the edge of town. Its fading yellow siding with white shutters was a welcome sight after the stone-silent ride from Nell's. Maybe once Tink was home she'd open up and tell me what happened at the party.

I'd barely stopped the car when she jumped out, grabbed her stuff out of the back, and hurried up the front walk. By the time I caught up with her, her sleeping bag and backpack lay carelessly tossed by the front door. Tink knelt on the floor with her arms wrapped tightly around my dog, Lady's, neck. Her face was buried in Lady's thick white fur.

Lady cocked her head, and two eyes, one brown, one blue, shot a look at me that seemed to say, *What do I do now?*

"Got me," I muttered to myself.

I walked over and reached out tentatively toward Tink. "Sweetie, don't you want to tell me what happened?" I asked gently.

Violet eyes, shimmering with tears, stared up at me. "No." She popped up like a jack-in-the box, wheeled away, and fled up the stairs before I could utter a word.

Lady scrambled after her.

Moments later I heard the door to her bedroom slam shut.

I stood in the hallway and looked around while my brain scrambled for a way to help Tink.

This motherhood gig was harder than it looked, I thought. And "just love them" wasn't going to solve this problem.

Two

"Something happened with Tink this weekend." I stood behind the counter at the library, pulling the library cards out of the file. My assistant, Darci, lounged two feet away.

Blue eyes, big blond hair, and a very curvy figure were the first things one noticed about her. In the past she'd always played up those attributes, but lately things had changed. The bloodred fingernails were now painted a subdued pink, the hair was less "big," and her clothes didn't seem to hug her curves as they once had.

Darci tapped one of those pink nails thoughtfully on her chin. "Did she have a tiff with Nell?"

"No, I don't think so. I know Nell called several times yesterday. Her number was on the caller ID."

"What about with one of the other girls?"

I shook my head in dismay. "I don't know. I tried several times to get her to talk about the party, but she kept shutting me out." A sigh escaped. "I don't think even Chinese water torture would've made her spill what happened at the party."

Darci giggled. "Teenagers can be stubborn. I don't—"

The rest of her words were muffled by a roar coming from

outside the building. We ran to the window and pulled up the ancient blinds to peer out.

Limestone buildings, erected at the turn of the century, lined the streets of our quiet Iowa town. Three motorcycles rumbled past them, on the way to the four-way stop. Chrome wheels gleamed in the bright May sun, and the black bodies of the bikes were polished to a mirror image. Their riders rode with an easy grace, their arms spread wide as they gripped the shining handlebars. Each wore a jacket with a coiled snake on the back and the words, EL SERPIENTE: The Snake. Wrapped around their heads were bandannas, with each biker wearing one of different color. Dark sunglasses wrapped around their faces, hiding their eyes. They looked tough and they looked mean. Modern day cowboys completely out of place against the backdrop of the old buildings.

I glanced at Darci and saw her lips tighten into a frown.

"This is not good," she said emphatically.

I turned away from the window and walked back to the counter. "It's just a bunch of bikers," I said over my shoulder, "trying to look big and bad."

She followed. "Haven't you noticed there's more and more of them hanging around town?"

"No."

"Honestly, Ophelia, you need to pay more attention to what's happening around here." Darci leaned against the counter.

Yeah, right. Like I didn't have enough on my plate right now? I had a teenage medium on my hands who seemed to be having some kind of crisis that I didn't know how to handle. A full-time job. And to top it off, there was the other little matter of trying to deal with my own psychic talent. More than enough to occupy my time, I'd say.

Darci continued. "Haven't you read Ned's latest editorial?"

"No, I haven't had time to read *The Courier* yet. Why?"

"He made some pretty strong comments about their presence in town."

"That sounds like Ned—"

Darci cut me off. "But he hasn't said anything about what they're doing."

"I suppose you know all about what's going on." I gave her a skeptical look.

"I've heard stories," she said, not meeting my eyes.

I snorted. "From your friend Georgia, no doubt." Turning away, I crossed to the shelves and picked up a stack of returned books. Setting them on the counter, I began slipping the cards back into the pockets.

Darci made no reply and still stood leaning against the counter with a faraway look on her face.

I knew I should let the topic drop, but now Darci had piqued my curiosity. "Okay, I'll bite. What have you heard?"

"What?" Her gaze focused back on me.

"I said, 'What have you heard?'"

"Umm . . . well," she said, and stood straight. "You know that old roadhouse on the edge of town?"

"Of course, it's only a mile from my house. Some guy from over in Polk County bought it and has made it into a bar and restaurant. What's he calling it?" I snapped my fingers. "Oh, yeah, 'The Viper's Nest.' I'm not too crazy about having a place called 'The Viper' so close to my house, but it seems harmless. I've seen a lot of semis pulled in there."

"It's not all that harmless. These bikers are using it as kind of a clubhouse after regular business hours." She shook her head. "There are rumors that what they've been doing at The Viper isn't exactly legal."

"Oh yeah, like what?" I picked up a stack of books.

"Like their women are providing comfort to the lonely truckers after business hours," she said with raised eyebrows.

"I don't understand," I replied, puzzled.

Darci rolled her eyes at my ignorance. "Prostitution," she hissed.

The stack of books slipped from my hands and tumbled to the counter. "What? Why hasn't anyone arrested them?"

She lifted a shoulder. "There's no proof; only rumors."

Fisting my hands on my hips, I stared at her. "You're telling me that a house of ill repute is operating not a mile from my home?"

"I said you need to pay more attention." She picked up the books I'd dropped and left the counter to return them to the shelves.

I darted around the counter and caught up with her. "Who did you hear this rumor from?"

A deep blush started at Darci's neckline and crept up to her face, staining her cheeks a bright red. "Danny kind of—"

Right—Danny, the new police officer in town. Dark hair, dark eyes, and dimples. Mr. Wonderful. And Darci's new boyfriend.

I broke in. "Danny said there's prostitution going on at The Viper?"

"Well, not exactly," she said, shoving a book onto the shelf. "Georgia told me that rumor. But Danny said not to go out there. That someone might get the wrong idea. I assumed he meant with the way I look and all, I might be mistaken for 'one of the girls.'"

"That's ridiculous," I huffed. "No one could mistake you for a biker babe. Or a hooker."

"I don't know," she said in an uncertain tone. "I did dress a little over the top. Danny made me realize that."

"Did he say that?"

"No. Danny's really good to me. He'd never criticize me, he—"

"He'd better not," I interrupted, drawing myself up to all of my five-foot-four height.

A quick smile flitted across Darci's face. "You don't have to rush out and defend me, Ophelia." The smile faded as she lifted her chin. "But he's commented on other women, how they dress, how they wear their makeup, so I thought I'd tone it down a bit."

That explained the recent change in Darci's appearance. *Who does this guy think he is?* ricocheted through my brain. The words almost popped out of my mouth before I had time to stop them. Darci obviously cared a great deal for Danny, and snide remarks from me could damage our friendship. I tried to frame what I wanted to say carefully in my mind, but before I could speak, Darci broke into my thoughts.

"I know what you're thinking," she said with a small laugh. "You're feelings are written all over your face, Ophelia."

"It's—"

She didn't let me finish. "I know," she said. "Why do I care about what Danny thinks? It shouldn't matter to him how I dress, right?"

I gave a quick nod. "Yeah."

"It doesn't, but I was ready for a change. All my life most people have never seen past the way I looked. I'm tired of being written off as an airhead, so I thought maybe if I changed the way I dress, the way I wear my hair and makeup, I'd get more respect."

"Darci, how long have you felt this way?"

"Oh, I don't know." She paused. "Always, I guess. I understand how Tink must be feeling right now. Me and my family were always outsiders in this town, too. Dad worked at the plant in Des Moines and Mom stayed home with all us kids. We never had much growing up." Darci stared off into space, shaking her head. "My brothers and sisters couldn't wait to get out of Summerset as soon as they graduated from high school."

"But you stayed to help your mom."

"Yeah, I was the only one left at home when Dad got sick, and Mom needed me."

"He's been gone several years, hasn't he?"

I saw tears gather in the corner of Darci's eyes. "Ten," she said softly.

"Was that when she moved in with your sister?"

She swiped a hand across both cheeks and nodded. "Yeah. She helps out with my nieces and nephews while my sister works. She's happy—she loves taking care of the grandkids, and the arrangement saves my sister a lot of money in day care."

"I've never asked you this, Darci, but why didn't you leave, too?"

"And do what?" she scoffed.

"I don't know." I hesitated. "Go to school; get an education."

"School was hard for me. I didn't know it back then, but I have a mild form of dyslexia, and—"

I jumped in. "You're kidding?"

She cocked her head at me. "No, I'm not."

"Why didn't you ever mention it?"

"It's just part of who I am, so I really don't even think about it much anymore. When I was in school, no one ever thought about testing me. They just thought I was stupid. I didn't figure out what the problem was until after I'd graduated." She grinned as her eyes traveled over the stacks of novels. "I guess that's why I love books, love working in the library, so much now. For all those years, books were my enemies, but once I learned how to deal with the dyslexia and reading became easier, books opened up a whole new world to me."

"Wow, Darci, I've worked with you all this time and never knew about this," I said in a shocked voice.

She laid a hand on my arm. "It's okay, Ophelia, not very many people know I ever had a problem. I don't talk about it much."

"Yeah, but still . . ." My voice trailed off as I tried to absorb what Darci had told me.

"It's okay, really," she said with a hint of amusement in her voice. "I know I'm not dumb, but sometimes it bugs me that other people don't realize it. It would be nice to have the same kind of respect that your family has."

"My family?"

"Well, Abby . . ." She pursed her lips and her forehead crinkled. "You kind of spook people out; it's the way you seem to trip over dead bodies and all." Her face brightened. "But look what happened last spring when Abby was hurt— half the people in town turned out to welcome her home."

Darci was right. Abby had always been careful about hiding her peculiar talents, but there was this aura of peace around her that drew people to her. Nothing shook her, and as her granddaughter, I'd learned a long time ago, ninety-nine percent of the time Abby was right. It could be annoying.

"Yeah, but Darci, Abby's had over seventy years to work on earning people's respect, and—"

I was interrupted by Edna Walters charging in through the handicapped entrance. Her walker thumped across the floor as she hurried toward us, making the book bag hanging from the handle swing wildly. The polyester pants she wore seemed to whistle with her rapid movements.

"Did you girls hear about it?" she asked in an excited voice, her false teeth clacking.

"Hear about what?"

"They found Percy Gordon in his garage this morning. The car doors were locked and the motor was running. He was dead." She fixed a suspicious look on me. "I'm surprised you weren't there, Ophelia."

"Hey," I replied in a defensive voice. "I've been here all morning."

First Darci, and now Edna, I thought. Darci mentioning it was okay—she understood—but I didn't appreciate Edna's veiled reference to my recent habit of finding dead people. After all, I'd only stumbled across two bodies—not so very many.

Three, said a little voice in my head, correcting me. But the murder last summer happened in Minnesota, so Edna didn't know about that one. It was still only *two* here in Summerset.

"A suicide?" Darci asked.

Edna's head bobbed up and down in agreement, making her double chin quiver.

"Do they know why? Did he leave a note?" I asked.

"No. Only thing I heard was that he's been calling in sick a lot at the bank." Edna gripped her walker and leaned forward. "And that he'd had a run-in with one of those bikers at the convenience store last week."

My eyes met Darci's from across the counter. And the feeling that I'd told Abby about on Saturday? The feeling that something was up? It glided up my spine, leaving in its wake a sense of foreboding.

Three

All afternoon I fought the feeling that had wrapped around me like a shadow after learning about the suicide. *Was it really a suicide?* Percy Gordon had been one of the most unassuming men I'd ever met. A confrontation with bikers would have made the poor man wet himself. Middle aged, with a growing bald spot that he desperately tried to cover with his remaining hair, Percy waited on customers at the bank quickly and quietly. What was there about his life that made him despondent enough to kill himself? The thought nibbled at the corner of my mind.

I was so focused on it that I missed Darci's speculative looks until it was too late. She cornered me in my basement office late that afternoon while I was trying to type a report for the library board.

"Ophelia," she said, strolling in the door and plopping down in a chair. "I've been thinking about what Edna said. You know you *are* a psychic—"

I shot out of my chair. "Nope. No way," I said, holding up my hand. "Not going to do it."

Darci leaned forward. "Do what?" she asked sweetly.

I narrowed my eyes and glared at her. "Don't pull that

innocent crap on me. I know how your mind works, Darci West. You were going to propose I use my talents to figure out what really happened to Percy."

"Ah ha," she exclaimed, thrusting a finger in the air. "You've been thinking the same thing I have. It might not be a suicide; it might be murder."

"That's not our concern," I replied emphatically.

"Oh, come on—aren't you curious?"

"No," I said, sitting back down in my chair and turning my attention to the keyboard.

Darci sat back in her chair, too, and crossed her long legs. "I don't believe you."

"Well, I'm not," I said, typing furiously.

thw expenktures orf Une, July, akd Aughret appeared on the computer screen.

My eyes skimmed over the gibberish I'd typed. "Dang." I pounded the backspace key and looked at Darci.

Raising an eyebrow, she crossed her arms over her chest and said nothing.

"Okay, okay." I sighed deeply. "Maybe I am a *little* curious, but it doesn't mean I'm going to blunder into a murder investigation. If it *is* a murder investigation." I gave her a tight smile. "Remember? The last time I did, Bill and Henry Comacho almost arrested me."

"Since Bill's the county sheriff, and Percy's death was within the city limits, he won't be involved. Brett and Danny will be investigating. And Henry? He's in Iraq, isn't he?"

"Yeah." My tone was curt.

My friendship with Henry had gone full circle. We had started out as enemies when, as primary investigator on my friend Brian's murder several years ago, he suspected me of lying. Last spring a killer had stalked the town of Summerset, and Henry was assigned to the case as an officer with the Iowa Department of Crime Investigation. I'd earned his grudging respect, but in the end Henry's skepticism wouldn't allow him to accept who and what I was. The last I'd heard, he'd traveled to the Mideast to work with Iraqis setting up their security forces.

I looked back at the computer screen. "We're not the Sleuth Sisters, and we're not getting involved." I gave Darci a determined stare. "That's my final word. I've got enough going on right now."

A disappointed look crossed her face, and I could feel her mind searching for a different approach. Suddenly, inspiration hit me with a way to distract Darci from the suicide.

"What about you? Isn't your cousin coming this weekend for your birthday party?"

Darci perked up. "She is." She nodded quickly. "She's getting in from California Thursday night and staying for a whole week." Her face broke into a broad smile. "I haven't seen Becca in three years. This is going to be great. We were always close, until she moved to California four years ago." Darci's smile dropped. "I've missed her."

I sat back in my chair. "I'm glad you're going to be able to spend time with her."

"Yeah, thanks for the time off, by the way."

"My pleasure. Claire is more than happy to fill in."

Claire Canyon was the president of our library board and a real go-getter. Her causes were many and her enthusiasm great. Only problem was, she'd probably have the entire library rearranged by the time Darci returned from her week off. Hmm, maybe I could talk Claire into organizing the automation program for the library. The pesky little program that would allow us to scan all the books as people checked them out lay neglected on my desk. Every single book's bar code had to be entered into the computer. It was a gargantuan task I'd been working on for the last six months.

I smiled with satisfaction. Yes indeed, it was a terrific job for Claire.

I looked at the clock. *Jeez, after five already.*

"Time to go, Darci. I bet Brenda's already locked up. I need to pick up Tink from Abby's." I closed down the file I'd been working on. The report would have to wait until tomorrow.

Grabbing my backpack, I followed Darci past the children's books and up the stairs to the main floor of the library. Sure enough, the lights were off and the doors locked. We made our way through the dim light to the front door. I unlocked it with my keys, stepped through, and held it open for Darci. But before I could turn and relock the door, Darci gripped my arm.

"Look," she said, pointing.

Down the block, a police car sat with its lights flashing. Two men stood in front of the car—one dressed in police blues and the other in a black leather jacket. A motorcycle was parked directly in front of the police cruiser. Even at this distance, I could see the coiled snake on the back of the man's jacket every time the flashing light hit it. And the police officer? His hand rested protectively on the gun he wore at his side.

Next to me I heard Darci gasp when the light hit the officer's face.

"Danny."

She made a move down the stairs but I grabbed her arm. "It's just a traffic stop, Darci. Let Danny do his job."

She shook my hand off. "If these bikers are as dangerous as Danny says, he could be in trouble." Darci took a step.

"Wait. There's not going to be a shootout on Main Street,

but if you go charging over there, you might complicate things."

Darci stopped. We watched while Danny removed a notebook and pen from his pocket. He quickly wrote something down, ripped off the paper, and handed it to the biker. The biker glanced at the paper, then shoved it in the back pocket of his jeans. Without a word, he turned on his heel and walked to his bike. A moment later he zoomed into the gathering twilight.

Darci sighed in relief and ran down the steps toward Danny. Paying no mind to any oncoming cars, she hurried across the street to the patrol car and to her boyfriend.

When she reached him, I saw Danny raise his hand and pat her face as one would a child.

A simple gesture, really. But for some reason it sent the alarms inside my head clanging.

I paused at the door of Abby's greenhouse. The smell of damp earth hung in the humid air. And there were long trays of new plants ready for sale everywhere. Marigolds, petunias, lavender, and salvia lined the tables, their colors reminding me of a rainbow.

In the corner, Abby sat on a workbench. Sitting at her feet was Tink, her face lifted toward Abby while she listened to my grandmother with a look of total concentration. A long ponytail drifted over Tink's skinny shoulders, and the strap of the overalls she wore had slipped down her arm. From my place by the door, I saw a swipe of dirt across one pale cheek.

A smile twitched at the corner of Abby's mouth as she looked down at Tink. Her silver braid wound around her head like a crown, and her green eyes sparkled with memories. I couldn't hear the words, but I knew Abby was sharing stories of her life in the mountains of Appalachia.

Tales of magick, of misty hollows, of soft mountain peaks covered in wildflowers, of the old ways followed by the women in my family for over a hundred years. Once, I had been the young girl sitting at Abby's feet, listening to the stories, but I'd tried to ignore them. In my foolishness and arrogance, I hadn't allowed Abby to train me as she wanted. How much easier my life would have been if I'd paid attention. I hoped that Tink wouldn't make the same mistake, though judging from her rapt attention, it didn't seem so.

They turned and looked at me simultaneously. Even though sixty years separated them, there was something identical about them. Maybe it was the energy that seemed to dance in the air around them. Maybe it was the considerable talent they both possessed. I don't know, but even though they shared no blood, they looked like they belonged together.

And me? Did I belong? I resembled my dad's side of the family far more than my mom's and Abby's. Brown hair, brown eyes, average height, average weight. Nothing remarkable about me at all. My mom, whom our family's heritage had passed by, had always complained about feeling left out whenever Abby and I were together. Now I understood what she meant.

"Hey guys, how's it going?" I said, walking toward them.

Tink's face broke into a big smile. "Abby was telling me stories about her mother and her aunts. She said maybe someday we could visit where she grew up."

I gave Tink's ponytail a playful tug. "Yeah, maybe we can." My eyes traveled to Abby. "Two aunts are still living, aren't they?"

"Um-hum," Abby replied with a grin. "My aunts Dot and Mary still live in the cabin where I grew up."

Ah yes, the much mentioned Aunt Mary, the one who

talked to spooks and did astral traveling. I'd met her once when I was a kid. Tall and thin, with an air of complete authority, she'd scared the pants off me.

As if reading my mind, Abby laughed. She stood to throw an arm around my shoulder. "Mary's in her late nineties now. She's mellowed quite a bit."

I looked at her skeptically.

She laughed again. "She has! Her letters aren't nearly as bossy as they once were. It would make an interesting trip, I think. Maybe we can go this summer."

Tink rose with the grace only the young possess. "Really?"

Abby placed her other hand on Tink's shoulder. "We'll see." She released us and picked up her gardening tools. Wiping them off with the corner of her old flannel shirt, she set them carefully in her toolbox and walked toward the door.

Tink skipped after her, still excited about the possibility of a trip to the mountains.

I followed a few steps behind, watching Tink. After the silent girl I'd lived with for the last two days, it was good to see her happy again. How long would it last?

An hour later Tink and I were home. The pets had been cared for and supper was on the table. Grilled cheese sandwiches and tomato soup—one of Tink's favorite meals. I wondered if maybe now would be a good time to bring up the slumber party. Or would talking about it ruin Tink's good mood? Before I reached a solution, out of the blue Tink asked a question.

"You think Ouija boards are bad, right?" she said, cocking her head.

Caught completely off guard, I stumbled over my words. "Uh, well, yeah." Laying down my spoon, I looked across the table at her. "Why?"

Tink suddenly found her soup fascinating and didn't meet my eyes. "Just wondering."

I slid my bowl away and crossed my arms on the table. "Tink, have you been playing with a Ouija board?"

She swirled her soup with her spoon. "No."

"Then why are you wondering about Ouija boards?"

She put down her spoon and sat back in her chair with a long sigh. "Okay, here's the deal. Melinda brought one to the slumber party—"

"Great," I interrupted. "Both Abby and I have told you how dangerous they are," I started lecturing. "Especially for people like us. They open doorways, and unless you have a lot of control, you don't know who, or *what,* might come through." I paused to take a breath. "With your talent, Tink, what if you'd summoned up some psychic nasty? Do you think you have the ability to deal with something like that?"

"Hey, I didn't mess with it," she replied defensively.

Somewhat mollified, I pulled a hand through my hair. "Look, I'm sorry. I didn't mean to rant at you. It's just that they're not a toy, and it frightens me to think what you, of all people, might unleash by fooling around with one."

"I could handle it," she mumbled, staring at a spot over the top of my head. "You use runes to foretell things."

Now I was on the defensive. "But they're not the same as a Ouija board. They have power, sure, but I don't use them to call forth spirits like a Ouija board does."

"You could, though, right?"

Stalling for time to work this one through, I picked up my bowl and carried it over to the sink. How did I explain the runes? Yes, they had power. I felt their energy hum every time I handled them. The strange series of twenty-four glyphs made sense to me instinctively. They seemed to speak to me, bringing clarity to my psychic intuition. According to my great-grandmother's journal, I *could* use them to create spells, but I never had. Summoning spirits? Great-Grandma didn't mention that in her journal. And I had no intention of experimenting to see if I could.

My best bet was to be honest. I turned and watched Tink carefully. "I don't know. I've never thought of using them that way. I respect what they can do too much."

"I don't get what the difference is," she said with a stubborn look on her face. "Why are runes okay but not Ouija boards?"

All right, she wasn't going to let this one go. Now was the time to pull out the old saying every mother had used since the beginning of time.

"Because I said so."

Four

I lay in bed thinking. My thoughts bombarded me in rapid succession. Suicide or murder? Why were bikers suddenly in Summerset? Was The Viper's Nest a front for prostitution? And what really happened at Nell's slumber party?

When I finally did sleep, I dreamt of Tink being chased across an empty field by Melinda, Mandy, and Mindy. As they ran after her, they hurled planchettes—the small triangle pieces that move around the Ouija board—at her. Trails of flames marked the path they ran.

In the dream, a circle of large stones resembling Stonehenge, sat in a clearing directly ahead of Tink. A rune towering several feet high was carved on each stone. Each rune pulsated with a purple light that seemed to glow from the very heart of the stone.

I knew that symbol—Algiz—the yew; a symbol of protection and sanctuary.

The faster Tink ran, the faster the shimmering light flashed, a beacon lighting her way to safety.

The dream never ended, but haunted me all night. When I woke in the early morning light, my first instinct was to go to Tink. I stumbled out of bed and made my way to her room. Softly, I opened the door and peered in.

She lay sprawled on her bed with one arm flung across the toy cat she had said reminded her of Queenie. She looked so defenseless, so young. I knew then that I'd do whatever it took to protect this child from harm, from hurt. The strength of my feelings for her swamped me.

She stirred then, and before I could tiptoe out of her room, her eyes opened and she saw me.

"Hey, I didn't mean to wake you," I said quietly.

She rubbed a hand over her eyes and stretched. "That's okay."

I walked to her bed, sat down and smoothed the fine hair away from her forehead.

The violet eyes watching me were serious. "I didn't play with the Ouija board. Honest," she said in a small voice.

I met her gaze. "I believe you, Tink."

She lowered her eyes and plucked at the blanket covering her. "Melinda, Mandy, and Mindy gave me a hard time 'cause I refused. Said I was a chicken."

"Did you try telling them I'd forbidden you to use one?" I asked.

"They wouldn't have cared. And if I'd said that, they would've just made fun of you, too." A snort slipped out. "I could've told them you were a psychic witch and that you know what a Ouija board can *really* do." She looked at me and smiled. "But I didn't think I'd better."

I returned her smile. "No, that wouldn't have been wise."

She hunched her shoulders. "I made it sound like I thought a Ouija board was just a stupid kid's game. Nell sided with me, so we left the room and watched a movie downstairs instead."

"Nell's a good friend, isn't she?" I asked while silently thanking the girl for helping Tink.

"Yeah, she told them to knock it off when they started in calling me a chicken the next morning, too. But they wouldn't stop, so I called you."

"I'm sorry those girls were mean to you, sweetie, but does it really matter so much what they think?"

Tink scooted up in bed. "Sort of. They've spread the story around school, and now they've got other kids calling me chicken, too." She plucked at the blanket again. "Someone even taped a picture of one on my locker yesterday."

My temper flashed. *How dare they gang up on her like that!*

"I suppose they're also giving Nell a hard time?" I tried to keep the anger out of my voice.

Tink flipped her hair over one shoulder. "Of course not. Nell's dad is one of Mr. Polaski's biggest customers. He sends all the trucks he uses in his roofing business to Polaski's Garage. Melinda wouldn't want Nell's dad to get mad and take away his business."

"But you're fair game?" I asked through clenched teeth.

"I guess."

Taking a deep breath, I hesitated, then picked up one of Tink's hands. "Sweetie, I'm so sorry. Maybe if I talked to the school—"

"No." She jerked her hand away and leaned forward. "Don't go to the school. You'll just make it worse. I can tough it out." Her voice was earnest. "Sooner or later the three M's will find someone else to pick on."

"But that's not right, Tink. These girls shouldn't be allowed to ride the other kids, either."

She leaned back on her pillows. "I know, but that's the way it is." She stared at me intently. "Promise me, Ophelia, you won't come to school and make a big deal out of this?"

I hated the idea of letting those little tyrants get away with making her life miserable, but what could I do? Tink was determined I stay away from the school.

"Okay, I promise," I said reluctantly.

She threw her arms around me and gave me a hug. "Thanks."

I patted her back. "I just want you to be happy, Tink."

"I am," she said, settling back in her bed and giving me a cheeky grin. "Most of the time."

"It's getting late. Breakfast is in ten minutes, so you'd better scoot," I said in my sternest voice, but my smile belied my tone.

On the way downstairs to make my coffee and Tink's breakfast, I thought about the situation with the three M's, and my temper soared again. Tink had had enough problems in her young life, and with her talent, Lord only knew what challenges she'd face in the future. She deserved a decent childhood; it was up to me to see that she got it.

I paused at the bottom of the stairs. I'd promised Tink not to talk to the school, but I hadn't said anything about Melinda's parents. Melinda obviously thought enough of her father that she didn't want to cost him any business by teasing Nell. Maybe he could rein in his daughter.

Instead of going home for lunch, I left the library and headed for Polaski's Garage, located at the opposite edge of town. Pete Polaski had bought the old building for his business four years ago when he and his family had moved to Summerset.

Though I didn't know them well, they seemed to be nice people. I tried to remember what Mrs. Polaski looked like, but the only image the came to mind was of her standing on the sidelines at a junior high softball game wearing shorts that a woman her size shouldn't. Cellulite had made her thighs as lumpy as cottage cheese, and the denim shorts had been stretched to the max across her rear end. But she was involved in the PTA and was always volunteering to act as a chaperone for school activities. They both attended all the programs, concerts, and sporting events starring their daughter, and their pride in her was obvious.

I needed to handle my conversation with Pete delicately, so as not to offend him. Right, Jensen, and you do that so well, I scoffed. Maybe I should have asked Abby to come with me. She was an expert at diplomacy. I shrugged. Too late now.

I left my car and entered the garage. The smell of rubber, grease, and gasoline tickled my nose. The far wall held a Nascar calendar amidst tools hanging on hooks in neat rows. Stepping over a shiny black spot on the concrete floor, I crossed to the man working on a car.

Pete Polaski stood at the side of the old vehicle with out-of-state plates. The hood was popped, and he leaned forward looking at the engine. One muscular arm rested on the edge of the car and the other held a light high.

"Mr. Polaski?" I said walking up to him. "Hi, I'm Ophelia Jensen."

He turned, putting down the light and looking at me in surprise. Instead of taking my outstretched hand, he quickly rolled down the sleeves of his faded blue work shirt, his fingers making greasy marks on the material.

He may have turned his sleeves down swiftly, but not before I noticed the scars puckering the skin of both arms. Not wanting to make him uncomfortable, I quickly looked away and dropped my hand.

"Sorry," he said with a bob of his head, and showed me a grimy hand. "Hazard of the job. Pleased to meet you. You're the librarian, aren't you?"

"Ah yes, I am," I said with a nod of my own. "I'm also Tink Harrison's foster mother. Tink is just a nickname. Her real name is Titania. Maybe Melinda's mentioned her? They're in the same class." I realized I was rambling, so I clasped my lips tightly together to stop.

He pushed at his thick glasses, leaving a black smudge on his nose. "No, no, I don't think I've heard that name from Melinda." He gestured toward a room at the back of the building. "Let's talk in my office. It's cleaner."

I followed him and took a seat in front of the battered desk. The wall behind his chair was lined with pictures of his wife and Melinda. Mrs. Polaski had put on weight over the years. In each picture she seemed to grow a little heavier and a little more somber.

Not only was Mrs. Polaski's weight gain documented on the wall of pictures, but so was Melinda's passage through the stages of babyhood to adolescence. I noticed her posed in birthday hats, in front of the yearly Christmas tree, fishing with her dad, wearing various sport uniforms. The kid's entire life had to be on that wall.

Pete's hazel eyes shone with delight as he caught my attention, and he smiled. "She's my pride and joy," he said. "She was sickly as a baby, and we thought we were going to lose her several times."

Peachy—I was about to tell this poor man that his precious child was making mine's life miserable. There wasn't enough tact in the world to handle this situation gracefully. I thought about excusing myself and letting the matter drop, but I then I remembered Tink's tears.

"Ah, Mr. Polaski—"

"Please call me Pete," he interrupted.

"Ah, Pete." I smiled nervously. "Did Melinda say anything about the slumber party last weekend at Nell's?"

"No." He gave me a quizzical look.

"Umm, ah, the girls had a Ouija board—"

"Not Melinda," he said, not letting me finish. "One of the other girls must have brought it. She knows how I feel about all the paranormal occult stuff." His hands, lying on top of the desk, clenched and his hazel eyes seemed to bug from behind his thick glasses. "Work of the devil, pure and simple. And those psychics, nothing but a bunch of charlatans in Satan's grasp. I watched my grandmother lose her life savings to one of those quacks," he finished emphatically.

I looked down quickly to hide my shocked expression. I wondered what he would have thought if he knew he was talking to one of those "charlatans" now. But the only devils I'd seen walk on two legs and didn't have horns or a tail. They looked like anyone else in town. And I should know—one of them tried to kill me.

I kept my thoughts to myself, and when I looked up I found Pete staring at me with a puzzled expression on his face.

"I'm sure you're right. It must have been one of the other girls who brought it to the party." *Let him find Melinda's little toy on his own.* "But you see, Mr. Polaski . . . er, Pete . . ." I smiled gratuitously. "When Tink refused to participate, the others accused her of being a chicken, and now it's gotten around school and is causing her problems."

Pete gave me a look that said, "So? What am I supposed to do about it, lady?"

Oh man, how did I get myself out of this one without telling him exactly what I thought of his daughter? It occurred to me I should've brought Abby with me. She would have known how to handle this doting father.

I had one chance to save face—feed his ego.

Leaning forward, I gave him a conspiratorial look. "These kids are always following the leader." I winked and tried not to choke on my next words. "I know how well respected your daughter is by the rest of the class, and if you could encourage her to get them to lay off Tink, I'd sure appreciate it."

Pete nodded. "Sure, no problem. I'll ask Melinda to use her influence to persuade the girls to be nice."

I stood. "Thanks. You know how it is—it's tough fitting in."

Pete looked perplexed and shook his head. "No, I don't," he said, standing and following me out the door. "Melinda's never had problems at school. She's always made friends so easily."

Trying not to gag, I smiled tightly. "I'm sure Melinda is very special." At the entrance to the garage, I turned and gave Pete my hand. "Thanks again for your help."

He shook it briefly, bobbing his head as he did. "Melinda has a kind heart. I'm sure she'll do everything she can to help your daughter."

I had a sense of futility as I walked to my car. Melinda was the golden child in her father's eyes, and I doubted if anything I said had penetrated Pete's veil of delusion. The girl would continue to dictate to everyone in that class until someone stood up to her.

The familiar growl of motorcycles cruising by broke into my thoughts as I got into my car. Watching in the rearview mirror, I saw three riders slow their bikes to a crawl while they drove past Pete's Garage. They all turned and looked toward the building.

Kind of odd, but so what? Maybe they were just look-ing for a place that worked on motorcycles? Driving into the street, I glanced in my rearview mirror again.

The bikers had turned around and were headed straight toward Pete's. Without signaling, they pulled into the parking lot and came to a stop.

I watched as all three riders got off their bikes and leisurely walked into the building.

Five

"You promised me you'd stay out of it!" Tink's eyes were flashing fire.

And the flames were directed at me.

She'd barged through the front door, threw her backpack on the floor, and now stood glaring. Her arms hugged her narrow body, as if to stop it from shaking.

I'd never seen her so upset. "What are you talking about?" I asked, crossing over to where she stood. I laid a hand on her shoulder, but she jerked away.

"Melinda! You promised you'd stay out of it! Then you went and talked to her dad." Her voice rang with accusations.

"Yes, I did. I promised I won't go to the school, and I thought Mr. Polaski might convince Melinda and the others to lay off. I had to do something."

"Well, it didn't work. Mr. Polaski found the Ouija board. Now Melinda's grounded for a month." Tink's eyes flooded with tears. "You made it worse. They're saying I'm a chicken *and* a rat."

"Tink, I'm sorry. I wanted them to leave you alone." I tried to lay my hand on her shoulder again, but she stepped away from me.

"We had to watch a film in biology class today, and a rat came on the screen." Tink's mouth twisted into a bitter line. "Melinda says 'Oh, look, there's Tink.' And the whole class laughed." Tears ran down her cheeks. "I wanted to die."

"Oh, Tink." I took a step forward, but she edged toward the stairs. I stepped back. "What did the teacher do?"

Tink hugged herself tighter. "Oh, he told her that wasn't nice and to stay after class, but I know nothing happened. She'd just act all sorry and stuff and worm her way out of it. They won't do anything to *her*."

"I'm so sorry that little bi—er, girl is making fun of you. I was only trying to help," I repeated.

Tink threw her arms down. "Next time, don't!" She spun around and ran up the stairs.

Oh, brother, had I made a mess of things. I should've just stayed out of it and let Tink handle it on her own. But how was I to know? I was new at this whole motherhood thing.

I dragged my feet into the kitchen, picked up the phone and called Abby.

"So you see, I made the whole thing worse," I said after explaining what had happened.

"Don't worry, dear," came her soothing voice on the other end of the line. "It'll all blow over."

Holding the cordless phone tight to my ear with my shoulder, I shoved clean pans back into the cupboard. "Maybe, but I really stirred things up by talking to Pete Polaski."

On the other end, Abby paused. "It's an unfortunate situation, but Tink will survive. She's a strong girl." Another pause. "Maybe a spell of protection would help," she said thoughtfully.

I made a derisive noise. "You wouldn't consider doing a little hex instead, would you? Nothing major, just make all of Melinda's hair fall out or something?"

"Ophelia," she said in a shocked voice. "However tempting that may be, it's unethical. Tink will have to deal with her tormentors in a normal way."

"Right, Mr. Polaski wouldn't appreciate us siccing the devil on his precious daughter."

"The devil? What in the world are you talking about? Devils don't have anything to do with our magick."

"I know, but tell that to Pete Polaski."

"Did you tell him about us?" she asked in a troubled voice.

"Of course not. But when I told him about the Ouija board, he freaked. He launched into a tirade about psychics and all things paranormal being in league with the devil."

"Nonsense. He doesn't know what he's talking about."

Her tone was short, and I could imagine the look on her face. Abby hated narrow, judgmental attitudes, especially when they were a result of ignorance.

"You're right, but I think there are a lot of things Pete Polaski doesn't understand. One being what kind of a person his daughter's becoming."

"Well, that's his problem. Our concern is Tink."

"I agree," I said, walking over to the window and staring out at the trees ringing my backyard. "Got any suggestions? Darci's party is tonight at Stumpy's, and right now I think I should stay home with Tink."

"She's angry, dear; she's not going to talk to you tonight. Why don't you call Nell's parents and ask if Nell can spend the night?" she advised calmly.

"You don't think they'd mind the girls staying alone while I go to the party?"

"No, if they trust Nell enough to allow her to babysit young children, I'm sure they won't mind her spending a few hours unsupervised at your house. Explain that you'll be checking in on them. The girls will be fine alone for a while."

"Okay, if you're sure," I said, hesitating.

"I am. It will give Tink a chance to vent to Nell about what a mean person you are and how you don't understand."

"What? I'm not mean," I grumbled.

Abby laughed. "I know that, but right now Tink thinks you are because she's angry. She'll complain to Nell, Nell will commiserate with her about how parents just don't get it, and by morning all will be well."

"You're sure?" I said, skeptical. "All will be well?"

"Yes."

Little did I know this time Abby would be wrong.

The party was in full swing by the time I arrived at Stumpy's Bar and Billiards, owned by Abby's octogenarian boyfriend, Stumpy, or Arthur, as she preferred to call him.

Nell's parents had agreed to her spending the night, so I'd picked her up and dropped her by my house. Before leaving the girls, I gave them every phone number I could think of— Abby's cell phone, Darci's cell phone, plus the main number for Stumpy's—just in case my phone failed to ring. I'd left explicit instructions: Don't make prank calls; keep the door locked and don't open it; don't invite anyone else over; don't stay up past midnight. The list went on and on, but I still felt a little ill at ease about leaving the girls alone while I attended Darci's party. Abby had said all would be well, and I told myself to trust her judgment.

Tink seemed glad to see Nell. By now I was sure they were both ensconced in Tink's room, talking about what a meanie I was.

I paused at the door of Stumpy's and let the noise surround me. The place was packed. Near the windows, the

booths were full of customers enjoying a late night supper. Patrons waited three deep at the bar, and from where I
stood, I saw Abby helping Stumpy and two bartenders serve
drinks. Behind her, Stumpy's collection of mounted antlers
hung around the old, smoky mirror. Half full bottles containing liquor sparkled on the shelves. Over the din of so many
voices, I heard the strains of the country group Confederate
Railroad. Their song "Trashy Women" played on the juke-
box.

The faces of regulars, people who spent every night telling the bartender their tale of woe, mixed with those who
came for Darci's birthday. Danny was there, his arm resting
protectively on Darci's shoulders as she sat at a table talking to someone whose face I couldn't see. Helium balloons,
drifting on currents of smoke-filled air, decorated Darci's table. And to her left I spied a big birthday cake covered with
candles.

In the back, around the pool table, I saw three guys and
a shapely blonde. I noticed they were the only ones back
there. Strange. Usually, a crowd gathered around the table to
watch the game. I glanced at the chairs near the pool table.
Carefully draped across the chair was a black leather jacket,
and even from the door I could see the coiled snake on the
jacket's back.

Bikers. Why were they hanging out at Stumpy's instead
of The Viper's Nest? I took a step and craned my neck for a
better look.

Two men watched their companion take a shot. His
shaggy hair brushed the collar of his T-shirt as he aimed
his cue stick. His biceps bunched when he drew back the
cue, making the tattoo on his arm jump. With a smooth,
easy motion he sent the ball careening into the others. A
look of satisfaction crossed his face as a red ball rolled

across the green felt and into one of the pockets. He straightened. Taller than his companions, his black T-shirt strained across a well-developed chest. An air of danger hung around him.

One of his buddies stepped forward to offer him a high five. This guy was about as wide as he was tall. His stomach hung over his belt in front, making the buckle invisible. The ponderous roll of fat jiggled when he moved away from the table, giving his buddy room for the next shot.

The last of the three bikers was built as well as the one shooting pool, but he was much shorter. A crop of dark red hair covered his head, and a pack of cigarettes were rolled up in the sleeve of his T-shirt. One dangled precariously from his lips, making the smoke drift into his face. His arm was wrapped tightly around the blonde draped at his side.

The blonde wore a tube top—totally unsuitable for Iowa at this time of year—and a skirt that showed a goodly stretch of long leg.

My gosh, I hope she isn't playing pool, too, I thought. If she bends over the table, she'll moon everyone in the place.

Sandals with three inch heels added to her height, and she stood at least two inches taller than her friend. Teased and curled hair floated around her head like a cloud. She was stunning, in an obvious sort of way. I hadn't expected a biker babe to be so attractive.

I pushed past the crowd to the bar and ordered a beer from Abby. When she placed the frosty mug in front of me, I jerked my head toward the back. "What are they doing here?"

Her green eye flicked toward the bikers and her mouth turned down. "I don't know. Arthur said they've been coming in a lot. They're not disruptive, keep to themselves shooting pool, so . . ." Her voice trailed off.

I glanced over my shoulder at the bikers and noticed the

tall one crossing the room to the bar. Our eyes locked for an instant before I quickly looked back at Abby. "Arthur can't kick them out?" I asked.

"No," she said with a shake of her head. "I—"

Before she could finish, someone at the end of the bar ordered a beer. She gave my hand a quick squeeze and moved away.

I'd lifted my mug to take a drink when my elbow was nudged, sloshing the beer on me. "Hey," I said, turning to see who'd jostled me.

It was the tall biker. Our eyes met for a second. Gray eyes as cold as sleet sized me up. The danger I'd sensed earlier was closing in. I felt like running, but it was a point of honor to hold my ground. I wouldn't let this guy intimidate me.

He turned away and called out to Stumpy, "Hey, pops, how about a beer?"

Surveying my spilled beer in disgust, I grabbed a napkin and wiped the side of my mug.

"What's got you in a twist, lady?" the biker asked sarcastically.

I turned narrowed eyes on him, trying to give this jerk my most scathing look. *He didn't need to know I was shaking in my boots, right?*

"I beg your pardon?" I asked in a chilly voice.

A smirk crossed his face, but before he could answer, Mr. Roly-Poly shoved in beside us. "Hey, Cobra, get me one, too," he said to his pal, eyeing the beer Arthur set on bar.

"Sure thing, Rattles." He jerked his head toward his buddy. "Pop, we need another beer."

Rattles? Cobra? Oh, I got it. The gang was called El Serpiente—The Snake—so all their nicknames were snake re-

lated. And they hung out at a place called The Viper's Nest.
How cute, I thought with scorn. The feeling faded, replaced
by a coldness that curled in my stomach when I realized their
names were those of *poisonous* snakes.

I felt a hand grab my arm and heard a shriek.

"Ophelia!"

"Happy Birthday, Darci," I said, moving away from the
bar and giving her a hug. I reached into my purse, took out
a small, heavy box and handed it to her. "It's not much, but I
thought you might like it."

She tore into the package, scattering bits of paper across
the bar. After ripping the box open, she removed the black
velvet pouch nestled inside, opened it, and let her gift roll
into her hands. "A crystal sphere!" Darci threw an arm
around my neck. "It's wonderful. Thank you."

I hugged her and took a step back, glancing down at the
stone in her open palm. Little flecks of mica sparkled from
the depths of the green stone. "It's made from adventurine.
A good crystal for here." I patted my chest. "Makes the heart
strong and helps you be who you were meant to be. It's a
stone of courage."

Rolling the sphere in her hand and feeling the weight of
it, she smiled. "I love it."

Darci was lit up like a Christmas tree. I didn't know if
it was from the booze or if she was just excited about her
party.

"You've got to meet my cousin," she said abruptly. Still
holding the sphere tightly in one hand, she grabbed my arm
with the other and pulled me away from the bar.

I gripped my mug and allowed her to steer me to the pool
table.

When we approached, the blonde peeled herself off Mr.
Cigarette and walked toward us. She stopped directly in front

of Darci, planting her high heels wide and settling her hands on her hips.

"Ophelia," Darci said in a rush. "This is Becca."

My mouth dropped. She wasn't a biker babe—she was Darci's cousin.

Six

She'd had more work done on her than Frankenstein's monster, but with much better results. Up close, Becca was older than I'd originally thought, but she was gorgeous, in a plastic kind of way. Darci looked almost frumpy standing next to her. Wow, if Darci looked plain, I could only imagine what I looked like in comparison. Self-consciously, I glanced down at my turtleneck sweater and jeans. Respectable was the most flattering term that came to my mind.

Darci threw her arms around the both of us and led Becca and me over to a table, away from the bikers. Becca cast a longing glance in the direction of Mr. Cigarette even as she followed Darci.

On our way to Darci's table, Cobra and Rattles strolled past us. I took a step to the side to avoid bumping into them. Cobra paused and his eyes briefly met mine. A sneer played at the corner of his mouth as if he was waiting to see if I would say something. My lips tightened and I lifted my chin. A grin flashed across his face, showing straight white teeth. He slapped his friend on the back and they continued on their way.

I released the breath I hadn't realized I was holding.

Darci guided us toward her table, where we three took our place around the chipped Formica top.

Becca leaned forward—making her cleavage even more pronounced, and the tube top slip dangerously low. She gave it a quick tug and smiled. "I'm so glad I was able to visit Darci this week."

Darci beamed at her. "Me, too," she said, and turned to me. "We're going to have so much fun this week."

I worked hard at smiling back at her. "What do you have planned?"

Darci wiggled in her chair like a little kid. "Tomorrow I'm taking Becca to the new mall in Des Moines, and we're going to shop till we drop. When we were younger, we never could afford to do that, right, Becca?"

"Right," Becca said with a brightness that didn't ring true.

"But now we can," Darci continued, smiling broadly. "Then tomorrow night, we're going to dinner with Danny."

Becca's eyes dropped and she traced a scratch in the table-top. She said nothing.

Darci didn't notice Becca's lack of enthusiasm, but I got the distinct impression that going to dinner with Danny was *not* Becca's idea of fun. The feeling was reinforced when she stole a glance over her shoulder toward the pool table, and a hungry look marred her features.

"So," I said, drawing her attention to me. "What do you do in California?"

"I work for an insurance company." The hungry look was replaced by a tight, almost bitter expression. "I went there to be an actress, but now . . ." She shrugged. " . . . I'm too old."

"You are not," Darci exclaimed, patting Becca's hand.

"Yes, I am, cuz. Los Angeles is full of girls a lot younger

than I am. All looking for that big break." She tossed her head. "I can't compete."

"Are you kidding? You're the prettiest woman here tonight."

Becca's eyes traveled the room, and by the look on her face, I could see she didn't think that was saying much. Her eyes settled on Mr. Cigarette, the red-haired biker, and I saw him wink and lift his glass in a toast to her. She perked up.

In my mind's eye a stop light blinked on and off, flashing a warning. Danger ahead? Wow, no kidding. I didn't need my psychic abilities to tell me those bikers were bad news, and Becca would be playing with fire if she got mixed up with them. I rubbed my forehead, trying to chase away the blinking red light. The vision wouldn't disappear.

I didn't understand. Tink wasn't the only one who'd been working with Abby and learning to control her abilities. I had, too. And now the images didn't drift in and out unless I allowed them. I hadn't opened my mind, so why was this happening? Was all the noise and confusion around me making it hard to maintain control? Was Abby having problems, too? I glanced over to where she stood behind the bar, talking with Danny.

Her face was clear and she appeared relaxed. Her green eyes twinkled with amusement while she talked to him. And by the look on Danny's face, he was totally charmed by my grandmother.

Watching them, I thought Darci wasn't the only one who envied Abby's ability to put people at ease. I did, too. It was a talent I didn't think I'd ever possess. It just wasn't in my nature—I worried too much, as Abby repeatedly told me, and I was too uptight about things. No matter how much I practiced my meditation, it was hard for me to loosen up. I knew that as a result I often came across as a little cold to people who didn't know me. And then there were my trust issues . . .

I shook myself out of my self-examination and turned my attention back to Darci and Becca. They were chatting away about their plans for the week, oblivious to the fact that I'd spaced out for a while.

Becca caught my eye and smiled.

Stop, stop, stop, flashed the light in my head.

As the night wore on and the booze flowed freely, the bar became louder and louder. I stepped out several times to call home and check on the girls. Each time, I was assured that everything was fine—doors were locked, no one else was there, and no, they hadn't been playing with the telephone. Finally, Tink informed me that I didn't have to keep calling; after all, they *were* thirteen years old and could stay by themselves. I decided I would have to trust them and tried to relax.

Even though Stumpy's was a respectable place, the bar scene had never really been my thing, even in college. I sat at the corner of the bar, talking to Abby when she had a spare moment, and watched.

Becca had ditched Darci and was back at the pool table with her love of the night, Mr. Cigarette. Every so often when my eyes drifted around the room, I'd find the guy named Cobra watching me. It made me uncomfortable, and I'd quickly look away.

Over in the corner sat several of our regulars from the library. Housewives enjoying a night out with their husbands.

"Spying on people, Slugger?"

I whirled around to see Ned Thomas, editor of *The Courier,* standing next to me. "I'm not spying," I said indignantly while Ned's green eyes shone with glee.

Lean and tall, Ned was one of the town's most eligible bachelors. He was also good looking, with a great sense humor; the town matchmakers had us linked in a hot romance last year, but the attachment existed only in their minds. Ned and I enjoyed an easy friendship, and I valued his opinion.

"What are you doing here?" I asked. "Covering the society beat?"

He laughed. "Summerset isn't big enough to have 'society.' I'm here to wish Darci a Happy Birthday." Watching Darci flit from table to table, his smile grew broader. "She's having a good time, isn't she?"

I nodded. "She's been worked up over this party all week." I felt my face tighten. "That, and her cousin coming for a visit."

"Don't like the cousin?" Ned asked, picking up on my mood.

"It's not that I don't like her; she's not what I expected."

Ned's eyes traveled to Becca and her friend. "Um-hmm. I see what you mean. She's more interested in the biker than celebrating Darci's birthday."

I slapped my hand on the bar. "Exactly. After not seeing Darci for four years, don't you think Becca should be paying more attention to her?"

Ned raised an eyebrow. "I think Becca would rather everyone be focused on her, instead of Darci."

"See—and that's not right. This is Darci's party."

Ned gave me a playful poke in the arm. "You'd better not let Darci see your irritation, Slugger. She evidently loves her cousin, and I think it would be wise if you didn't voice your opinion."

"Okay, okay," I muttered. "You're right, and I don't want to ruin her party."

"Smart girl," he said with another poke.

"I heard you've been vocal about Summerset's latest residents," I said with a jerk toward the pool table.

Ned's playful tone disappeared. "It's like a cancer has invaded Summerset." With a shake of his head, he frowned. "But so far there's no proof that they're doing anything illegal."

"And until there is, we're stuck with them?"

"'Fraid so," he replied, and took a sip of his beer.

I laid my hand on his arm. "Listen, Ned, if they're as dangerous as everyone says, you need to be careful."

A quick smile dashed across his face. "This is a switch—you telling me to be careful. Usually it's the other way around." He patted my hand. "Don't worry, Slugger, I'll watch my back."

After Ned left, I continued scanning the bar. My eyes widened when I saw Pete Polaski talking to Danny in a booth at the front of the room. They were in deep conversation, and Pete's face wore a heavy frown. He shook his head and took a long drink from his glass. With a serious expression on his face, Danny leaned in and said something, and in response, Pete's eyes shifted toward the pool table and he squirmed uncomfortably in his seat.

Had the bikers stopped at his shop the day I saw them driving by? Had something happened to make Pete nervous? Dang, I would have loved to know what they were saying. I strained to pick up their voices over the crowd, but there was too much noise. Did I turn my radar on them? All night I'd had problems blocking impressions. Could I narrow them down to Pete and Danny? No, there were too many people in too small a space for me to sort out all the emotions that would beep across my internal screen.

With a fleeting look at the bikers, Danny rose and walked

to where Darci stood talking to Georgia and a group of friends at another table. Darci had been wandering around the bar all night gathering good wishes and shots. When Georgia handed her a shot glass, I saw Danny shake his head no. Darci's mouth formed a little pout, then she smiled and tossed back the shot, to the cheers of Georgia and the group at the table.

I shook my head and grinned. The way she was drinking, she was going to have the mother of all hangovers tomorrow, but that was okay. Darci worked hard, and she deserved to cut loose a little. After all, it was her birthday.

Danny finally gave up on Darci and, holding his glass, made his way over to where I sat at the bar. I'd never talked much to Danny, but I could see why Darci was attracted to him. With thick dark hair and dark eyes with eyelashes most women would kill for, he was a knockout.

"Having fun?" I asked, and sipped my beer.

He set his empty glass on the bar and motioned for another Coke. "Not really. I'm only here to keep an eye on Darci."

Jeez, the way he said it made it sound like she needed a babysitter. The remark hit me the wrong way.

"Darci can take care of herself," I said, lifting an eyebrow.

His eyes flicked over to where Darci stood talking to Georgia, and his face tightened.

Before I could stop myself, the words slipped out. "Don't you like Georgia?"

A flash of surprise crossed his face. "I think Darci could do better in her selection of friends."

Does that include me? I wondered.

Danny continued, "Darci's a sweet girl, but she lacks direction."

I bit my lip to keep from asking if he was the one who intended to give it to her. I was beginning to think maybe Danny wasn't so attractive after all.

He took a drink from the Coke he'd been served. "She needs to decide what her goals are," he said, setting the glass down. "Maybe if she did, people would show her more respect."

He sounded so judgmental that I couldn't keep my mouth shut any longer. I placed an arm on the bar and leaned toward him.

"I like Darci just the way she is. You'd have a hard time finding anyone to say a bad word about her. Our patrons love her."

From the look on his face, I saw that he realized he'd gone too far. He turned on a megawatt smile. "Of course they love her. She's a great person. But it bothers her that some people treat her like a ditz. I'm trying to help her change that."

I wondered if he understood the difference between helping and controlling.

From the corner of my eye, I saw the bikers saunter across the bar to the door. The crowd seemed to part as they approached. I turned to see where Becca was.

She sat at a table with Darci, looking bored now that her friend had left. She leaned over to Darci and whispered something in her ear. The smile left Darci's face and she shook her head. Becca leaned in closer. Darci's eyes drifted down and she listened intently. Finally she lifted her head, rolled her eyes, and stood up. Leaving the table, she crossed to where Danny and I were sitting at the bar.

"Ophelia," she said, not looking at Danny. "I have a problem. Becca wants to go to The Viper's Nest—"

"No," Danny butted in.

She cast him a helpless look and returned her attention

to me. "If I don't take her, someone else will. A bunch of people are leaving soon to go out there. At least if I'm with her, I can keep her out of trouble."

"Darci, I told you to stay away from that place," Danny said, his voice rising.

Darci stood straight and I watched the emotions play across her face. She was torn between pleasing her boyfriend and loyalty to her cousin.

She might have chosen placating Danny if he'd only known when to keep his mouth shut.

"Look," he said touching her arm. "The Viper's Nest may be okay for a woman like Becca, but not you. You're—"

He didn't have a chance to finish. Darci narrowed her eyes and glared at him. "What do you mean 'a woman like Becca'? You just met her. You don't know what kind of a person she is."

"I've seen her type before."

Darci shook off his hand and turned her back to him. "Ophelia, I've had too much to drink, and I can't drive. Neither can Becca. Will you go with us?"

Danny jerked away from the bar and huffed off.

A hurt look crossed Darci's face, but she didn't comment on Danny's behavior. "Please?"

The Viper's Nest was the last place I wanted to go. Others in town might like to walk on the wild side, but not me. But what could I do? Darci was my friend, and she was in a spot.

Grabbing my bag, I slid my mug across the bar. "Okay, let's go."

Seven

The parking lot of the roadhouse was packed. Semis, SUVs, and motorcycles sat side by side in the crowded lot. Several of the vehicles belonged to Summerset's residents. What drove them to frequent a place like The Viper's Nest? Was it curiosity? Did they want to see if the rumors were true? Or did the idea of "slumming" add an element of danger to their normally quiet lives? I didn't know and really didn't care. I couldn't think of a place I'd rather *not* be than there. At least I didn't need to be concerned about Tink and Nell—Abby had left Stumpy's the same time we had, and offered to go to my house and spend the rest of the night with the girls. Becca assured us that she just wanted to take a look and then we could leave. I intended to hold her to her promise.

Inside the bar, smoke from a hundred cigarettes hung in the air, casting the room in a blue haze. A stage, with a live band performing, took up the far side of the room, and the heavy metal sound reverberated around me. It seemed to pound in my head. I took a deep breath, clutched my bag closer to my waist and followed Becca and Darci into the bar.

Becca led the way like a racehorse out of the gate and

made straight toward her new friend, who stood drinking with his buddies. When he spied Becca, he left his pals and went up to her. Throwing an arm around her waist, he drew her close and escorted her to his friends. Darci and I spied an empty table in a dark corner and headed toward it. The last thing we wanted to do was draw the attention of all the bikers littering the bar. Moments later a waitress with tired eyes approached the table to take our orders.

"What'll it be," she asked in a voice as weary as her eyes.

No way was I going to have any alcohol in this place. "Coffee for me," I replied.

"Same here," Darci said, her eyes never leaving Becca.

The waitress shrugged and left the table to fetch our order.

Darci wiggled uncomfortably in her seat. "I need to use the restroom."

"Darci, I swear, you pick the worst times," I hissed, casting an eye at a group of bikers gathered near the sign saying RESTROOMS. "Why didn't you—"

"I know, I know," she said in a helpless voice, "but I didn't need to at Stumpy's. Now I've got to wedge my way past all those guys."

So much for not drawing any attention.

"I'd better go with you." I started to stand but she waved me down.

"No, you stay here and keep an eye on Becca."

"Okay," I said reluctantly. "But if you're not back in five minutes, I'm calling the cops." To make my point, I reached in my bag and put my cell phone on the table.

Darci crossed the room to the hall leading back to the restrooms. As she did, several men cast an appraising look her way, but she held her head high and ignored them.

With a sigh, I looked at my watch. We'd been there fifteen minutes. Out of the corner of my eye, I saw a coffee cup appear in front of me. I reached in my bag and pulled out a couple of dollars. I looked up, about to hand the waitress my money. Only it wasn't the waitress, it was the guy they called Cobra.

Without an invitation, he pulled out a chair and sat. "Janet asked me to bring these over," he said, sliding the cup closer to me.

"Thanks," I mumbled, laying the bills on the table.

"So what's your story, lady?" he asked.

I scooted back in my chair and crossed my arms. "What do you mean?"

"What are you doing here?" He watched my face with those cold gray eyes.

My eyes traveled to Becca standing at the bar.

"I get it. You're watching out for your friend." He snorted. "You're going to have trouble with that one, lady. Looks to me she's old enough to make her own decisions, and she's decided on Adder."

"Adder?"

He jerked his head toward them. "The guy she's with."

Right, back to the snake thing.

Cobra lifted his glass and took a long swallow. As he did, I noticed another tattoo on his forearm. Not a snake, but a *one* with a percent sign after it.

My curiosity got the best of me. "What's the one percent for?" I asked, pointing to the tattoo.

He glanced down at his arm and a sneer darted across his face. "This? Haven't you heard that ninety-nine percent of the members of motorcycle clubs are good guys?"

"But it's a one percent sign," I said, puzzled. Then the lightbulb went off in my head. "I get it. If ninety-nine percent are good guys, then one percent are . . ." My voice trailed away.

"The bad guys," he said, finishing my sentence for me. He stood and leaned in close. His cold gray eyes sent a chill through me. "You'd do well to remember that, lady. I suggest you gather up your friends and get the hell out of here." With that, he turned and strolled away.

I clutched my bag tighter and scanned the room nervously. Crap, I couldn't see Becca or her friend anywhere. I stood and peered through the smoke filled room. Darci was going to kill me. Some babysitter I was. How long had she been gone? A sudden tap on my shoulder made me jump. I whirled around to see Darci standing beside me.

"Where's Becca?"

"Don't know." I cast my eyes down.

"What do you mean 'you don't know'? Did she leave?"

"I guess so," I muttered.

"Ophelia—"

"I know," I said quickly. "I'm sorry. But that Cobra guy came over and started talking to me. He distracted me." I clutched Darci's arm. "He said for us to leave."

Concern ran across Darci's face. "We can't go home without Becca."

"What do you suggest we do? Sit here all night waiting for her to come back?"

"No." She tugged on her bottom lip. "We could go look for her."

I sighed. "And where do you think we should look?" Shaking my head, I looked at the bar. "Maybe we should go ask the guys there if they have any ideas."

Darci picked up on my sarcasm. "Okay, so we can't do that." She pulled a hand through her hair. "I don't know what to do. I can't leave without her."

The waitress walked by with drinks for the next table. An idea hit me. Reaching into my purse, I took out a twenty. "Hey, listen," I said, loud enough to draw her attention. The waitress stopped and looked at me. "Our friend, the blonde who was at the bar with Adder? They left. Any idea where they might have gone?"

She gave me a derisive look. "Try any one of the motels between here and Des Moines."

"Please, we're worried about our friend. She might be in over her head." I took her hand and pressed the twenty into her palm. "Does he have a favorite?"

With a nervous glance over her shoulder at the bar, she swiftly tucked the twenty in the pocket of her jeans. "I've heard he frequents the one over in Akin."

Great, that was about fifteen miles away.

"What kind of a bike does he ride?"

"A black Harley with a shovel head."

I wouldn't know a Harley from a Yamaha. And what in the heck was a "shovel head"? "Is there anything else distinctive about Adder's bike?" I asked hopefully.

The waitress thought for a moment. "Yeah, he has a rubber snake tied on the back."

Okay, there couldn't be too many of those cruising the countryside. Maybe we could find them. I didn't know what we were going to do if we *did* find them, but I'd worry about that one later.

"Come on," I said, hustling Darci out of the bar.

Even without looking, I felt Cobra's gray eyes drilling a hole in my back.

Three hours later Darci and I were pulling up in front of her house. When we hadn't found Adder's bike at the motel in Akin, we checked others in the small towns around

Summerset. No sign of the bike at any of them. Darci had been so desperate, I'd even tried using my psychic abilities to pinpoint where they might be, but all I saw in my mind's eye was the same flashing stop light I'd seen all evening. Now the image had faded, leaving in its place a dull headache, and all I wanted to do was go home and crawl into bed.

As I made the turn into Darci's driveway, the headlights drifted across the face of the dark house and settled on a bike parked by the back door.

Instantly, Darci's anger seemed to fill the car. "She brought him here." Her hand was on the door handle before the car even came to a stop.

"Wait," I said stopping her. "Maybe you should call Danny before you go in? This Adder might not appreciate you kicking him out of your house."

"Are you kidding?" She turned blazing eyes toward me. "He's ticked off that we went out there in the first place. No way am I going to call him now."

"But Darci—"

"No," she said stubbornly.

I took a deep breath and blew it out. "Okay." I reached for my door handle.

"What are you doing?"

"I'm not letting you go in there by yourself," I said, opening my door. "By the way, you don't have a baseball bat, do you? Just in case?"

"Very funny," she said, then followed me out of the car and up the walk. "You don't have to do this, you know."

"I know, but you might need help getting that guy out of here."

"I can handle it." Darci passed me, marched up the front porch, and shoved her key in the door.

"I still think you should call Danny," I muttered under my breath.

With a backward look at me, she swung the door open.

We walked into the dark house, enveloped by a deadly quiet. Heavy, oppressive, it pushed down on us. I felt a rush of adrenaline, a rush of fear.

"Wait." I grabbed Darci's arm as she reached for the light switch. "We need to—"

The sudden images cascading through my head stopped my words. *Becca laughing. Becca and the biker stumbling toward the bed.* I fought the images. I didn't want to watch the scene unfolding in my mind. They faded, only to rush back with the force of a tidal wave. I staggered and would have fallen if I hadn't been clutching Darci's arm in a desperate grip.

She grabbed my shoulder to steady me. "Ophelia, what's wrong?" Her voice echoed the fear I felt.

A scream rent the air. Darci released me and took off at a dead run toward the back of the house.

I stumbled after her, knocking my shin on the coffee table, almost tripping over the couch, and staggering like a drunk until I reached the back bedroom.

Darci's hands braced the door frame and her body went rigid. Over her shoulder I saw Becca sitting in the room lit only by one single candle glowing brightly from the top of the chest of drawers.

Becca was on her knees, in the middle of the bed, clad only in her underwear. Sprawled next to her was the biker, his arms flung wide. One leg draped out from underneath the red, soggy sheet covering the lower part of his body.

Becca held a knife in her hand. A knife she stared at with an expression of absolute terror on her face. A knife that in the warm glow of the candlelight dripped blood.

Eight

Pale morning light filtered in the long window at the end of the hospital corridor, and the aroma of food from breakfast trays drifted in the air. My stomach rumbled at the scent. When was the last time I'd eaten? I couldn't remember. Memories of the past few hours jumbled through my mind, making it difficult to put events in their proper sequence. Darci having fun at Stumpy's. The tired eyes of the waitress from The Viper. And the blood. My God, there'd been so much blood in the tiny bedroom. I didn't know a human body held that much.

I rubbed my temple with trembling fingers as I talked to Abby on my cell phone.

"We got Becca out of the room and called 911," I explained. "Brett was on duty last night, so he was the first to arrive, along with the paramedics. Bill and Alan showed up a little later." I pressed a hand against my grumbling stomach. "Brett must've called them from the patrol car."

"Well, the sheriff's department does have more training in murder investigations. It was murder, wasn't it?" Abby asked.

"Oh yeah." My voice rang with certainty. "I heard someone say the femoral artery had been sliced. The guy would've been dead within minutes."

"How terrible," Abby exclaimed. "What about Becca?"

I shook my head. "She said she doesn't remember anything." I paused and took a deep breath. "The paramedics said she's suffering from shock, so they rushed her here to the hospital. She does seem disoriented and confused . . ." My voice faded away.

"How's Darci holding up?"

"She's pretty shaky, too, but she's keeping it together so far. She's in the examination room with Becca right now. Abby, how are the girls?" I asked, switching the subject.

"They're fine. Still asleep when I checked on them a few minutes ago," she said with confidence.

I thought of the two teens innocently sleeping in Tink's bedroom. Oh, how I'd like to protect them from all this ugliness that seemed to be rearing its head in our peaceful little town, but within hours news of Adder's murder would be burning the phone lines and be the main subject of discussion at many a breakfast table. Several hypotheses would be debated, and conclusions would be leapt to. By the time the rumor mill was finished with what happened, the facts would be distorted to Lord only knew what. The girls would hear all about it Monday at school. Since I was one of those who found the body, I only hoped Tink wouldn't be singled out as a source of information. She had enough problems right now without getting grilled by her classmates.

I tucked my worries away. I'd think about it later. Right now I needed to know my grandmother's thoughts.

"Abby, have you sensed anything at all lately?"

"No. No, I haven't." She sounded confused. "And I don't understand it. Usually an event of this magnitude sets off some kind of warning. You did say you felt something was 'off.'"

"But I didn't think it would be a murder," I said emphatically. "I thought my feelings stemmed from concern over Tink."

"You didn't have any kind of premonitions last night?"

"Well, yeah. Flashing red lights kept going off in my head. Big deal. And when we walked in the house, a sense of danger overwhelmed me. But once again," my voice was laced with frustration, "it came too late to change what happened."

"Ophelia, some things are meant to be," Abby replied gently. "And we can't change them."

Her words touched a sore spot with me. One of the things I hated about my psychic talents was the fact that visions are no good if they can't be used to help people, to prevent catastrophes. Abby accepted the way her abilities worked—I didn't. It seemed I was always fighting the rules.

"I don't know why," I muttered, staring down at the floor.

"It's not the way our gift works." Abby's voice was gentle.

"Well, it should—" I broke off when a shadow fell across the shiny linoleum at my feet. I looked up to find Bill Wilson, our county sheriff, standing over me. "Got to go," I said quickly and snapped my phone shut. "Hey, Bill."

"Ophelia," Bill said cautiously, and took a seat next to me. He removed his hat and rubbed his bald head. "Do you want—"

I held up my hand, stopping him. "I didn't find the body this time."

"No," he said, saying the word slowly, as if talking to a child. "Technically, you didn't. Darci did, but you were there. That's almost the same thing."

I opened my mouth to argue, but closed it quickly after seeing the look on Bill's face. I waited for him to continue.

"What happened?" he asked, and flipped open the notebook in his hand.

I gave him a rundown on Stumpy's and why we went to The Viper's Nest. His face tightened into a frown when I mentioned the bikers' hangout.

"You shouldn't have gone there."

"No fooling," I replied.

"It's a dangerous place."

I twisted on the bench to face him. "Why hasn't someone shut it down?"

"There's something called 'probable cause,' Ophelia." He sounded like he was talking to a kid again. "Without it, we can't touch them." Bill studied his notebook. "Did you witness Becca leaving with the biker?"

"No."

"How much time elapsed before you reached Darci's?"

"I don't know . . ." I tried to remember if I'd looked at the clock in my car and couldn't recall. "A couple of hours, maybe more. It's all kind of a blur. Why? Is it important?"

"We're trying to put a time frame on the chain of events. The autopsy will help decide the time of death. That, and the condition of the blood on the sheets."

Bad mental image. Suddenly, the smell of the food in the hallway made my stomach lurch.

"Do you think Becca did it?" I asked, trying to wipe the image of those soggy sheets from my brain.

Bill snapped his notebook shut and stood. "You know I can't comment on that."

"Why do you think she was so disoriented?" I persisted.

"Shock."

"But she says she doesn't remember anything."

Bill looked down at me skeptically. "What do you expect her to say?"

"You think she did it. Are you going to arrest her?"

"We haven't found any signs of forced entry. You and Darci both said the doors were locked when you arrived," he said without thinking. Realizing he was giving me too much information, he pointed a finger at me. "I didn't say we were going to arrest her."

I wasn't going to let it go. "There has to be an explanation. Have you questioned his buddies?"

"Alan's out there now." Bill narrowed his eyes while he looked down at me. "And that's all I'm going to tell you." He snapped his fingers. "Oh, one more thing—I'm going to warn you once, Ophelia Jensen—stay out of this. Or you'll be a guest of the county, not Becca."

Left alone with my thoughts, the minutes seemed to drag by. A deep weariness settled over me, and I understood Abby's saying, "bone tired." It felt as if the fatigue penetrated every muscle of my body, going straight to my marrow. I leaned my head back against the wall and let my mind drift. I heard the hum of the hospital, the soft squish of nurses' rubber soled shoes, the clicking of the food carts as they rolled from room to room, the creak of the vinyl bench as someone sat down next to me.

My eyes flew open to see Darci sitting there.

Black smudges circled her eyes, eyes shot with red. I didn't know if the tiny red lines were caused by the same weariness I felt or by crying.

"How are you doing, my friend?" I asked, patting her leg.

She shook her head while tears formed in her weary eyes. Closing them and pressing her fingertips against the lids, she was silent for a moment. "I'll be okay," she said, opening her eyes again. "I'm worried about Becca. The doctors want to keep her overnight for observation and do more blood and urine tests."

"Why all the lab work?"

"They think she might have been drugged."

"Drugged?"

She nodded. "Yeah. One of those date rape drugs."

"Oh, my God, Darci," I stammered.

The tears rushed to her eyes again. "They're going to arrest her, Ophelia," she said in a helpless voice. "I know they are. The doors were locked, there wasn't a sign of forced entry, no footprints, tire tracks, nothing to show that anyone else had been in the house."

"They've called in a forensics team from Des Moines, haven't they? Maybe they'll find something."

She brushed away the tears. "Like what?"

My mind scrambled over every crime show I'd ever watched on TV. "Fibers, a hair? I don't know—something." My voice sounded uncertain even to me.

"I know you weren't impressed with Becca." She hesitated, not meeting my eyes. "I'm not stupid, and you're not very good at hiding your feelings. But there's another Becca—"

"You don't have to explain," I interrupted.

"Yes, I do." Darci stared off into space. "She's five years older than me, and I've always looked up to her." Her lips formed a tight smile. "She helped me get ready for my first date. The first time my heart was broken by some pimply teenage boy, she was the one who made me feel better. Whenever her brothers or one of the other cousins picked on me, Becca would rush to my defense. She was fearless and she was my hero." The smile left her face. "You know I've always envied the closeness you have with Abby. I've never had that with anyone . . . except Becca."

At a loss for words, I patted her leg again and wished I had the magick to take away her pain, to make everything right. But I didn't.

"Even when she moved to California, I knew she was only a phone call away." A tear slowly slid down Darci's face. "She didn't do it, Ophelia."

I was having trouble reconciling the woman Darci just described with the person I'd met last night, when I heard rapid footsteps approach from down the hall. Looking up, I watched Danny making directly for us.

He took a seat next to Darci and without a word gathered her in his arms. With her head resting on his shoulder, he whispered in her ear.

I squirmed in my seat, uncomfortable at this show of intimacy. Talk about a fifth wheel.

"Ah . . . I think I'll go get some coffee." I made a move to stand.

Darci raised her head and looked at me. "No, stay, Ophelia." She scooted away from Danny's hug and turned her attention to him. "What's going on at my house?"

"Baby, you know I can't talk about the investigation," he replied gently.

"Are the people from the crime lab still there?" she asked.

"Yes. And officers from the Iowa Department of Crime Investigation."

Darci clutched Danny's hand. "Becca didn't kill that biker." She squeezed his hand. "You have to help her, prove she didn't do it."

Danny shook his head. "Darci, I'm not going to be involved in the investigation. It would be a conflict of interest because of you."

"But you can keep an eye on what's going on, right?" she asked hopefully.

"Darci." His voice was gentle. "Maybe they'll find it was self-defense. You know, things got rough and—" He hesitated.

Darci rushed in. "And what? She ran downstairs, grabbed one of my kitchen knives, ran back upstairs and stabbed him?"

A surprised look crossed Danny's face.

"You didn't think I'd recognize one of my own knives?"

He rubbed his jeans nervously. "Umm, well . . ."

"Danny, I don't keep knives in my bedrooms. She would've had to get the knife from the kitchen." She wrapped her arms tightly around herself. "That would make it kind of hard to plead self-defense, now wouldn't it?"

"Darci, baby, let the investigators do their job. If she's innocent, they'll prove it."

"But you're already convinced she did it, aren't you?" Anger flashed in her eyes. "And you're not going to do a thing to help show otherwise, are you?"

"I can't, Darci."

Darci stood up swiftly, and grabbing my arm, pulled me to my feet. "Well, that's okay," she said, standing straight. "Ophelia will establish that Becca didn't do it."

With that she turned on her heel and marched down the hall, dragging me with her.

Nine

After checking on Becca, I persuaded Darci to return with me to my house. I let the remark about me proving Becca's innocence lay. I was too tired to deal with the idea of murder. Once home, we both crashed.

Five hours later I woke up groggy. Opening one eye cautiously, I struggled to get my bearings. The other eye popped open when I noticed Tink sitting quietly in the armchair by the window.

"Hey kiddo," I said, scooting up in bed. I patted the edge and motioned her over. "How's it going?"

Tink wandered to the bed and sat. "Fine." She kept her face averted, and with the directness only kids possess said, "There's been a murder."

It wasn't a question.

"Yes," I answered, but had no intention of giving her the gory details. She would hear about them soon enough.

"At Darci's house?"

"Yes."

Tink turned toward me and her violet eyes bore into mine. "Are you going to solve it?"

"No. That's the job of the police."

"You and Abby solved the one in Minnesota."

I squirmed under her direct stare. "But there were extenuating circumstances last summer, Tink. We hadn't planned on getting involved in that case."

"But your gift led you to the solution." She broke her stare and looked down at the old comforter covering my bed. She made lazy circles around the wedding ring pattern. "If you can use your talent this time to help a friend," her voice dropped, "shouldn't you?"

She had a point. Darci had been a good friend to me over the years, even when I didn't want her to be. The situation with Becca was tearing her up inside, and I could sense her desperation, and her determination. Then I remembered Bill's warning.

Taking Tink's hand in mine, I said gently, "Honey, I'm not a trained investigator. It's dangerous to blunder around in a murder investigation." I squeezed it. "Especially this one. These bikers are not nice people."

I studied Tink's profile as I spoke and was struck by what a lovely girl she was. A trickle of fear skittered through me.

"They haven't bothered you, have they?" My hand closed around hers a little tighter.

Her face puckered in a frown. "What do you mean?"

What did I mean? "Ah, well, you know, stopped and talked to you. Asked you if you wanted a ride on their bikes—"

"Are you kidding?" She snorted. "They're old. They've got to be at least in their thirties or forties."

Ah, my age. A smile chased away my fears.

"Melinda's talked to them, though," she said suddenly.

"What?"

Tink's mouth turned down with distaste. "She's been

bragging about it at school." She flipped her hair over her shoulder. "I guess they were at her dad's garage. She met them one day after school."

"What did she say about it?"

Tink shrugged. "I don't know—she thinks it's cool her dad knows a bunch of tough guys."

"Did she say he knew them?"

"She made it sound like he does."

Pete Polaski had seemed too easygoing and too smart a businessman to get mixed up with a bunch of outlaws. Had they stopped to check out his garage? Have their bikes worked on? Had it been the day I'd watched them drive by the garage?

"Tink . . ." I leaned forward. "It's not cool. I suspect they really are bad guys. I just hope the police can prove it."

"If you could, would you?" she asked earnestly.

I sighed. "Sweetie, you can't find someone guilty based on dreams and premonitions." I grinned at her. "They don't hold up well in a court of law." My grin dropped away. "The best I could do would be to try and steer the investigation in the right direction . . ." I hesitated, thinking it over. "But to do that, I'd have to let the police in on our little secret, in on our heritage. Summerset is too small of a town, and if I did, soon everyone would know about us."

Tink watched me closely again. "Don't you think everyone would be impressed?"

"Ha. More likely scared," I said emphatically. "People fear what they don't understand. The whole town would probably leave us alone."

"That can be good sometimes," she said softly.

I had to agree. It was good to be left alone at times. I thought about my life back in the days when it contained only Abby and my pets. My world was a lot simpler then, but it was empty, too.

I tipped Tink's face toward me. "You really don't want that. Life would be lonely without Darci, Nell, Arthur, and all the other people that care about us, wouldn't it?"

She wiggled on the bed. "I suppose. But isn't it a lie when you don't let people know who and what you are?"

"No, it's not." I hugged her. "Someday you'll learn how to use your talents in a subtle way. Like Abby. You'll be able to help people without broadcasting how."

She leaned away from me. "That's what Abby says."

"See?" I gave her a big smile. "Have you ever known Abby to be wrong?"

I busied myself in the kitchen rounding up something to eat. Peering in my fridge, I grabbed eggs, milk, and butter. Scrambled eggs would be good. For what? I looked over at the clock. Too late for lunch. Too early for dinner. Whatever. All I knew was I needed food.

As I cracked the eggs and whipped them in the bowl, Tink's words pecked at me. Was it my responsibility to help Darci? In the past, Abby had guided me in decisions like that. She'd pointed the way with her insight. But this time her only comment had been, "Some things are meant to be." Not a very helpful statement.

What did my own intuition tell me? Not much, I thought wryly. Did my lack of inspiration mean I should sit this one out? Or had the signs been there and I'd missed them? Was I too focused on my new role as a mother to see what was in front of me? What *had* I seen?

Flashing red lights. Big deal. That could've been either a sign not to go to The Viper's Nest or it could've meant we'd find trouble if we did. Another possibility—maybe it indicated I should stay out of whatever was happening this time.

I took my frustration out on the poor eggs in the skillet, splattering the stove as I whisked them around. Moving the pan off the burner, I made my decision. After Darci left for the hospital, I'd go to Abby's. We were going to hash this situation over. I felt better immediately, and was able to give Darci an honest smile when she entered the kitchen a few minutes later.

"Hungry?" I asked while dishing the eggs onto plates.

"Not really." Her tone was listless.

"You have to eat something."

She eased onto a chair at the table. "Danny called."

"He did?" I kept my voice reserved.

"Yeah. He apologized for what happened at the hospital."

"Did you forgive him?"

She nodded, a small smile on her face. "I do understand he's in a tight spot with the department, and maybe I over-reacted a bit."

"You're worried about your cousin," I said, placing a plate in front of her. "Eat."

She picked up a fork and slid the eggs around on her plate. "I called the hospital. They still plan on releasing Becca to-morrow morning, but she's out of it right now."

"That's probably for the best." I joined her at the table with my own plate. "Maybe when she wakes up she can tell the police what happened."

"I hope so." She took a tiny bite and swallowed. "Danny said it's going to be a couple of days before I can go home." A shudder shook her. "I don't know if I can even then."

"Darci, you and Becca are welcome to stay here."

She reached across the table and patted my hand. "That's

kind of you, but I know how you are about your private space. I don't want to impose."

"Really, Darci, I don't mind."

She smiled. "Ophelia, right now Becca isn't one of your favorite people." Her words rushed out before I could interrupt her. "And that's okay. I understand why. I called Georgia; it's slow at the bed and breakfast right now, so we're going to stay there for a few days."

"Are you sure?"

"Yeah, we'll have more privacy, and so will you." Her fork stopped midway to her mouth and she let out a small giggle.

"What?" I asked, surprised.

"I just remembered how prickly you used to be. A year ago the last thing you would've wanted was two house guests."

I grimaced. She was right. Darci and Abby had dragged me kicking and screaming out of the safe little world that I'd created for myself.

"Darci, I've never asked you this . . ." I hesitated. "Why did you try so hard to be my friend?"

She laid down her fork and gave me a big smile. "Because, silly, I knew what a good person you were on the inside. You only pretended to be hard to protect yourself. Like me, you used how people saw you to keep them at arm's length."

I looked at her. Even without much sleep and no makeup, dressed in a pair of my baggy pajamas, Darci looked fresh and pretty. I thought of how I appeared—sweats, a crummy T-shirt, my brown hair in an untidy twist on the top of my head. I laughed. "Gee, Darce, who'd have thought we had so much in common?"

She grinned back at me and took a bigger bite of food. "Where's Tink?"

I scooped up a forkful of eggs. "She's spending the night at Nell's. I swear, sometimes it's like those girls are joined at the hip." I paused my fork. "Why?"

"Because after we're finished eating, I want you to do a rune reading to find Adder's killer."

My fork clattered onto my plate.

Ten

"I have it all figured out," Darci said with excitement. "While I'm at the hospital visiting Becca, you can get ready." She leaned forward, pushing her plate to the side. "There's stuff you've got to do, right? Go in a trance or something?"

I rolled my eyes. "Where *do* you get your information about psychics? I don't go into a trance," I said emphatically. "I do have to prepare mentally—center my energy—and a purifying bath helps my concentration. But I don't do a bunch of mumbo-jumbo."

"Sorry." She shrugged a shoulder. "Okay, so you do your thing while I'm at the hospital. When I get back, we'll do the reading."

I picked up my plate and carried it to the sink. "I don't know if I'm supposed to get involved with this."

She stood and crossed over to me. "Why?"

Scraping the leftover eggs down the garbage disposal, I framed my words carefully. "Except for the danger I felt when we walked into your house, I haven't picked anything up, Darci." I thought about the red lights. "The only thing that's popped through has been flashing red lights. It could mean that this time I should stay out of it."

Her face dropped in disappointment. "You're not going to help me." Her voice sounded flat. "Abby? Does she have any insight?"

I shook my head. "Nope. Nothing. Nada. Zip." I turned and placed my hand on Darci's shoulder. "I'm sorry."

Big blue eyes stared back at me with tears threatening to fall. "Danny can't help. You and Abby can't help. What am I going to do?"

I felt my resolve weakening. What would it hurt to do a little reading? Maybe the runes might show something.

She sensed her advantage and pressed. "Please?"

"Darci . . ." I stopped.

A mutinous expression crossed her face. "Okay, be that way." She crossed her arms over her chest. "I've helped you find killers before. I know how to snoop. I'll discover who killed Adder on my own."

Darci looked about as helpless as a new puppy. And people underestimated her. I didn't. I knew if she made up her mind to do something, she'd either accomplish her goal or die trying. Not a good resolution to the problem.

I caved. "Okay. I'll do it," I said with resignation.

"Ophelia," she squealed, throwing her arms around my neck. "Thank you."

I thought of Bill's warning. "Yeah, well, we'll see if you're still thanking me when we're in jail, guests of the county," I grumbled. "I've heard that at least Bill feeds his prisoners well."

She stepped back. "You're so silly," she said with a big grin. "After all, it's only a rune reading."

Two hours later Darci was back and we were in my office. Candles shone from my desk and my bookcases. My collection of crystals caught the candlelight and glowed with the colors of the rainbow. Darci and I—dressed in my white robe—sat in the center of the circle of salt I'd created, facing each other. I unfolded a linen square and placed it between us. A single white candle sat to my left. I held a chunk of unpolished amethyst in my hand to help channel my psychic gift.

With my mind clear, and feeling centered, I watched Darci in the candlelight. "Okay, ask your question."

"Who killed Adder?" she asked in a somber voice.

Picking up the wooden cup holding the runes, I took a deep, cleansing breath and cast the runes on the linen square. For once, they all fell facedown. Moving my finger slowly over the stones, I waited for Darci to tell me to stop.

Her brown wrinkled with concentration. "Stop," she whispered.

I picked up the rune, and as I did, a tingle of energy shot up my arm. After placing the stone to the side in the exact position as it was on the linen square, we repeated the process two more times.

The pattern of the reading would be the three sisters—the Norns. The past, the present, the future. I had thought about doing the more difficult Celtic Cross, using five runes. But although the runes did seem to speak to me, I didn't have enough confidence in my ability to interpret the complicated cross pattern correctly.

Scooping up the remaining runes, I put them back in their worn leather pouch that had been their home for decades.

I moved the runes once again, this time placing them directly in front of me, careful not to switch their positions. Flipping the first one—the past—over.

"Perthro," I said, pronouncing it phonetically: *Perth-row*.

Ah yes, I'd seen that one before. Magick, the occult. It had turned up many times in my readings. No surprise, given my folk magick heritage. Only this time the glyph was reversed—murk stave, according to my great-grandmother's journal. It looked like a cup with the opening turned to the left. I frowned. Not good.

Darci watched me with a somber expression. "What?" she said, noticing my frown.

"Hmm," I said, studying the rune. "Not the best since it's facing the wrong way."

A fearful look crossed Darci's face.

I briefly touched her knee in reassurance. "It's okay, considering that we're dealing with a murder. When placed in this position, it means disappointment, dangerous secrets. Things are hidden and not what they appear to be."

She seized on my last remark. "'Things not what they appear to be,' it's got to mean Becca didn't kill him."

"Not necessarily," I said, hating to burst her bubble. "It can also represent the occult, magick, but since it's turned wrong, it would mean bad magick." I scratched my head. "I don't see how that plays into the question, but maybe the other stones will clarify the meaning."

I turned over the next rune representing the present. "Tiwaz." Again I pronounced it as the rune sounded: *Teawawz.*

I faltered. Another rune upside down. Tiwaz looks like an arrow, and the point was down. So far this reading was negative. Not a good sign for Becca.

Darci picked up on my hesitation. "Another bad one?"

"It's not bad." I vacillated. "Tiwaz, right side up, can represent justice—"

"But," Darci broke in, "it's upside down. So does it represent injustice?"

"Maybe. It's also a masculine sign, and since it's pointing down, it would mean the man *is not* a good one."

"Well, Adder was involved in the biker gang. And if half the stories are true, they're definitely not good men."

"True. Let's see what the last rune is." I flipped it over.

"Jera." *Yare-awe.* I studied the glyph. "Well, at least Jera has no reverse. That's good. It means 'harvest.' But just as one can't force the seeds from the ground, one can't force Jera."

"That's a pretty oblique statement." Darci sounded irritated.

"Sorry." I sighed, trying to think of a better way to explain. "A harvest is ready in its season, after a lot of hard work. When the time is right. And it's a reaping of what's been sowed, sort of."

She looked puzzled.

"Okay, look at it this way—if you plant weeds, you're going to get weeds—"

"But if you sow flowers, you'll get flowers." Her face lightened. "You get what you deserve based on your past." She wrinkled her nose. "Does that mean Adder's murder was justified?"

"No." I shook my head. "No, I don't think Jera means that in this case. I can't imagine the runes indicating that anyone should be murdered. I think it represents justice—hard won justice." My eyes were drawn back to Perthro. The stone seemed to glow from the inside. I felt my lids slowly drift shut. Playing before my closed eyes, I saw the shining cup flip and cascade blood onto an arrow pointing down.

My eyes flew open. "I've got it. The answer lies in Adder's past. Find out his secrets and you'll find justice."

Eleven

Sunday morning, after Darci left to pick up Becca at the hospital, I pulled my hair back in a scrunchy and got dressed. Wearing jeans and an old sweatshirt, I was ready to face the day. I hurried out of the house and jumped in the car to fetch Tink from Nell's. I hadn't had a chance to talk to Abby yesterday, but I'd already spoken with her on the phone. A detour to her house before returning home would work. Plus, she'd informed me she had a surprise for Tink.

After I picked Tink up, she looked somber while I explained we were stopping by Abby's. Dark shadows circled her violet eyes, and she seemed listless, worn-out.

"You look tired," I said with a quick glance. "Did you stay up all night?"

"No. I don't feel good. Do I have to go to Abby's with you?" she asked in a weary voice.

"Yes. She said she has something to show you." I stole a swift look at her. "Think you're coming down with a cold?"

"No."

"Does your stomach hurt?"

"No."

"Do you have a headache?"

"No." From out of the corner of my eye I saw her face turn a pale pink. "If you must know, I'm having cramps."

"Oh, ahh, well—" I stuttered.

She slunk down in the seat. "Nell had what I needed."

"Okay, well, that's good. I think I have some over the counter stuff at home that will help with the cramps."

"It's okay. I already took some at Nell's," she said in a short voice.

"Since you don't feel good, Abby would understand if I dropped you off."

She sighed. "No. I don't want to hurt her feelings."

"She wouldn't be upset."

"That's okay. We won't stay long, will we?"

"No, I promise. Let Abby show you her surprise, then we'll go home. I think I've got a heating pad somewhere. It might help."

"Okay," she mumbled.

A few minutes later we were driving up Abby's long lane, past the gardens. Straight green rows of Abby's sweet corn, tomatoes, squash, and pumpkins grew in the rich black soil. Vegetables to be sold in the coming months to anxious customers.

She stood on her wide front porch, waiting for us. Dressed in one of her old flannel shirts, jeans, and clogs, excitement seemed to float around her. Her hands were clutched in front and it was as if she could barely stand still. A big grin lit her face.

"Hello," she said as soon as we got out of the car. She held out an arm to Tink.

Tink flew up the walk to Abby and received a big hug and a peck on the cheek.

After giving me the same, she looked at Tink with her

eyes sparkling with mischief. "I have a surprise for you in the kitchen."

Tink perked up immediately, and the listlessness that had hung around her earlier seemed to dissipate. "Really?" she asked, shifting from one foot to the other.

"Yes," Abby said, throwing an arm around her shoulder, then leading her down the hallway into the kitchen.

I followed a few steps behind them. Taking a deep breath, I inhaled the same smells that always greeted me when I walked into Abby's house. Wood smoke, coffee, drying herbs, beeswax candles—it smelled like . . . like . . . home. The worry that I'd felt over the past couple of days drifted away and was replaced by a sense of peace.

Abby led Tink over to a cardboard box sitting by the old cook stove.

Curled up in the box with its round, little tummy full, lay a black and white spotted puppy.

Before I could question Abby about this new addition to her household, Tink shrieked.

"A puppy!" she exclaimed. "Is it for me?"

Abby, her face bright with love, nodded.

Startled by all the commotion, the puppy lifted its head, and with round brown eyes stared at a spot over Tink's shoulder.

I turned to see what the puppy found so fascinating, but nothing was there.

The dog's gaze traveled to Tink. It scrambled to its feet and barked furiously in short, high-pitched yips.

Tink pulled back and her face dropped in disappointment. "I don't think he likes me."

"Nonsense," Abby said, bending down and picking it up. "He was just surprised to see you." She stroked the dog's short black and white fur, murmuring soft words to him.

The puppy's yelps settled down to pitiful whimpers.

Abby handed the dog to Tink. "Here. Why don't you take him out back and you can get to know each other," she said with a smile of encouragement.

Tink hesitantly took the puppy from her arms and slowly petted him as she walked out the back door.

Once I heard the back screen safely slam shut, I turned to Abby. "Why didn't you ask me about the puppy?"

She waved my concerns away and crossed to the coffee-pot on the stove. "Every child should have a pet."

Sitting down at the table, I watched her pour two cups and bring them to the table. "Abby, we already have Queenie and Lady."

"But they're your pets—"

"Lady's very attached to Tink," I interjected.

"Yes, but this puppy is hers. Something of her own." She took a sip of coffee.

I sat back in my chair and crossed my arms. "Doesn't seem to me that they're off to a very good start. The dog didn't like Tink."

"Don't be silly. She startled him, that's all."

I could see my objections were falling on deaf ears. And unless I wanted to make a big stink about it, it looked like I was stuck with a new dog. The peace that I'd felt earlier slipped away.

"Please tell me he's house broken?"

She smiled.

"Oh, that's just great," I exclaimed. "When do you suggest I find the time to train a dog?"

"You'll manage."

Her cavalier attitude about the dog irritated me. "I really think you should've asked me about the dog first," I grumbled.

She sipped her coffee again. "They'll bond. Don't worry about it."

Letting the subject of the dog go, I looked over my shoulder at the back door. "We can't stay long. Tink's having cramps, and I need to—"

Abby shot out of her chair before I could finish and walked over to the cupboards, where she removed a small packet of herbs. Crossing to the table, she placed them in front of me. "Here. Make her a tea out of this."

I opened the packet and sniffed. Yuck. I remembered that aroma from when I was a girl. Abby made me drink it whenever I felt crampy. *Ooh—nasty stuff*. I shuddered.

I slid the packet away from me. "She's already taken over the counter meds at Nell's."

Abby's mouth twisted in disapproval. "The junk they sell at drugstores is no good. Tink doesn't need a bunch of manufactured chemicals in her system." She moved the packet back in front of me.

It looked like I'd lost this battle, too. We were getting into some real boundary issues here. In fact, Abby was starting to remind me of Margaret Mary Jensen, my dear mother, safely retired with my father in Florida, two thousand miles away. It wasn't that I didn't love my mother—I did, with all my heart. But she never did understand the meaning of "back off." I was beginning to see where she got it.

I knew it wouldn't do any good to fight with Abby, so I grudgingly picked up the packet and swallowed my words.

A satisfied expression crossed her face and she resumed her place at the table.

"Look, I need to talk to you before Tink comes back," I said with a hurried glance at the back door. "Are you sensing anything at all to do with this Adder's murder?"

"No."

I quickly told her about my rune reading for Darci.

"What are you going to do?" Abby asked.

Swirling the coffee round and round in my cup, I stared at the dark swirls. "I don't know. I can't very well tell Bill to check into Adder's past."

"Wouldn't that be part of their investigation anyway?"

"I don't know." I tugged at my lip. "I've got the feeling they think they've already found their killer, so I don't know how hard they'll check into other possibilities."

"But what can you do about it?"

Looking up at Abby, I shrugged. "I suppose I could try and find the waitress we talked with at The Viper's Nest. Ask her what she knows about Adder."

Abby sat back in her chair. "Do you think she'll tell you anything?"

"It's worth a shot."

Abby leaned forward and watched me intently. "As sorry as I am to say this, have you considered that maybe Bill's right?"

I frowned. "You mean that Becca *did* kill him?"

"Yes," she said, weighing her words. "Maybe the runes meant that a secret in Becca's past led her to commit the crime."

Her words didn't ring true with me. "No, Tiwaz indicates a male. I think the rune was indicating Adder, not Becca."

"Maybe the actions of another man, a bad man, led Becca to do what she did?"

I looked at her in surprise. "You think she did it, too, don't you?"

"It is what it is," she replied sadly.

Her fatalistic approach grated on my nerves. "Abby, it will crush Darci if you're right. We owe—"

The back door slamming stopped me. Tink entered the

kitchen carrying the whimpering puppy. "Abby, he won't stop crying." Her brow was wrinkled with distress.

Abby held out a hand to Tink. "He'll be okay after he gets to know you. Just talk to him and play with him."

"Okay," she said, not disguising her doubts.

We left Abby in the kitchen and walked out to the car. The puppy squirmed and whimpered, but settled down after the car started. He curled up in a ball in Tink's lap and slept. Maybe Abby was right after all.

I had just pulled in the driveway when the engine clunked, sputtered, and quit running.

Peachy. Crying puppies, murder, an interfering grandmother, and now a dead car.

Twelve

I stomped up the walk, while Tink followed me with the wiggling puppy. Pete's Garage was the only place in town that did repairs, but today was Sunday and it wasn't open. I would have to wait until tomorrow morning to call and have my car towed. That left me with the problem of how I was going to make it to the library the next morning. Guess I'd be walking.

Queenie and Lady were waiting for us at the door when I opened it. The puppy took one look at the two of them and wiggled so vigorously, Tink lost her grip on his fat little body. He dropped to the floor, immediately righted himself and began yapping. He bounced on his tiny feet as his high-pitched yips echoed through the house, reminding me of one of those annoying wind-up toys.

Queenie didn't care for the intruder in her realm. She arched her back till her black fur ridged down her spine. Her green eyes narrowed into slits and she emitted a low rumbling growl.

Lady, bewildered by all the commotion, looked first at Queenie, then at the yapping puppy. Cocking her head, she watched the two of them square off. When the puppy's bouncing brought him too close to Queenie, Lady had had enough. With one loud bark, she silenced the both of them.

A look of surprise crossed the now silent puppy's face, and a yellow puddle appeared at his feet.

"No!" I yelled. "Bad dog, bad dog."

He glanced at me with frightened eyes and took off down the hall, with Tink in hot pursuit.

"Catch him before he has another accident," I called after her.

Queenie, satisfied that she'd vanquished the stranger, strolled sedately into the living room and curled up in her favorite spot by the window.

Lady gave me a look that seemed to say, "Hey, I tried." She joined Queenie in the living room, lying down a short distance away. With a sigh, she put her head on her paws and shut her eyes, too tired to deal with the situation.

I watched the puddle spreading across the floor. Swearing under my breath, I marched into the kitchen, grabbed the paper towels and the spray cleaner from underneath the sink. Back in the hall and on my knees, I swiped at the puddle. Dang it, Abby, why couldn't you just mind your own business? I thought, my temper boiling. I took my frustration out on the spray bottle, squirting the floor till the bottle was empty.

Oh, for the good old days. Life was simpler—no teenage angst, no piddling puppies, no friends with murderous cousins. I ripped another paper towel off the roll. A movement beside me startled me out of my thoughts. Tink was on her knees beside me.

"I couldn't find him," she said with an unhappy frown. "I'm sorry he made a mess." Tearing off her own towel, she scrubbed the floor with quick, jerky movements. "I don't know why the puppy doesn't like me. I guess he thinks I'm weird, just like everybody else."

Poor Tink. First she was catching crap at school, and now her own dog didn't like her. I sat back on my heels. When I was a child, my mother would drag out a self-help parenting book that was popular at the moment. She'd scan through it, searching for the answer to whatever problem she had with me. Wonder if there were any books now that explained how to handle a teenage medium with low self-esteem? The thought made me smile.

I gave Tink a playful shove. "Hey, we can't keep calling him 'the puppy.' Do you have a name for him?"

"I don't know," she said, staring at the floor.

"You know names are important. Abby says animals live up to their names." I waved toward Queenie and Lady. "Just look at them. Queenie thinks she rules all she surveys. And Lady's polite and well-mannered. What name do you think will fit your dog?"

Her face cleared and she gave a mischievous look at the wet paper towels piled beside us.

"No," I said, smiling, "don't go there. We don't want to encourage this kind of behavior."

Her lips twitched. "Okay, how about 'Chicken'? He's scared of everything."

I laughed. "No, we don't want to reinforce that, either. How about something brave?"

"Bruiser, Crusher, Fang," Tink said, rattling off macho sounding names. She shook her head. "No, those don't fit, either. For now I'm just going to call him 'T.P.'"

"T.P.?"

"Yeah, 'The Puppy.' Maybe after I get to know him better, I'll come up with a better name."

I looked over my shoulder. "Speaking of which, we'd better find him."

Tink and I scooped up the paper towels, wrapped them

in plastic, and disposed of them in the garbage. After washing our hands thoroughly with soap and water, we wandered around the house calling for the puppy. Lady and Queenie joined the hunt.

I was searching my office in the back of the house when I heard Tink call from upstairs.

"Ophelia, you'd better come here."

I flew up the stairs to find Tink, Lady, and Queenie gathered at the door to the bathroom. Peering around Tink, I saw the floor was littered with itsy-bitsy pieces of white paper. It looked like a snowstorm had whirled through the room.

Lying by the stool with a roll of half-eaten toilet paper between his paws, T.P. chewed merrily away.

I pulled a hand through my hair and gave Tink a wry glance. "What did I tell you about names? You've got to think of something else." I looked back at the mess. "And soon."

"I'm sorry, Mr. Carroll. I ordered your book from the regional library, but it's not in yet," I said to the man whose elderly face was becoming redder with each passing moment.

He yanked at the waistband of his pants in disgust, pulling them higher on his bony body.

I turned to Claire, my eyes making a silent plea for her to help me with the fuming Mr. Carroll.

Claire stood at the counter stamping SUMMERSET PUBLIC LIBRARY inside the cover of our newly arrived books and ignored me. Head down, her glasses were perched precariously on the end of her nose while she concentrated on her task. Normally Claire wasn't shy about expressing opinions, but not even she wanted to tackle the irate Mr. Carroll.

Boy, did I miss Darci. Within twenty seconds she would have soothed Mr. Carroll's ruffled feathers and had him away from the counter, interested in another selection. I didn't have Darci's talent. And Claire wasn't about to run interference with him.

"Claire," I said, "have you picked up the mail at the post office yet?"

"Yes," she replied in a clipped voice, keeping her eyes on the book in front of her. "No packages." She snatched up a few of the new books and bustled away from the counter to place them on the shelves.

I lifted my hands helplessly. "Sorry," I said trying to placate Mr. Carroll.

His bushy white eyebrows knitted together in a tight frown. "And just when may I expect my book to be here?"

"Soon. I promise we'll call you when it's in." I tried to keep my tone even, but he was beginning to frazzle me.

"Humph." He hitched up his pants even higher. If he kept at it, pretty soon they'd be under his armpits. He must have thought that if he stood there long enough the book he wanted would miraculously appear on the counter.

"Mr. Carroll, I can't give you something we don't have." I pulled a couple of the books still lying on the counter toward me. "Here's one by Carolyn Hart and one by Jo Dereske. Read these until your book comes in."

He gave the novels a disgruntled look while his mouth curled down. "I don't hold with women authors."

Annoyed, I flipped the books open. I wondered how Jo Dereske's protagonist, Miss Zukas—a no-nonsense librarian, and my personal hero—would handle a grumpy old man like Mr. Carroll. The thought made me smile.

"That's too bad. You're missing out on a lot of wonderful stories," I said, taking the cards out of the pockets and stamping the due date a little harder than necessary on the inside. I shoved the books toward him. "Here," I said tapping on the top book. "This is Carolyn Hart's *Letters from Home*. It won an Agatha Award. Read it."

Done with persnickety old men, I turned away from the counter and spied Edna Walters, with her back toward me, talking with Agnes McPhearson. Edna's head with its tight gray curls leaned in close to Agnes. From over Edna's shoulder I saw Agnes's small brown eyes dart from Edna's face to me and back again. Their voices were hushed and I couldn't pick up what they were saying.

But I didn't need to hear the words. I knew what they were doing. They were going over their plan of attack. They wanted the dirt and they wanted it now. And I was expected to give it to them—everything I knew about Adder's murder. If I didn't make myself scarce, they'd corner me and subject me to a grilling I wouldn't soon forget.

The scene played out it my head.

"How awful for you my dear, stumbling across another body like that."

"Yes. We heard there was a lot of blood?"

"Is it true they were both naked?"

"Darci's cousin is from California, isn't she? You never know what to expect from people out there."

"Were there drugs?"

I shuddered while my eyes raced around the library looking for a place to run. They landed on the school house clock above the door: 11:00 A.M. A little too early to leave for lunch. I tapped my chin. Claire had been to the post office, so I couldn't use that as an excuse to leave.

Suddenly Edna and Agnes turned, and in unison they began to hobble toward me. Edna's walker thudded along in front of them, and with each thud, I saw my avenue of escape diminish.

The stairs. Edna couldn't make it down the stairs with her

walker. "Claire, I'll be in my office," I called out in a hurried voice while I flew around the counter, then beat it down the stairs.

Once safely in my office, away from the inquiring minds of Agnes and Edna, I leaned against the closed door in relief. If I had to be holed up in my office for the rest of the day, I might as well tackle the bar coding project. Going to my desk, I removed my jacket and booted up the computer. When it had finished, my eyes were immediately drawn to the Internet icon on the computer's desktop.

The runes had indicated that the answer to the murder lay in the past. Becca's past, as Abby thought, or Adder's? My knowledge of biker gangs would fill less than a page. Nothing in my life up to that point had taught me anything about them. Thank goodness. But now I needed information. I clicked on the Internet and typed in *outlaw biker gangs*. Thousands of Web sites were listed. Too many.

I typed in *El Serpiente*. Not so many. I opened the first—an old story from the archives of a newspaper in California. The story told of extortion, prostitution, turf wars, and murder. The gang had had such a hold on several counties in the state that the governor appointed a special task force to investigate. Finally, one of the leaders was murdered by a rival gang. The ones responsible for the killing were currently serving time in a federal prison. I printed out the story.

The name of the rival gang was "The Rogues." I typed that name in next and went to the first link—another news article.

This one told of two teen hitchhikers who were last seen alive being picked up by three Rogue gang members. Their bodies were found two weeks later in another state. The same task force charged the three bikers who'd picked up the girls with murder. They, too, were found guilty and sentenced to a federal facility.

A grainy black and white picture accompanied the story. Squinting my eyes, I studied the picture of the three men. They all wore shaggy beards that obscured the lower part of their faces. Stringy hair hung around their shoulders. Their hands were cuffed in front of them, and they had what appeared to be matching tattoos on their forearms. I leaned forward as I tried to make out the tattoos, but the picture was too blurry to distinguish them.

Again I hit Print. I picked up a pen and tapped it on the desktop while I waited. Who were these people? And why had they picked Summerset? Did they think we were a bunch of country rubes, too stupid to catch on to their illegal activities?

In the distance, I heard the noon whistle. Lunchtime. My car was at Pete's Garage, so I had no way to run home and eat. Instead, I could catch Ned at *The Courier.* I wanted to hear his opinion about the news articles I'd found.

Tossing the pen on my desk, I shoved the articles into my bag, hurried up the stairs and out of the building. The two eating places in Summerset—Joe's Café, doing a booming lunchtime business as usual, and Stumpy's—were down the street from the library. Not wanting to stop and engage in conversation, I walked quickly by Joe's with my head down and ignored the cars lining the street. I'd almost passed Stumpy's when I walked straight into a solid body. My bag swung off my arm at the impact and hit the sidewalk. Its contents scattered at my feet.

With my eyes never leaving my dumped bag, I crouched quickly to gather my stuff. My hand hovered over the news articles and I raised my head long enough to mutter an apology to whomever I bumped into. I did a double take.

It was the biker named Cobra.

A sudden gust ruffled the pages, and before I could grab them, the newspaper articles skittered away from me. I watched Cobra take two steps and slam a booted foot down to prevent them from blowing under a nearby car. He reached down and picked up the pages.

Still kneeling on the sidewalk, I watched helplessly as he leaned against the hood of the car and skimmed the articles.

I shot to my feet and stared at him defiantly. "Those belong to me," I said, stretching out my hand.

He said nothing, but held up the pages with a challenging look.

My anger got the best of me and I stomped over to him. Grabbing the pages out of his hands, I pivoted on my heel and headed for the newspaper office. As I walked, I felt the hair on the back of my neck prickle, and I fought the desire to look over my shoulder. Clutching my bag and the pages tightly to my body, my pace quickened. I all but ran down the block and across the street. Finally, when I was safely at the door to *The Courier,* I allowed myself a furtive look.

Cobra had moved from the car to his motorcycle. His long legs were stretched out in front of him as he rested against the bike. His arms were crossed over his chest and his eyes, cold and gray, stared straight at me.

Thirteen

"What?" Ned looked at me in surprise as I stumbled through the door of *The Courier*. "The devil on your heels?"

I released the death grip on my bag and gave him a shaky smile. "You could say that." I scanned the room. All of his staff seemed busy, but . . . I jerked my head in the direction of his private office. "May I talk to you for a minute?"

A puzzled look crossed Ned's face. "Sure," he said, motioning toward the back.

Once in his office, he sank into the cushy chair behind his desk while I seated myself across from him. Without a word, I handed him the crumpled pages and watched while his eyes traveled quickly down one of them and then went on to another. His jaw clenched as he continued to read in silence. A couple of times he stopped and flipped back to a previous page, his eyes narrowing as he reread the words, and he'd shake his head sadly. Finished, he laid the pages down and studied my face. "Find these articles on the Internet?"

I nodded. "You said these gangs are a cancer. I guess you were right."

Ned leaned back in his chair. "I've read more, and worse,

stories than these," he said in an even voice. An angry look crossed his face as his eyes fell to a folded piece of paper lying on the corner of his desk. "I even thought about running a couple of them, but I couldn't get permission to reprint."

"Ned, why are they in Summerset?"

"I wish I knew, Ophelia." Leaning forward, he clasped his hands on top of the desk. "We do sit close to the east-west interstate, and we have the north-south blacktop that connects to two other major highways running across the state—"

"Transportation?" I said, butting in.

"Yeah, from Summerset a drug drop can easily be moved north, south, east, or west."

"So Summerset might be 'drug' central?"

"It's a possibility."

"Bill said there's nothing they can do right now."

Ned spread his hands wide. "Without probable cause . . ."

"They can't get warrants," I finished for him.

"Right."

I scooted to the edge of my chair. "What about Percy Gordon's death? Do you think it was really a suicide?"

Ned tugged at his lip. "If I share something with you, do you promise to keep quiet about it?"

I made a cross over my heart and raised my hand. "I swear."

"There were auditors at the bank last Monday. They found a shortage of several thousand dollars."

"Percy embezzling?" I asked in a shocked voice. "He was so quiet, so unobtrusive. I can't imagine him doing something illegal."

Ned spread his hands again. "People do crazy things when they're desperate."

"But how could Percy be in financial trouble? He always seemed to me to lead a modest life."

"Seemed that way to me, too, but for some reason his credit cards were maxed out, and he'd taken out a second mortgage on his house."

"Why?"

"No one knows. Maybe he was into drugs, or gambling. I heard through the rumor mill he'd been seen at The Viper's Nest several times."

"Percy had a tie to El Serpiente?" I was incredulous. The idea of mild mannered Percy hanging with bikers blew my mind. My eyes fell to the papers lying on Ned's desk. "These articles mention extortion as a gang's favorite money-maker," I said, tapping the pages. "Do you think someone at The Viper's Nest was blackmailing Percy? Edna did mention some kind of confrontation at the convenience store."

Ned leaned back and folded his arms. "Could be. It's all supposition right now. I've tried untangling all these rumors, but all I get from Bill is 'No comment.'"

"In your opinion, could Percy's death be tied to Adder's murder in any way?" I asked, rubbing my chin thoughtfully.

"Wait a second, Slugger." He sat forward in alarm. "I see where you're going with this. I know you want to help Darci, but stay out of it."

"That's what everyone keeps telling me," I grumbled.

"They're right. You warned me to be careful. Take your own advice. Let Bill and Brett handle this. That's what I'm doing now." His eyes fell to the folded piece of paper on the corner of the desk again.

"What do you mean?"

His eyes returned to me. "As much as it goes against the grain, I'm backing off on the editorials for a while."

"That's not like you, Ned."

He exhaled slowly. "You're right, but Bill asked me to while they're investigating the murder. He's afraid I'll add fuel to an already hot fire. He's worried about vendettas."

A chill ran up my arm. "What? Someone in town starting one, or the bikers?"

"The bikers—"

"Wait a second," I interjected. "Are you saying there's a possibility that they might go after Becca?"

"Two things are important to these guys—their bikes and the brotherhood." Ned picked up the news articles and waved them at me. "You think these are bad? I read a story about a woman who, according to informants, disrespected the leader of one of these gangs. Not El Serpiente, but a gang like them. She wound up in a swamp in Florida, cut up in little pieces." He tossed the pages down. "If they'd do that to a woman for insulting a brother, what would they do to a woman for *killing* a brother?"

"But if Becca didn't do it . . ." I paused.

"I don't imagine they'd worry about 'innocent until proven guilty,' do you?" he asked with cynicism.

"No, no, I don't suppose they would," I stuttered while I mulled over what Ned was suggesting. "Do you know if Bill or Brett will put Becca in protective custody?"

"They might, if the situation gets worse."

How much worse could it be? Unexplained suicides, unsolved murders, hints of extortion and drugs? The chill I'd felt earlier seemed to wrap around me with icy fingers. And in my mind, the flashing red lights beat with a relentless rhythm.

The afternoon wore on slowly, and I couldn't shake the anxiety Ned's words had caused. Staring blankly at the computer screen in my office, I thought about his warnings. If El Serpiente targeted Becca for revenge, who else might be caught in the cross fire? Georgia? Darci? And what could I do to help protect them? As a psychic, it seemed I should be able to pick up on something—some clue, some hint—but all I could see in my mind were the flashing lights. Picking up a pen and clicking it rapidly, I pondered what significance red lights might have. *Stop; danger; warning.* Not exactly an enlightening message. Disgusted, I tossed the pen on my desk and grabbed the phone. A minute later I had Darci on the line.

"How's it going?" I asked.

"Fine." Her voice sounded tired. "Becca's sleeping right now, and we're still waiting for a call with the results from the urine and blood tests . . ." Her voice trailed off.

"Has Danny been by?"

"Yes, last night and again this morning. He's out of the investigation, you know."

"That's probably just as well, Darce," I said gently.

"Yeah, well." Her sigh sounded softly in my ear. "I was hoping Danny would help prove Becca's innocence."

"I know you were, but it will be better if Bill or the DCI discover the truth." I hesitated. "Has anyone said anything about keeping an eye on Becca?"

"You mean has anyone told her not to leave town?"

"Ahh, sort of . . ." I stumbled over my words. "Umm, are there patrol cars driving by?"

"I don't think so." I heard the surprise in Darci's voice. "Why?"

Great, I'd bungled that one. I didn't want to scare her, so how did I answer her question without telling her they could be in danger; that maybe Adder's friends might want to chop up Becca? I quivered at the gruesome image.

A solution flashed in my head. "You know how snoopy

everyone is. And it's all over town that you're staying at Georgia's. People might start dropping by, bothering you, trying to get the inside story. A car patrolling the street might deter them."

"Oh, I never thought about that," Darci exclaimed. "I'm supposed to call Bill when Becca wakes up. I'll mention the idea to him then."

"Great," I replied, trying to mask the relief in my voice.

Darci cut in. "What are the town gossips saying?"

Another question I didn't want to answer. "I don't know," I fabricated. "I've spent most of the day working on that dang bar coding program and getting chewed out by Mr. Carroll."

Darci giggled. "What else is new? You'll never please Mr. Carroll."

"Yeah, I know," I complained. "I wish that you'd been there to handle him. I—"

"Just a second," Darci broke in.

I heard muffled voices in the background while I waited for her to come back on the phone.

A minute later she returned. "I've got to go. Becca's awake now."

"Take care, okay?"

"I will. I'll call you later. I want to go over the rune thing again."

Darci hung up without hearing my groan.

By the time I finished working on the bar coding project, Claire had closed the library and I had the building to myself. I looked around my office at my pictures on the shelves; Abby, Tink, my parents, all stared happily at me from their frames. A couple of crystals, one for concentration and one for protection, sparkled in the fluorescent light. This was my space, and except for one night a year ago, I'd always felt safe here. But tonight feelings of security seemed to elude me. I felt antsy, as if something unknown hung over my shoulder, waiting to pounce.

Don't be a ditz, Jensen. You're letting tales of murder and dismembered bodies get to you. Right now the town's crawling with law enforcement—the DCI, county deputies, police officers. A person would have to be some kind of stupid to try anything now.

Rolling my shoulders, I tried to loosen my feelings of apprehension. I grabbed my backpack and headed out of my office and the library. Outside the building, I stood on the steps and took a deep breath of fresh air. The tension I'd felt leeched out of me.

It was a beautiful evening. The setting sun hung over the limestone buildings of Main Street, bathing them in a golden, mellow light. Shiny green leaves whispered in the faint breeze that carried with it the spicy scent of spring flowers.

I inhaled again. Abby was helping out Arthur with the supper crowd and had suggested I stop by after work. She said she'd give me a ride home, but the evening was so fresh, so clean, that I decided I'd rather walk home. Locking the door and swinging my backpack over my shoulder, I took off at a brisk pace.

The sun sank lower and shadows stretched across my path. I was only a couple blocks from my house when I heard a familiar growl in the distance, getting closer and closer. Images of the murdered teenage girls in California drifted into my consciousness and my edginess came crashing back.

Lowering my head, I walked faster as the rumbling bike drew alongside of me and slowed. Only one more block, I thought, fighting the urge to flee. The image of the young girls was quickly replaced with how I must have looked scurrying down the street.

No. I wasn't going to allow whoever was on that bike to scare me. I'd spent five years living in fear after Brian's death, and I wasn't going to do it again.

Lifting my chin, I ignored the biker and slowed my steps to a normal gait. Suddenly, the bike keeping pace with me roared to life and sped down the street.

Over the snarl of the engine, Cobra's laugh drifted on the light breeze.

Fourteen

By the time I reached my front porch, my heart had slowed to its normal rate. After rummaging through the backpack for my keys, I inserted them in the door. It wasn't locked.

Great. Tink had forgotten to lock the door when she left for the soccer meet. I made a mental note to talk to her about home safety as I opened the door.

Garbage lay from one end of the hall to the other. Shredded paper towels, used coffee filters, bits of chewed plastic. I picked my way over the mess and headed toward the kitchen. The culprit lay in the living room with one of my favorite shoes in his mouth, gnawing away. Lady and Queenie, from their respective distance, watched in fascination as he destroyed the shoe.

"Bad puppy," I shrieked, heading for T.P.

At the sound of my voice, Lady and Queenie beat a hasty retreat for the back of the house, while T.P. yelped and scrambled to his feet. He rushed past me toward the kitchen and the safety of his crate.

Fisting my hands on my hips, I surveyed the disaster. Who should I yell at first? I wondered. Tink for not shutting the door on the crate? Abby for giving us the dog in the first place? T.P. for acting like a puppy?

A low growl sounded in my throat as my anger boiled. Dropping my backpack, I marched into the kitchen and ripped a garbage bag off the roll under the sink. On the periphery I saw T.P. watching from his crate.

He whimpered once and put his head on his paws. Big brown eyes stared at me dejectedly.

"You'd better be sorry," I said, shaking my finger at him.

A soft whine changed my anger to guilt. It wasn't his fault the door to his crate had been left open.

I put the bag on the counter and sat cross-legged on the floor in front of him. Sensing the change in my mood, he scurried out of his crate and onto my lap. Propping his short legs on my chest, his wet pink tongue lashed out at my chin, while his stubby tail wiggled in delight.

Grasping his round body, I settled him on my lap. "Okay, you're forgiven," I said, stroking his soft fur. "Not your fault the door wasn't shut, right?"

I heard the front door open and shut.

"Oh no," came a voice from the hall.

At the sound, T.P. scampered off my lap and back into his crate.

A second later Tink stood in the kitchen doorway. "How did *he* get out?"

Frowning, I looked up at her. "I don't know. You tell me."

"But," her eyes flew from the dog crate to the mess in the hallway, "I shut the door."

"Then how did he get loose?" I stood and handed her the garbage bag.

Tink's head dropped and her eyes focused on a spot on the floor. "I don't know."

"You also forgot to lock the front door," I said sternly.

"No, I didn't," she mumbled, her eyes still fixed on the floor.

"Look, Tink, I want you to have fun, to be able to go places with Nell, but you have to be responsible." I took a step closer. "I can't—" Catching the distinct smell of cigarette smoke, I stepped back and crossed my arms over my chest. "Where have you been?"

Her head jerked up and she stared at me. "With Nell," she replied in a defiant voice. "Her dad gave me a ride home from the soccer game."

"Does he smoke?"

"No."

I sniffed and again smelled cigarettes. "Have you been smoking?" My voice rang with shock.

"No." Tink turned away and stomped into the hallway. She squatted and began to shove the strewn garbage into the bag.

I followed her. "Tink, you smell like cigarette smoke."

She stopped for a moment and smelled the sleeve of her jacket. "No, I don't."

I crossed over to her and, bending down, inhaled deeply. The stale smell of smoke was gone.

"I could've sworn I smelled smoke," I muttered in a puzzled voice.

Violet eyes looked at me like I was crazy.

Maybe she was right. Maybe I was finally losing it and beginning to see and smell things that weren't there.

"Okay, that's it." I reached down and pulled Tink to her feet.

"What?"

"Leave the bag," I said, taking the sack out of her hand and giving it a toss. "This trash has been lying here all day—

an hour more won't make a difference." With a tiny push, I headed her in the direction of the kitchen. "Get the leash I bought for T.P., and bring Lady's, too, while you're at it."

"Ophelia, what are you doing?" Now she really did think I'd gone nuts.

I crossed to where Tink stood in the kitchen doorway. Placing my hands on her shoulders, I looked into her troubled eyes. "Tink, for the past week it's been nothing but one thing after another. And I don't know about you, but I'm sick of worrying and waiting for the next catastrophe. We're taking the dogs and going for a walk. We'll stop at Joe's, get an order to go, and eat it in the park."

"But it's dark outside."

I squeezed her shoulders. "So? We'll take a candle."

The corner of her mouth twitched as she tried to mask her grin. "People will think we're crazy, having a picnic by candlelight."

"Honey, people have thought that about me for years," I said with a wink.

Her grin widened into a smile. "Okay, let's go."

T.P. whined when Tink pulled him out of his crate, but once the leash was attached to his collar and we were outside, his whining ceased and he sniffed the air in anticipation. Lady, after giving the puppy a long suffering look, took the lead, and off we went down the street.

The evening was beautiful. Above the old-fashioned streetlights, a thousand stars lit the heavens. A full moon hung dead center over Main Street like a huge orange ball in the night sky. As we walked, I shared with Tink all the folklore Abby had taught me over the years about the moon signs.

"Look." I pointed at the moon. "See the faint ring around it? I think it means rain will come soon."

"Abby plants by the moon signs, doesn't she?"

"Umm-hmm. When the moon is more than half full and waxing, she sows seeds for plants that grow aboveground, like tomatoes, green beans, squash. But if they grow below-ground like potatoes and carrots, she sows the seeds right after the full moon, when it's waning."

Tink tugged on T.P.'s leash. "That seems kind of silly."

I lifted a shoulder. "Oh, I don't know, it seems to work for her. Her vegetables always win blue ribbons every year at the county fair."

"Does she really talk them out of the ground?" Tink asked skeptically.

I turned to her in surprise. "What do you mean?"

"Abby told me plants are living things and you need to treat them kindly. And I've watched her walking around the greenhouse murmuring to the seedlings."

"With Abby, who knows," I said with a laugh. "It wouldn't surprise me. I know she talks to her bees, and she's got this strange thing going with animals . . ." I paused for a moment. "It's like she communicates with them, too." I shrugged again. "I don't know. As a girl, she learned a lot of things in the mountains. Things that I don't understand yet."

"Do you think you can do that?"

"Do what?"

"Talk seeds out of the ground?"

"What? Me croon over the chrysanthemums?" I asked, laughing again, and gave her a playful nudge. "I don't think so."

"Have you ever tried?"

"No, and I'm not planning on it. I'm having a hard enough time with what I can do."

Tink toyed with the end of T.P.'s leash. "What exactly are your talents? You never talk about them much."

"Ah, well . . ." I hesitated. "I've spent most of my life trying to ignore them, but they seem to be mostly clairvoyant and precognitive—"

"You see stuff?" she asked, breaking in.

"Yeah—sometimes it's the future, sometimes the past—but most of the time the message comes through as symbols." I watched Lady give T.P. a swat when the puppy tried to nip at her face. "Same thing with the runes, so then I have to figure out what the symbols mean. And I have dreams. But I'm not telepathic."

"You can't read someone's mind?"

"Right."

"And you don't see shadows like I do?" she asked in a small voice.

"No, I don't." I stroked her arm lightly. "Have you been having problems with the shadows, Tink?"

"No," she said, shaking her head quickly. "Every morning I picture the gold light surrounding me, like Abby taught me. The shadows don't like the light, and they leave me alone."

The idea of Tink experimenting on her own without Abby to guide her frightened me. "You haven't tried to let them reach you, have you?"

She kicked a stone lying on the sidewalk. "No."

"Well," I said, watching the moon. "For now, I think that's best. You need Abby to help you. Great-Aunt Mary is a medium like you are, and she lived in the same house as Abby when Abby was growing up. Abby can use that experience to teach you how to handle your talent."

Tink didn't reply.

We stopped and let the dogs inhale what they found to be delectable scents coming from under a neighbor's bushes. T.P. became excited and ran back to Tink with a happy puppy look on his face. He sat up on his hind legs and pawed at her legs.

"See," I said, "Abby was right. T.P. is warming up to you."

Tink bent down and scooped him up. He gave her face a quick swipe with his tongue, then wiggled to be put down. She set him on his feet, and he was off, back to sniffing the ground.

"Maybe, but when we're home, all he wants to do is stay in his crate." She stopped, and I could see the realization of what she'd said cross her face. "Except when he can play in the garbage," she continued with a rueful look. "And he hates it in my room."

I nodded toward the dog. "He's happy now. I know you're busy, with the end of the school year coming up, but if you'd spend more time with him, I think he'd adjust."

"I'll try."

After our impromptu picnic at the park we walked home slowly. Halfway there T.P.'s legs gave out and Tink had to carry him the rest of the way. He curled in a little ball in her arms and fell asleep. Still snoozing when we reached the house, Tink tucked him in his crate, and I checked the catch to ensure that it was fastened.

Together we made short work of cleaning up the remainders of T.P.'s playtime and were off to bed ourselves. An hour later the full moon gleaming in my bedroom window woke me. Unable to sleep with it shining in my eyes, I stumbled to the window to pull the blinds.

As I drew the cord, I gazed up at the sky. The ring around the moon's bright face had turned bloodred.

Fifteen

The next morning, I stumbled down the stairs to once again find T.P. in the living room, chewing on the same shoe as the day before. Standing there watching him, I scratched my head. How was that dog getting out of his crate? I'd checked the catch myself. Maybe a good name for this dog would be Houdini.

I scooped him up and walked out to the backyard in my nightgown. I put him on the ground and waited while he did his necessary business. Finished, he ran back to me and pawed at the air to be picked up. When I entered the kitchen, Tink was standing at the kitchen sink, mowing through a bowl of cereal.

"I'm late," she said, and shoved a spoonful of Cheerios in her mouth.

T.P. saw Tink and twisted in my arms. When I set him down, he scurried back into his crate, his stubby tail tucked down.

Noticing the dog's behavior, Tink arched an eyebrow at me. "See, what did I tell you? He wants to hide in there all the time," she said with a jerk toward the dog.

"He wasn't hiding when I got up. Did you let him out earlier?" I asked, filling the coffeepot with water.

"No. He was out of the crate again?" She rinsed out her bowl and shoved it in the dishwasher.

"Yup. And I checked the catch myself before we went to bed last night." I rolled my eyes. "It must be defective. I'll pick up a new crate at the hardware store today, after I get my car from the garage."

Dang, it seemed everything I touched lately was breaking. The car, the dog crate. What next?

Tink crossed to the kitchen table, opened her backpack and rummaged through it. "Is it okay if I go to Nell's after school? Semesters are next week and we're going to study."

"You're not working at the greenhouse tonight?"

"No. Abby said it was okay since I've got tests coming up." She zipped her bag shut and slung it on her shoulders.

Chewing on my lip, I gazed at her. "Are Nell's parents going to be home?"

"Her mom is," she said, shifting her weight and settling her hand on her hip.

"I guess." I looked away. "Ah, Tink—" I broke off, reluctant to bring up an unpleasant subject. "Are things better at school?"

Her head dropped. "You mean with the three M's?"

"Yeah."

She raised her head and looked at me. "Yes," she said quickly.

I studied her face. It sounded like she was telling the truth, but she had a funny expression around her eyes. Almost as if she was daring me to dispute her.

"Tink—"

At the sound of a car honking in the driveway, Tink's head whipped toward the door. "That's Nell's mom." She rushed over to me and gave me a quick peck on the cheek. "Got to run."

Before I could open my mouth, she rushed out of the kitchen. A minute later I heard the screen door slam.

I'd finished making the coffee and was in my bedroom, getting dressed, when I heard a voice call out.

"Knock, knock. Anyone home?"

Abby.

"Help yourself to some coffee," I hollered from the top of the stairs. "I'll be down in a minute."

I checked myself out quickly in the mirror. A little mascara, hair in a twist, T-shirt, and khaki pants. This was as good as it was going to get. After slipping on a pair of loafers, I hurried out of the room and down the stairs.

Abby sat hunched over by the kitchen table, laughing, with a cup of coffee in front of her. In her hand she held the end of my chewed-up shoe. T.P. had the other end in his mouth and was pulling for all he was worth. He shook his head, and as he did, he growled.

"Oh yeah, you're tough, aren't you?" I said, glancing at the dog and crossing to the coffee maker. After pouring a cup for myself, I joined Abby at the table.

She let go of the shoe, and T.P., happy that he'd won the tug of war, dragged it into his crate and set about adding more teeth marks to the soft leather.

"How's it going with the puppy?" she asked, motioning toward the crate.

"How do you think it's going?" I narrowed my eyes and fixed a look at her. "A puppy who isn't housebroken and chews on everything?"

A chagrined expression crossed her face.

"Did I mention that he also has a fondness for strewing garbage all over the house?" I said in an even tone, and took a sip of coffee.

Abby winced. "Maybe the puppy was a bad idea after all."

"Oh, it's okay," I said with a wave. "We took the dogs for a walk last night and had a good time. He seemed to bond a little with Tink while we were gone, so maybe . . ." I let my voice trail off. "Just have to give it time."

"Last night was a beautiful—"

"Yeah," I cut her off. "Did you see the moon? I pointed it out to Tink."

"You what?" she asked, alarmed.

"I pointed it out to Tink," I said, surprised at her reaction. "In fact, it was so bright, I couldn't sleep after I went to bed. The light hit me right in the face and woke me up. I had to pull the blinds."

"You slept with the moonlight in your face?"

I wrinkled my brow, perplexed at Abby's concern. "Yeah. Until I finally closed the blinds."

"And you pointed at it with your finger?"

Smiling, I sat back in my chair. "Of course with my finger. What else would I point with?"

Abby covered her face with her hands and shook her head. "Have I taught you nothing?" she mumbled into her palms.

Throwing up my hands, I stood and picked up my cup. Crossing to the sink, I took one last swallow and dumped the rest down the drain, then turned and looked at Abby. "I don't understand what the big deal is."

Abby lowered her hands and stared at me. "First you point at the moon, then you let its light shine in your face while you sleep—"

"So?" I interrupted.

"So? So?" she replied in a severe voice. "It's bad luck. Haven't you paid attention to any of the stories I've told you?"

I leaned against the counter and waved a hand, dismissing her words. "Those were just old wives' tales."

Abby's eyes narrowed. "Humph. Did you ever think those old *wives* may have been old *witches* who had an understanding of these things?"

"Oh, please," I scoffed.

She tapped her chin thoughtfully. "We need to do a 'banishing.' Maybe a little allspice and some clove."

"I don't want my house smelling like a pumpkin pie," I said indignantly.

"We'll add a few pots of marigolds to be on the safe side," she went on, ignoring me.

"Whoa, time out here." I made a sign like a referee at a football game. "I believe in your magick, Abby, I really do. But I don't believe in all those old superstitions. Come on, spilling salt, walking under a ladder, umbrellas opening in the house, a black cat crossing your path—"

"Black cats aren't unlucky for you." Her voice drowned out my litany of unlucky signs. "You own a black cat, so one crossing your path is a sign of good fortune."

I groaned and wrapped my arms around my chest. "Don't you think we have more important things to worry about? Real, tangible things? Not a bunch of old notions?"

"Like murder?"

"That's a start," I said with sarcasm. "And bikers, and suicides, and extortion, and—"

Abby sighed. "All the more reason to do a banishing."

"I give up." I threw my hands up in the air and changed the subject. "You still haven't picked up on anything?"

"No. And I'm somewhat puzzled by it, too. Usually I at least get a feeling, an inkling, that something's about to happen."

A mad idea flashed through my head. I wondered what

would happen if I took Abby to The Viper's Nest and she "read" one of those tough guys. I knew she could do it—she could pick up on events and emotions by touching people. Her readings always left the subject a little off kilter for a moment or two, though. A chuckle slipped out of me at a ludicrous image that snapped into my mind: a big bad biker, all dressed up in his leathers, with his brain scrambled by my proper grandmother.

I suddenly sobered. If half the stories about the bikers were true, I wouldn't want Abby to see the ugliness inside of them. Scratch that idea. I'd just have to think of another way to help Darci.

Noticing my worried expression, Abby stood and walked over to me. "Ophelia, I think our lack of premonitions means we're to stay out of the situation this time."

"I can't," I said. "Darci's my best friend and she's asked me for help. After I pick up my car tonight, I'm driving to Georgia's to talk to Becca. Maybe I can get a read on what's happening."

Her face tightened. "I don't think that's wise."

"I'm sorry you feel that way, but I'm going to help her, Abby," I said with determination.

Shoving away from the counter, I looked at the clock. Shoot, I was going to be late if I walked to work.

"Abby, can you give me a ride?" I smiled sweetly. "Please?"

Her stern look softened and she nodded.

I'd grabbed my bag and was following Abby out the door to her truck when I remembered a question I had for her.

"Since you're so into superstitions this morning, I thought of another one. A red ring around the moon means rain, right?"

Abby dropped her keys. "A red ring? Not yellow, or hazy?"

Jeez, was Abby suddenly hard of hearing? "Yes, a *red* ring. Means rain, doesn't it?"

"No," she answered slapping her forehead. "It means really *bad* luck."

Whoops. Maybe my house smelling like pumpkin pie wasn't such a terrible idea after all.

Sixteen

After work I caught a ride with Claire to Pete's Garage. When I got out and she drove off, a car sitting in Pete's lot caught my attention and I did a double take. It was Danny's personal vehicle. I recognized it from the nights he'd picked up Darci at the library. Boy, Pete sure was getting a lot of business lately.

I opened the door to the garage and peered inside. No one around. A car with out of state plates sat high in the air on the hoist, but I didn't see Pete or Danny. I stepped over the puddles of grease on the concrete floor and walked to the counter. An old-fashioned bell sat next to the cash register.

I rang the bell twice and was about to call out when Pete and Danny walked out of Pete's office. Pete's face registered surprise when he saw me.

"Hi," I said brightly.

It was Danny who replied. "Oh, hi, Ophelia," he said. "We didn't hear you come in." He pointed back toward the office. "Pete was setting up a time to get my car serviced."

I turned my attention to Pete and cocked my head. There was something different about him but I couldn't put my finger on it. I realized what it was when he reached into the pocket of his shirt and quickly pulled out his heavy glasses. He shoved them on his nose and exchanged a quick look with Danny.

Still smiling, I eyed them both. "What's wrong?" I asked, thinking of my car.

Pete looked at me in puzzlement as he rolled down his shirtsleeves. "Huh?"

"With my car?"

His eyes darted toward Danny again before settling on me. "Oh yeah, the alternator was fried and your battery wasn't charging," he said, walking behind the counter and opening his receipt book. "I put a new one in, so it should be fine now."

I nodded. "Great." I stole a look at Danny.

He stood silently, staring down at the floor.

Narrowing my eyes, I looked from him to Pete and back again. They reminded me of two little boys caught with their hands in the cookie jar.

Danny, perhaps feeling the weight of my stare, raised his head, and a grin flitted across his face before his expression turned serious. "Have you talked to Darci?"

Plopping my bag on the counter, I took out my checkbook. "Yes, as a matter of fact, I'm on my way to Georgia's right now."

"She's determined to prove Becca innocent, isn't she?" he asked in a hard voice.

"Yes," I said. "She loves her cousin, and Darci being Darci, will do whatever it takes to help her."

"I don't care for her attitude." He said the words as if it were up to him to decide how Darci should or shouldn't feel.

I ripped out the check I'd written and handed it to Pete. "Darci's a big girl," I said to Danny, trying not to grind my teeth. "She can decide for herself what she needs to do."

"Maybe." He tugged on his lip as he rested an arm on the counter. "You're not really going to get involved, are you?"

I lifted a shoulder casually.

"I think you should stay out of the investigation, Ophelia." He straightened, and his eyes, staring into mine, were somber.

I slapped my hand on the counter and gave him a cheerful grin. "You know, you're about the fourth person who's told me that. I don't know why everyone thinks I'm such a snoop."

A wry smile twisted the corners of his mouth. "Maybe they have a reason?" The smile vanished. "I know you've helped Bill before—"

"I don't think Bill considered it *helping*," I said, not letting him finish.

"Exactly my point."

The old scar in my side suddenly tingled, reminding me of what happened to amateur sleuths when they butted into police investigations. They get shot. Not as bad as dismemberment, I guess, like what happened to the biker's girlfriend in Florida, but dead's dead, no matter how you get that way.

I stole a look at Pete to gauge his reaction to our conversation.

Little beads of sweat stood out on his forehead. He grabbed a rag lying on the counter and gave his head a quick swipe.

I nudged Danny's arm in a friendly gesture. "Don't worry about it. All I'm doing is looking up background information about El Serpiente on the Internet." Rubbing my side, I smiled confidently. "That's pretty harmless."

"What do you hope to find?" Danny asked.

I thought about the newspaper articles I'd read. "Well, I've already found some stuff. El Serpiente had quite a turf war in California with another gang called The Rogues several years ago. These guys are really into vengeance, right? Maybe Adder's murder is tied to what happened in California."

Danny shook his head in amusement. "Ophelia," he said in a condescending voice. "There are three agencies looking into the murder. Don't you think they already know about an old turf war?"

"I suppose," I muttered.

"And I think you're going to find that's quite a stretch to imagine the two could be tied together. It happened how many years ago?"

"Seventeen," I said, shifting my weight from one foot to the other.

"And where did you say the turf war happened?"

I stared at a spot over his left shoulder. "California."

"And you think it's possible this rival gang tracked El Serpiente to a small town in Iowa and killed Adder to get even for something that happened seventeen years ago?" He watched me squirm as he systematically blew holes in my favorite theory.

I looked down at my feet. "Well, I guess since you put it that way, probably not."

Danny gave me a smug look. "I know you want to help Darci, but pursuing wild theories is just going to give her false hope."

I hid the shock that I felt. Danny not only didn't approve of Darci looking out for Becca, he'd already tried and convicted Becca in his mind.

Pete, who'd been silent through the whole conversation, cleared his throat and looked pointedly at the clock.

"Oh gosh, I'm sorry, Pete," I said, snatching my bag. "We're keeping you, aren't we?"

He mopped his brow again. "Supper is waiting, and I need to help Melinda study for her tests."

I felt a flash of guilt. What kind of mom was I? No supper waiting on the table at home for Tink. And studying? She had to count on Nell for help instead of me. The words *loser, loser* niggled in the corner of my mind.

My lips pressed into a tight smile. "Thanks, Pete," I said, turning away from the counter.

"If you have any problems," he called after me, "let me know."

"I will," I answered over my shoulder.

Danny fell into step beside me. "See you tomorrow, Pete," he said with a wave.

On the way to the car, I asked Danny, "Did you think Pete seemed a little nervous?"

"I don't know. Why do you ask?"

"He was sweating."

Danny chuckled. "Of course he was sweating. He wears those long-sleeve shirts all the time."

"Yeah, I noticed. He's so self-conscious about the scars on his arms. Wonder how he got them?"

"He said something once about sparks from a welder catching his shirt on fire."

I shook my head sadly. "It's too bad they bother him so much. Long-sleeve shirts must be miserable in the summer." I thought for a moment. "Call me crazy, but he really didn't start sweating until we were talking about El Serpiente."

"They're making a lot of people around town nervous, Ophelia."

I scuffed the gravel with the toe of my shoe. "I know they are. Did you know they've been at the garage?"

"How do you know?" Danny asked.

I shoved my hands in my pockets. "I saw them driving by

real slow, then Tink told me Melinda was bragging at school about her dad knowing tough guys."

We'd reached my car, and Danny now leaned against it. "They're probably just looking for someone to work on their bikes. Maybe it makes Pete nervous doing business with them."

The news articles flashed through my mind again. "But what if it's something more?"

He shook his head and crossed his arms over his chest. "Is this another wild theory?"

"Maybe not," I replied defensively. "The articles I read on the Internet said gangs rely on extortion—"

"What would they have on Pete?" Danny cut in. "He's harmless."

"But what if they're running a protection scam?" I asked, warming up to my latest supposition. "They do that, don't they?"

"You mean, 'Pay us money, or something bad will happen to your business'?"

"Yeah." My eyes widened in excitement. "You're a cop. Are there any rumors of them doing that?"

Danny shoved away from my car. "That's not a question I can answer," he replied shortly.

My eyes opened wider. "You didn't say no, Danny."

"No."

"Ha! I don't believe you." I tugged on his jacket. "Maybe they threatened the wrong person, and that person killed Adder."

"Who?" he asked. "Stumpy? Joe? Pete?" He ticked off their names on his fingers.

"No, they'd all come straight to you."

"Right."

Mentally I went up and down Main Street picturing the

businessmen. They were all a pretty average bunch, all law abiding citizens. My face fell.

Danny saw his advantage and pressed his point. "You can't think of anyone who might be capable of murder, can you?"

"No."

"Ophelia, I know a little about profiling, and believe me, this murder was personal. Stabbings usually are. The perp knew Adder, and had a reason for killing him."

"Becca."

Danny exhaled slowly. "Ophelia, leave it alone. You're not going to help Darci, or Becca, by coming up with all these crazy suppositions."

I tucked a strand of hair behind my ear and looked down at the ground. "I'm only trying to find the truth."

"I know," he said, patting me on the shoulder. "And Darci's lucky to have you for a friend."

"I don't know about that," I replied, rolling my eyes.

"She is." He leaned down until he could see into my face. "But by running around asking all these questions, you might make a bad situation worse. I don't think the boys in El Serpiente would appreciate your curiosity. They might get the wrong idea." He straightened and stared off into space. "At least they don't know you're looking them up on the Internet."

The picture of Cobra reading the newspaper articles that I printed flickered in my head. I turned away, refusing to look at Danny. Telling him about Cobra would only earn me another lecture. And to tell the truth, I was getting a little sick of them.

"Yup, that's right," I said, trying to sound perky. "Why would they suspect me of anything? I'm just a librarian."

Danny gave me a hard stare. "Might be a good idea if you tried to remember that."

Seventeen

Ten minutes later I was pulling into the driveway of Georgia's Bed and Breakfast. Sitting on the edge of town, the old house represented the best of the famous Victorian painted ladies. Lacy grillwork swirled around cupolas and towers, giving the house the appearance of a huge wedding cake.

I walked up the broad steps, across the front porch, past the wicker furniture covered in bright floral cushions, and rang the doorbell. It only took a moment for Georgia to swing the heavy oak-paneled door open.

"Hey, Ophelia," she greeted me as she wiped her hands on the old apron tied at her waist.

She made an incongruous picture. Her red hair was gathered in an old-fashioned bun on top of head, much like the women from the same era as her house. The apron fit that same period. Yet underneath the apron she wore blue jeans and a T-shirt advertising Summerset's Korn Karnival.

She swung the door wide. "Come on in," she said, motioning toward the parlor.

I shut the door behind me and followed her down the wide hallway. Large ceiling fans whirled high above us, spreading the delectable smell of Georgia's cooking through the house.

My nose detected the scent of pot roast wafting from the kitchen. Georgia not only had the reputation of being the biggest gossip in town, but also the best cook. The wonderful aroma made my stomach rumble loudly. Embarrassed, I pressed my hand against my middle.

Georgia flashed a grin at me over her shoulder. "Stay for supper, Ophelia?"

"Aaah—gee, I'd love to, but Tink's studying at Nell's, so I'll need to pick her up after I talk to Becca and Darci." I took a deep breath and thought about the wonderful meal I'd miss. The frozen pizza I'd planned for supper that night didn't quite stack up to Georgia's pot roast. The niggle of guilt I'd felt at Pete's came back. I felt I should be feeding Tink nutritious meals instead of frozen pizzas, takeout, and grilled cheese sandwiches. I made a silent vow to improve my cooking skills.

Georgia motioned toward the staircase. "Darci and Becca are in the violet room. Fourth door on the left."

I climbed the stairs and had almost reached the top when one of the treads creaked. Ah yes, the infamous third step from the top—I remembered it well. During my one attempt at burglary, the noise it made had almost given me a heart attack.

After stopping in front of the fourth door, I gave it a light rap. The door opened a crack and Darci peeked out. She gave a quick look behind her and stepped into the hallway, shutting the door.

"Is Becca sleeping?" I asked.

"No," she said softly. "I just wanted to fill you in before you saw her." Darci chewed on her lip. "The hospital called—Becca had flunitrazepam in her system."

"What's flu-flunitrazepam," I asked, stumbling over the unfamiliar word.

"Roofies."

I frowned and shook my head, still not getting what she meant.

Exasperation crossed Darci's face. "The date rape drug I mentioned in the hospital."

"Ohhh." The lightbulb finally went off. "How did Adder slip it to her?"

"She swears they didn't pop any pills, so he must have put it in her drink at The Viper's Nest."

"Wouldn't the drug have made her drink taste funny?"

"No, it's tasteless and odorless. I used Georgia's computer to look it up on the Internet."

Good old Internet.

"What else did you learn?"

Darci hugged herself tightly. "The drug takes effect in about thirty minutes and peaks at two hours, but can last much longer."

I reached out and rubbed her arm. "This is a good piece of information. If Becca was drugged and out of it, she couldn't have killed Adder."

Chewing on her bottom lip, a worried look darted across her face. "Not necessarily. Roofies affect everyone differently. In some people it can cause aggressive behavior."

I dropped my hand. "Aggressive enough to commit murder?"

She gazed up at the ceiling. "I don't know. What if Becca was so whacked out on the drug—" She stopped abruptly and shivered. "—things got out of hand, or she had some kind of a hallucination and killed him?" She lowered her eyes and stared at me bleakly. "It's what the police are going to think."

At a loss as what to say, I said nothing.

Giving me a weak smile, she opened the door and said

softly, "Maybe if you talk to Becca, you'll sense an answer." She pointed down the hallway. "I'll go ask Georgia for some ice tea. Tell Becca I'll be right back."

I entered the room to find Becca dressed in an oversized jersey and sweatpants, sitting by the window in a dark green velvet wing chair. Her hands were folded uselessly in her lap, and her hair was as flat as the expression on her face. With blank eyes she watched me cross the room and take a seat in a matching chair next to hers.

"Hi, Becca. Ah, Darci's bringing up some tea." I waved at the door, then leaned forward. "How are you feeling?"

A stupid question, I thought, but it was the only remark that came to mind.

"Ehh," she said in a low voice, and turned her head toward the window. "Okay, I guess."

The early evening light hit her square in the face and showed every wrinkle, every line, making her look older than her years. Gone was the sexy, biker babe, replaced by a worn shell of a woman. My heart turned in sympathy.

"I'm glad you're out of the hospital," I said, trying to look cheerful.

Blue eyes turned to me and the hopeless look of a caged animal flashed in their depths. "They're going to arrest me, you know," she said, turning back to the window. "I never thought my life would come to this."

"You don't know that. Bill is a pretty sharp guy. He'll get to the truth."

Becca gave a rusty laugh. "Come on, Ophelia, you're a smart woman. My fingerprints are all over that knife."

I scooted back in my chair. "Do you recall anything?"

Her brow wrinkled and she rubbed it with a shaky hand. "Not really. Snatches of images, like half-remembered dreams." She dropped her head. "I don't know if they really happened."

"Tell me what memories you do have."

She gripped the arms of the chair and laid her head back. "Adder buying me a drink at The Viper's Nest." Lifting her head, a hint of anger raced across her face. "He drugged me."

"Yeah, Darci told me."

"We left on his bike and went to Darci's. I remember going up the stairs and into the bedroom. It gets fuzzy after that. I know we . . ." She stumbled over the words. "Ah, you know . . ."

"Had sex?" I interrupted.

Her mouth twisted in a bitter line. "Yeah. I think I passed out." With a sigh, she leaned back again. "I woke up and felt really groggy. I remember looking over at Adder, thinking he was still asleep. I didn't notice the sheets."

"What happened next?" I gently prodded.

"I began to worry about what Darci would say when she found him in the house, so I slipped back into my underwear and tried to wake him up." She shuddered. "That's when I saw the knife and the blood on the sheets. Next thing I know, I started screaming."

"You don't recall picking up the knife?"

"No, but I must have. You and Darci found it in my hand."

"Do you remember where the knife was?"

She closed her eyes and thought for a moment. "It was on his chest."

"Did you see the knife lying anywhere when you walked in the room with Adder?"

"I wasn't exactly paying attention to my surroundings at that point, but no, I didn't see it." She scrubbed her face with her hands. "I wish I could remember."

Bill had voiced an opinion that Becca could be lying, but every sense in my body told me she wasn't. She truly didn't remember much of that night.

Becca lowered her hands and a tear rolled down her face. "There's a lot of things in my life that I'm not proud of. But this . . ." Her voice trailed away.

I had to ask the question lurking in the corner of my mind. "Becca, do you think you killed him?"

She swiped at her nose. "I don't think so." A terrified look lit her face. "But what if I did? What if I do have that kind of anger inside me?"

My hands rested feebly on my knees, and any words of comfort I had froze in my throat. I may not have liked Becca when I met her, but it didn't mean I thought she was capable of murder. What a mess. How could she mount a defense when the whole incident was no more than a mist in her mind?

A connection occurred to me. "El Serpiente was founded in California. Do you know any bikers who might belong to the gang out there?"

"I've met a lot of sleezes, but none of them associated with El Serpiente. At least, I don't think so."

"I don't mean to pry, but have you had any problems with the police in California?"

"No," she said shortly. "Like I said, I've done things that I'm not proud of, but nothing illegal." She shook her head sadly. "I went to California with such high hope of being an actress. Everyone had always told me how pretty I was, how talented. But you know something?" she asked, a steely look on her face. "The world's full of pretty, talented girls. It was like 'take a number and stand in line.' And I never reached the front of the line. I was too tall, too short, too fat, too thin—always too something."

"Becca, most women would give anything to look like you."

"Right," she scoffed. "It got to the point that every time I looked in the mirror, all I saw were flaws."

"But—"

She held up a hand, stopping me. "If you're told often enough that something's wrong with you, pretty soon you start believing it." Taking a deep breath, she turned to the window. "And instead of confidence, you have this big empty spot inside of you. It gets bigger and bigger every time you're rejected. For me the only thing that seemed to fill the hole was to be with some guy. Only the next morning the hole was back, larger and emptier than ever." Her head dropped. "I'm so tired of it all. Maybe getting locked up is what I deserve."

"Nonsense," I said, patting her leg. "The truth will come out. You need to have faith."

She raised her head and looked at me. "Do you know," she said, her voice cracking, "how long it's been since I've had faith in anything?"

"Becca, I *am* sorry."

She sniffed and tried to smile. "Thanks. I know you weren't that impressed with me when we met—"

I broke in. "But—"

She wouldn't let me finish. "No, it's okay, I understand why. I appreciate what you're trying to do now." The corner of her mouth twitched. "Darci thinks you're terrific, you know, and she's convinced you'll figure out who really killed Adder." She cocked her head and gave me a puzzled look. "She said something about you've had experience in solving murders?"

"Ah well," I stuttered. "You see—"

A sharp rap at the door interrupted me. It swung open to

reveal Darci standing in the doorway, three shades whiter than milk. Over her shoulder I saw Bill and Brett.

Bill walked around Darci and crossed the room. With hat in hand, he stopped directly in front of Becca.

"Becca West, you have the right to remain silent . . ."

Oh crap.

Eighteen

Darci insisted I leave while she accompanied Becca to the police station. She was right. There wasn't any reason for me to go other than to provide emotional support. I gave Darci a hug, patted Becca on the shoulder, and tried to say a few reassuring words.

After leaving Georgia's, I picked up Tink. Lost in the thoughts floating around in my head, not even the smell of the roast beef dinner she insisted on sending home with me was a distraction. I'd seen a different side of Becca during our conversation, and it told me she was innocent.

"Ophelia, did you hear me?" Tink said, drawing me out of my reverie.

"I'm sorry—I didn't. My brain's kind of fractured right now. So much has happened." I glanced at her out of the corner of my eye. "What did you say?"

"I asked about Becca being arrested."

Reluctant to talk to Tink about murder and casual sex, I hadn't said too much to her about that night. But now I was going to have to.

"Yes, Bill and Brett arrested her while I was there," I said in a noncommittal voice.

"How's Darci?"

"She was upset, but she's holding it together. She's going to call later. They've already hired an attorney, so he was going to meet them at the station . . ." I hesitated. "Ah, Tink, what are the kids saying about it at school?"

Maybe if the casual sex hadn't been discussed, I could avoid bringing it up.

She relaxed back in the seat. "That Becca killed the biker after a one-night stand."

So much for not talking about sex. My hands gripped the steering wheel tighter and I shifted in my seat. What should I say? How could I skirt the subject? I thought back to when I became a teenager. How did Margaret Mary handle it? Oh yeah, she gave me a book and said, "Here, read this, and if you have any questions, let me know."

I sat up straight and tried to loosen my grip on the wheel. "Well, Tink," I said in my wisest voice. "It's like this—"

"I know one-night stands aren't a good idea, Ophelia," she said, breaking in and turning toward me.

Her directness caught me by surprise, and I gave her a sideways glance. "You do?"

"Sure. Besides the risk of pregnancy, there's AIDS, STDs, and all kinds of nasty stuff."

My eyes widened in shock. "You know about sexually transmitted diseases?"

"Sure." Her voice rang with confidence. "We talked about them in health class."

I did a mental head slap. Oh yeah, the paper from school I signed that gave my permission for Tink to attend that class. She hadn't brought the subject up, so I'd forgotten about it. I thought I'd have more time before I had to deal with that particular issue. Guess not. I snuck a look at her.

She sat there unperturbed at the direction the conversation was taking. Why did I have the idea she could probably fill me in on a thing or two?

"Ahh, ahh, well . . ." I stumbled on my words. "That's good. You know if you have any questions, you can always talk to me or Abby."

Please, I prayed, *let it be Abby!*

I took my eyes off the road long enough to see a slight smile playing at the corner of her mouth.

"No problem. I'm not really interested in that stuff right now—"

"What stuff?" I interrupted.

"Oh you know, boys and all that."

I breathed a sigh of relief.

"They're okay," she continued, "but most of the time they're doing stupid, gross stuff. Yuck." She shook her head. "I don't know why some of the girls in my class think they have to have a boyfriend. They think they're a nobody without one."

"They're wrong."

She nodded. "I know. Look at you. You don't date."

"Well, yes, you're right." I searched for a way to explain to Tink why I haven't gone out much. "I have had relationships; I was even engaged once, but it didn't work out. And the past five years have been kind of tough. But maybe someday, if I find the right person . . ." I let my voice trail away.

"That's the trick, isn't it? Finding the right person?"

Her maturity caught me off guard, and I did a quick double take. She lifted her chin, and as I had many times in the past, I saw a glimpse of the woman she'd become. She was going to be a heartbreaker, and soon, probably before I was ready, boys would be chasing her, whether she wanted them to or not.

I gripped the wheel tighter and fidgeted in my seat.

Tink noticed my discomfort and gave me a pat. "Don't worry about it, Ophelia."

I laughed in spite of my thoughts. "You're beginning to sound like Abby," I said, pulling into the driveway.

Suddenly, Tink grabbed my arm. "Did you see that?" she asked, pointing toward the house.

Stopping the car, I peered at the house. "What?"

"I thought I saw someone in the living room. A shadow passed by the window."

"You're sure?"

"Yes." Her voice held a hint of fear.

"Stay in the car," I commanded. I reached into my bag, pulled out my can of pepper spray, and got out. I snuck up the front walk and onto the porch. Slowly, I tried turning the doorknob. Locked. *Whew.* Sidling off the porch, I walked around the side of the house, looking at the windows. They all appeared secure. My inspection took me to the backyard gate, which I opened and slipped through.

Lady and T.P. came running when they saw me. I reached down and scratched them both, and when I did, didn't sense any unease in either one of them. Gripping Lady's collar, I approached the back door and tried that knob, too. Still locked.

I wondered if the shadow Tink had seen might have been only a trick of light, played by the setting sun.

After unlocking the door with the spare key hidden under the back stoop, I entered the house and stopped, letting my mental shield drop and scanning with my mind for any disturbances in the energy. A slight tingle tickled the back of my neck, and I gripped Lady's collar tighter. A backward look out the door showed T.P. running across the yard, toward the bushes.

With the pepper spray ready in one hand and the other

securely holding onto Lady, I systematically walked through the downstairs, room by room, turning on lights as I went. All was as it should be.

Slowly, I climbed the stairs. In the bathroom, trigger finger ready, I yanked the shower curtain back to find the tub empty. I checked Tink's room next. Nothing out of place there, either.

One last room to check—my bedroom. My palms were sweating and my fingers were white from grasping Lady and the can of pepper spray. Cautiously, I eased into the room while my eyes flicked from corner to corner.

Okay, Jensen, if you were a burglar, where would you hide?

My glance landed on the closet door. I tiptoed across the room and stared at the door as if I had X-ray vision and could see if anyone lurked amid my T-shirts and skirts. With a finger on the trigger of the pepper spray, I let go of Lady and jerked the door open. Nothing. Pressing a hand over my heart thundering in my chest, I took a deep breath in relief.

Then I noticed that something smelled funny. I sniffed twice. Was that the faint odor of cigarettes? I took a deeper breath. Nope. Must be my overactive imagination, I thought.

I crossed to the center of the room and, with a hand on my hip, scanned the room one more time. As I did, I heard a motorcycle starting. I flew to the window then, but the trees blocked my view of the street.

I rushed out of the room and stumbled down the stairs. At the front door, my fingers fumbled with the lock. Finally, I managed to get it open. Rushing out the door, I ran to the car and wrenched the door open.

"Did you see anyone?" I asked Tink.

A surprised look crossed her face. "No. Is everything okay?"

I spied my cell phone clasped in her hand. "Yes, it's fine. Must have been a reflection," I said with a smile to reassure her.

From a distance, I heard the motorcycle again.

I frowned. *That's it,* I told myself. *I'm buying a baseball bat!*

After Tink went to bed, I sat in my office alone, with only the three animals keeping me company. Lady and Queenie were curled up in one corner, and T.P. sprawled in the center of the room, sound asleep. Tink had wanted the puppy in her room, but he cried and scratched at the door, so she had to let him out.

Bookshelves lined one wall, with my collection of crystals and candles nestled among the books. Little bowls of a special potpourri that Abby made sat on the surface of my desk and reading table. A lamp made from an antique kerosene lantern shone a soft light throughout. This room was my special place. A place where I did my magick.

No magick in the room tonight. The unease I'd felt earlier kept picking at the back of my mind. Had someone been in my house? I didn't think so. All the doors had been locked and the windows were secure. Was the tickle of energy that I'd felt only fear or something else?

I shook my head. Not easy being psychic. How did I know if what I experienced was normal human emotion or my talent at work? At times the difference was apparent, like the flashing stoplight in my head the night of the murder. But at other times it was subtle and hard to define.

Combing my fingers through my hair, I went back over my afternoon. I still thought it strange that Pete seemed so nerv-

ous during my conversation with Danny. Wait a second—
twice now I'd seen Danny and Pete together—all within the
last week. Once at Stumpy's the night of Darci's party, and
that day in the garage. He'd looked nervous at Stumpy's, too.
Danny had vehemently dismissed my theories of extortion,
but what if that was only to throw me off track? Danny might
not be involved in Adder's murder investigation, but that
didn't mean he wasn't up to his eyeballs in something else.

A book fell from the shelf then, startling me out of my
thoughts. It also surprised T.P. He yelped, and his little paws
struggled to gain purchase on the slick wooden floor. Once
on his feet, he flew out of the room, his toenails clicking
rapidly on the shiny surface.

I sighed and walked over to pick up the book. It occurred
to me that maybe "Chicken" would be a good name for that
dog. He seemed scared of everything.

Straightening, I caught the reflection of the room in the
window, and all the hair on my arms stood up. Whipping
around, I stared at the doorway. Nothing there. I could've
sworn I glimpsed a figure standing in the opening.

"Tink?" I called out, rubbing my arms.

Silence.

Shaking my head again at my nerves, I crossed back to
my desk and sat. I spied the old leather pouch holding my
runes lying on the corner of the desk. I'd told Tink that the
runes brought clarity to my thoughts. Maybe they would help
me tonight. It didn't need to be a full reading. Often, asking
a question and pulling out one rune would point me in the
right direction.

I picked up the bag, opened it, and ran my hand through
the stones as I framed my question. I'd ask the same one
Darci had: Who killed Adder? What would the runes say this
time?

Little needles of energy tickled my fingertips as I turned the runes in my hand and thought about the murder. Finally one stone seemed stronger, more insistent. I drew it out of the pouch and turned it over in my palm.

"Okay, I get it," I said out loud. "Tiwaz."

The same rune that had popped up in Darci's reading. And in the same position—upside down.

A bad man. Duh. Only one problem: With El Serpiente taking up residence in Summerset, it seemed to me the town was crawling with bad men. How did I figure out which one was the killer?

Nineteen

I opened the door and flashed a big smile at Danny and Darci standing on my front porch. As I did, I was struck again by what a handsome couple they made. Darci's blond hair and blue eyes complimented Danny's darkness. They were both dressed casually in jeans. Darci wore a loose fitting blue top that brought out the color of her eyes. And even after all she'd been through in the past few days, she looked terrific. With her hand held tightly in Danny's, she seemed relaxed and calm.

Danny, though out of uniform, still had *cop* written all over him. Mirrored sunglasses shielded his dark eyes, and the smile he gave me gleamed against the tan of his complexion. He held himself with confidence and an air of authority.

Not somebody that I'd want to go up against popped into my head.

"Thanks for coming over," I said, giving Darci a quick hug.

"Not a problem, Ophelia," Danny replied as he tucked his sunglasses into the pocket of his shirt. "You're concerned about your home security?"

"Yeah." I stepped back and motioned them both into the

house. "With everything that's been going on, I don't know if my safety measures are what they should be."

In the hallway, I heard Darci sniff a couple of times. Well aware of my aversion to anything that involved recipes and mixing bowls, she turned to me in surprise. "Have you been baking pumpkin pie, Ophelia?"

Not wanting to explain my grandmother's spell work in front of Danny, I gave my head a quick shake and mouthed, *Abby.*

The light of realization dawned in Darci's eyes and she nodded.

I guided them into the living room, where Lady, Queenie, and T.P. watched the newcomers with interest.

"Ophelia," Darci squealed, "when did you get a puppy?"

An unladylike snort slipped out. "Trust me, it wasn't my idea. Abby thought Tink needed her own dog." I grimaced. "Without asking me what I thought, I might add."

Darci crossed over to T.P. and picked him up. The puppy squirmed in delight. "He's adorable." She rubbed her chin on the dog's head. "What's his name?"

"T.P., as in 'the puppy,' for now," I said, walking up and scratching the dog's ears. "We're trying to think up a better name . . ." I hesitated. "He's kind of a pill, but I guess we're getting used to having him around."

She looked at Lady and Queenie with laughter in her eyes. "How do they like T.P.?"

"Lady tolerates him." I chuckled. "But Queenie? He gives her a wide berth. I think she nailed him on the nose, so he keeps his distance."

At the mention of her name, Queenie turned her head slowly and gave me a regal stare from her position on the windowsill. With a graceful flick of her tail, she stood, arched her back in an easy stretch, and hopped down. A minute later she was rubbing up against Darci's leg, demanding her share of attention.

Darci set T.P. on his feet as she bent to pet Queenie. He gave the cat one fearful look and took off for the safety of his crate.

"See what I mean?" I said, laughing.

Danny watched the scene with the pets without comment. Stealing a look at him, I noticed his lips in a tight line, not frowning, but not smiling, either.

He glanced at his watch quickly. "Baby, we don't have time to play with Ophelia's pets if you want to make the movie in Des Moines."

My eyes shifted from Danny to Darci.

It was like a shutter dropped over the light in Darci's eyes as she stood. "You're right. I'm sorry." She turned to me. "Danny thought it would be good for me to get out of town for the evening, so he's taking me to a movie."

"That sounds like a good idea."

Darci lowered her head. "I guess, but I feel guilty, going out while Becca's sitting in jail—"

"Baby, we talked about this," he cut in, crossing over to her and taking her hand. "There's nothing you can do for her. Let her attorney handle things."

She lifted her face and her eyes flared. "I'm not going to abandon her."

"Of course not, I'm not asking you to," he said in a soothing tone. "But you still have to live your own life, don't you?"

"I guess." The stubborn look on her face contradicted her words.

"'I guess'?" he asked, lifting an eyebrow.

Her stubborn expression faded, replaced by one of contrition. "You're right."

"That's my baby." He threw an arm around her shoulder and pulled her next to him. "Ouch," he said as Darci's purse thumped against his leg. "What do you have in that thing?"

She opened it and pulled out the gift I'd given her for her birthday. "It's a crystal," she said proudly.

He stroked her head like she was his pet. "Baby, do you really need to carry rocks around in your bag? I know it's pretty, but wouldn't you be better off leaving it in your room?"

I wanted to hurl! Once again I was struck by his condescending attitude toward her. I opened my mouth, but shut it quickly when a little voice inside my head said, *Boundaries, Jensen, boundaries*. I didn't want to pull an Abby and offer unasked-for advice, but what Danny was doing to Darci's self-esteem grated on me.

Rolling my eyes, I plastered a fake smile on my face and said brightly, "Do you want to walk around outside, Danny? Point out how I can make the house more secure?"

"Sure."

Outside, the three of us walked around the house, Danny pointing out the things that would deter a burglar and what wouldn't.

"The truth is," he said, standing in the center of the backyard with his hands on his hips, surveying the trees and bushes, "unless you spend a lot of money on an expensive security system, nothing's going to stop a pro. But you can protect your house from amateurs. That's what you really want to do. It's the amateurs that lose their heads and hurt you. Pros want in and out quickly with no fuss, no muss." He gave me a knowing look. "You have a key hidden outside, like everyone else in town?"

Shifting my weight, I shoved my hands in my pockets. "Yes, under the back stoop."

"At least it's not in the flower pot, like at Georgia's." His mouth pushed into a forced grin. "I suggest you put one in a magnetic key holder and place it in the garage. Do you have a place you could hide one?"

"Yes, I've got metal shelves on the back wall. I could put it underneath one of them."

"That would work," he said as he glanced at his watch again. "We've got to get going, baby." Danny headed toward the back gate with Darci following several paces behind him.

I gritted my teeth and caught up with her. "Are you going back to your house soon?"

"No—"

Danny whirled around. "Yes."

"But Danny, the place gives me the creeps." She shuddered. "You didn't see the room, see all the blood."

"Baby, I see that kind of stuff every day. What if I decided I couldn't go to work because of what I might find?"

Come on, give me a break, I thought as I watched Darci's reaction. Summerset didn't have a fatality once a day.

"I have to do my job, don't I?" Danny continued.

"Yes," Darci said in a small voice.

"And remember, baby, we talked about how you need to face what happened and put it behind you?"

"Yes," she mumbled.

"Come here." He motioned her over to him. Again he threw an arm around her shoulders and yanked her body next to his. He bent his head close to her ear. "I'll be there to help you, baby. You can count on me. When I'm with you, you're not afraid, are you?"

"No," she whispered, hanging her head.

Crap—she wasn't going to let Danny take up residence in her house, was she?

* * *

The remains of the dinner Abby had prepared for Tink and me were all put away. Tink was out in the front yard playing with T.P., and Abby and I had just about finished doing dishes. The meal at Abby's had been a nice break from all the drama I'd witnessed between Danny and Darci.

"But Abby," I said, handing her the last plate to dry. "He treats her like a little kid. And it's almost like he's trying to separate her from those she cares about."

She wiped the plate carefully as she thought about that. "Unfortunately, some men are like that. They want to be the center of their partner's universe, and they see anyone else as a threat to that position."

"I wouldn't want to be in a relationship like that." I swirled the washcloth around in the soapy water.

"I don't imagine you would, but it's Darci's business, not yours."

"I know," I admitted grudgingly. "I hope she doesn't let him move in with her." I turned and looked at her. "I told you I think that's what Danny has in mind?"

Abby nodded.

"He's using Becca's trouble as an excuse," I continued, "but he won't take Darci's conviction that Becca's innocent seriously." I fished the silverware out of the water and scrubbed them furiously until they shone. Rinsing them off, I placed them in the drainer.

"Again, Ophelia, that's Darci's concern." She picked up the silverware, dried them quickly, and put them away.

"That may be, but somebody needs to help her," I mumbled, more to myself than to Abby.

"So you intend to proceed with your meddling?"

My head whipped toward Abby. I was shocked at her choice of words. *Meddle*? From a woman who bought a dog without talking to me about it first? Now *that* was meddling.

"It's not meddling," I replied indignantly. "I'm supporting my friend."

Abby's lips were pursed in disapproval, showing me what she really thought. Her attitude ticked me off, and I tossed the dishcloth in the sink, splashing water onto the window above it.

Bracing my wet hands on my hips, I stared at her. "*What* is up with you? In the past, you've always encouraged me to 'follow my destiny,' to 'use my talent to help others.' Plus, you're usually the first one who wants to rush into a mess like this." I paused and took a deep breath, but before I could speak Abby made the most of my silence.

"Not this time," she said, her tone abrupt.

"Why?"

She turned on her heel and walked away from me. "You'll bring more misfortune onto your house."

I leaned against the counter and stared at her back. "How do you know? You said you didn't sense anything."

"I'm not, but you've already brought bad luck by pointing at the moon—"

My groan cut her off. "We're not back to that moon thing, are we?" I asked.

She whirled around, her eyes angry. "Don't you dare scoff at the old ways," she said, shaking a finger at me. "You'll only bring more bad luck."

I grabbed my head. *Man, was she stuck on this bad luck thing, or what?* Lowering my hands, I said in a calm voice, "I know you did a spell when I wasn't home. My house reeks of allspice and cloves, so what's—"

"I'm not sure the spell will work—"

"Your spells always work," I said with confidence.

She shook her head slowly as she twisted her hands together. "I felt like something was interfering with my intention."

I pushed away from the counter. "Are you saying someone's hexing me?"

Been there, done that, didn't like it. In fact, the hex had actually made me physically ill, until Abby broke it with a little magick of her own.

"No." She rubbed her forehead. "I don't know what was blocking me, but it felt as if something was."

Smiling, I took a step forward. "You're always telling me not to worry, that everything will be okay—"

"No, it won't," she said, dropping her hand and glaring at me.

My eyes flew wide at the look on her face. "Jeez, Abby, don't you think you're overreacting a bit? I'm sorry I violated one of your superstitions, but—"

"You are so stubborn. You're going to blunder around willy-nilly." She tapped her foot in irritation. "You won't listen, will you?"

Her words sparked my temper. "It's not that I won't listen, but I think I'm old enough to make a few decisions for myself—"

"Right, like during Brian's murder—"

"Hold it right there," I said, and started to point my finger at her. I caught myself in time and clasped my hands behind my back. "Brian's death doesn't have anything to do with what's happening now."

"No?" she asked. "You refused to listen then, and look what happened? You had a breakdown."

I gripped my hands tighter. "That's not why I had a breakdown. I—"

She cut me off with a wave of her hand. "You've got no

sense, no sense at all." Her voice slipped deeper into a drawl and the vernacular of the mountains. "You don't care nothin' about raisin' that child in a cursed house."

"Curse? What curse?" My voice rose with my temper. "All I did was point at the moon, for Pete's sake! This is crazy."

She stomped her foot in anger.

In all my years with Abby, I'd never seen her do that.

"Do you understand what forces you're playin' around with? No," she said, her voice emphatic. "You don't know spit. For years I've tried to help you, but you won't pay attention. You—"

I held up a hand, stopping her. "Okay, we're leaving now. I don't understand what your problem is, but I'm getting out of here before we both say something we'll regret." I strode out of the kitchen, leaving Abby to swirl in her fury.

"Ophelia Mette Marie Jensen, y'all get back in here, right this instant," she called after me.

For the first time in my life, I ignored my grandmother.

Twenty

All night long I did a little swirling of my own—I didn't like being angry at Abby, and I liked it even less when she was mad at me. But I didn't see a resolution to the problem. Something was eating at her, and whatever it was, it was coming out sideways. Until she wanted to talk, my best bet was to lay low. That, and try and solve the situation with Becca as quickly as possible so we could get on with our lives. Maybe then Abby would quit muttering about bad luck and curses. One thing for sure, I knew I'd never point at the moon again. Not in this lifetime.

I sat in bed, propped against my pillows. Drawing my knees to my chest, I rested my chin on them and thought about what I did know. Not much. Darci's rune reading kept circling in my mind.

When Abby had given me the runes, she said they didn't lie. Okay, so what did they tell me? They said a bad man, the past, and that justice will be served. As I pondered her remark about how my reading meant the murder was triggered by something that had happened in Becca's past, I came to acknowledge the possibility that she was right. After what she'd told me about her life in California and her experiences with men, I could understand how she might have some deep-seated anger against men in general. Maybe Adder did something to bring that anger out, and in her drugged state, she killed him.

No, I thought, rubbing my chin on my knees, that answer didn't feel right. Back to the bad man angle.

I already knew the bikers were bad news, so was it possible that one of Adder's "brothers" killed him? Maybe. I needed a motive to make that theory fly, and I didn't know enough about El Serpiente to make a judgment.

Scooting down in bed, I shut off the lamp and stared at the dark ceiling. Could Adder have betrayed one of the brothers? From what I'd read, loyalty meant everything, so to go against the gang would really tick them off. Enough to kill? Yeah. I thought of the woman in Florida. And Danny had said killing with a knife is personal. Can't get more personal than betrayal. So who would have committed the crime? An evil thought occurred to me—I remembered Cobra's cold gray eyes, and the way he stared at me. It wouldn't break my heart to see him hauled off in handcuffs.

I turned on my side and tucked an arm under my pillow. I still favored the idea of a rival gang doing the deed, but Danny had shot holes clear through that theory. The articles said the power of The Rogues had been broken when their leaders were arrested for the murder of the two hitchhikers. And those men were all doing time in a federal prison. Guess they had air-tight alibis.

Flipping over on my stomach, I felt my eyelids drift shut as sleep carried me away from thoughts of murder.

In my dream, I floated just above the ground. Ahead lay the clearing I'd seen before in another dream, and in the clearing, as before, were the circle of stones. The rune Algiz was again carved on each one, and glowed with the same purple light. Only this time Tink was huddled in the center of the circle. Her white night gown looked lavender in the purple light from the glowing runes and she hugged her knees to her chest. Her head was tipped toward the heavens while she watched planchettes streaming fire fly in the night sky above her.

The planchettes dipped and weaved around the circle as if seeking a way to get at Tink, but the power of protection from Algiz stopped them. They hurled themselves in a fiery ball toward the purple light, only to bounce back when they hit the wall of color.

The look of terror on Tink's face made my heart pound. I struggled in my dream to float toward her, to join her in the circle and protect her, but an invisible force kept me in place. I could only watch helplessly as the planchettes beat against the light.

The dream shifted suddenly, and I was no longer in the clearing with Tink, but floating along a ribbon of highway. The full moon above lit scrub pine trees lining the road, and from a distance I heard the waves hitting the shore. California—I was in California, and I knew what I'd see next.

Wake up, wake up! I screamed inside my head, but the dream held me fast.

I saw three motorcycles slow down to a stop next to the two teenagers standing alongside the road. The girls smiled at each other, and I watched them both nod and then climb on the back of two bikes.

A cloud crossed the moon, obscuring the riders' faces, but not before I made out the tattoos on their forearms: a one percent sign on one arm and a Jolly Roger on the other. One of the bikers turned his head in profile and said something to the girl seated behind him. She giggled and wrapped her arms tighter around his waist.

There was something familiar about that profile, but I couldn't place it.

He glanced over his shoulder once more, and this time I saw his eyes. They were the eyes of a predator, and they were gray and as cold as sleet.

The next morning, I may have appeared to be walking sedately up the steps to the library, but in my mind I did a happy dance worthy of a Fred Astaire and Ginger Rogers movie. I glided and pirouetted with the best of them, and instead of loafers and linen pants, in my head I wore a floating evening gown with a feather boa. Maybe it wasn't the most appropriate reaction, but I *knew* who the killer was. Cobra was younger in my dream, but I'd have recognized those chilly gray eyes anywhere. I'd solved the case. Hip hip hooray for Ophelia.

I paused on the top step and slipped out of my reverie. *One problem there, Jensen,* said the realistic little voice in my head. *Now you have to prove it.* Another thought silenced the voice: Cobra had read the articles from the Internet. The killer knew what I was up to. My happy dance wasn't so happy anymore.

And what was up with those flying planchettes? The circle of stones, Algiz glowing with a purple light—I slapped my forehead. Purple was the color of the third eye chakra, the seat, many believed, of all psychic abilities. Algiz was a rune of protection. Did the dream mean Tink's psychic talent would protect her? Or would it be mine? Or Abby's? Maybe it would be best if I sent Tink to stay with her until Cobra had been arrested? Abby was angry with me now, but if Tink needed her, she'd be there. *Yes, good idea.*

I entered the library and went straight to my office, leaving Claire to deal with the counter. I had a plan; no more worrying, no more dithering around. First on my agenda was a late lunch at Stumpy's. Danny had lied to me about the extortion, I knew he had. And who best to grill but one of the more successful businessmen on Main Street? Stumpy.

The morning flew by swiftly as I tackled the bar coding program. Finally, at one o'clock, I made my way out the door and down the street to the bar. No bikes lined the parking spaces along the street, and I didn't spy Abby's pickup parked in its usual spot.

With a deep breath, I pushed the door open and sauntered in. I gave the bar a quick scan and was happy to see it empty.

Stumpy stood behind the bar washing glasses. Hearing me enter, he turned and peered through his thick glasses. "Ophelia, is that you?" he asked, squinting against the light shining in the wide windows behind me.

I headed toward the bar. "Hi, Arthur. How's it going?"

His eyelids behind the thick lenses fluttered rapidly and he seemed uncomfortable. "Abby's not here," he replied with hesitation.

"Actually, I'm here to see you," I said with what I hoped was an engaging smile, and hopped up on a bar stool.

Arthur put down the dish towel and leaned against the bar. "If this is about what happened between you and Abby—" he started to say.

Ah-ha. Abby had done some venting about ungrateful granddaughters. That accounted for his discomfort.

I held up a hand, stopping him. "No, this visit isn't about Abby. It's—"

"About that murder, isn't it?" he broke in. He shook his bald head slowly. "I don't think I should encourage you."

I picked up a bar napkin and began to pleat it. "Come on, I'm not doing anything dangerous. Just asking people I trust a few questions." I put emphasis on the word "trust."

He relaxed a little but still eyed me suspiciously. "What do you want to know?"

"Do members of El Serpiente come here often?"

"Some."

"Do you know their names?"

"No."

"Have they caused any trouble?"

"No."

Great, he wasn't going to make this easy for me, and I didn't feel like playing twenty questions. I cut to the chase. "Have they tried to extort money from you?"

Arthur turned his back to me. "Leave it alone," he said in a short voice.

Excited, I jumped off the bar stool and ran around the corner of the bar. "They have, haven't they?" I tugged at his sleeve.

Arthur's owl-like eyes shifted away from me. "Not supposed to talk about it," he muttered.

"Oh, come on, we're almost family," I pleaded.

A faint blush stained his weathered face. "Abby won't like it."

"I won't tell her, I promise."

"She'll know," he said, nodding his head wisely. "She always knows."

"No, she won't," I argued.

I wasn't aware of how much Abby had told him about our family's peculiar gifts, but I decided to take a chance.

I narrowed my eyes and gave him an even look. "You know I have ways of finding out the information I want."

His eyes traveled to the row of bottles lined up neatly

on the shelves, and I heard him softly mumble a few swear words.

Maybe I could scam him into telling me what I wanted to know? Like a TV psychic, I let my eyelids drift shut and placed my fingertips on my temples while I pretended to read his mind.

"Knock it off, Ophelia," he said, startling me out of my play-acting. "I know you're not one of them telepaths."

Dang. He called my bluff.

My eyes flew open and I gave him a sheepish grin. "Please?"

"You won't tell Abby I said anything? Or Danny?"

"I swear."

"Okay," he grumbled. He looked swiftly around the bar and his voice dropped. "They came in here 'bout this time of day. Didn't exactly threaten to hurt me or the business, but they made sure I understood they could. Offered to 'protect' me without really saying so."

I was elated. My suspicions were correct, and I bet if I could find a way to worm the information out of him, I'd learn they'd done the same thing to Pete.

Arthur's lips twisted indignantly. "They thought they were going to intimidate an old man." He reached under the bar and pulled something out. Waving it in front of my nose, he continued, "Boy let me tell you, they hightailed it outta here when I showed 'em this. They still come in here, but they don't try messing with me now."

The engraved lettering was worn and faded, but the wood's patina still shone in the dim light of the bar as Arthur slapped the object against his open palm.

My eyes widened with lust. It was his Louisville Slugger.

I cocked my head and stared at the baseball bat. "Say, Arthur—where can I buy one of those?"

Twenty-One

For the rest of the afternoon it was hard to concentrate. I'd convinced myself—no, scratch that, *knew*—the killer was Cobra. However, now that my initial excitement over my discovery had faded, I saw a few holes in my favorite theory.

I leaned back in the chair at my desk, picked up a pen and did some deep thinking. Number one, according to the news article, Cobra was supposed to be in prison. Number two, Danny was right, ten years is a long time to hold a grudge. Number three, how did Cobra know where to find Adder that night? If Cobra had wanted to find him, wouldn't it have been logical for him to visit the same motels we did? We didn't see or hear any motorcycles during our goose chase.

But what if Adder told him where they were going? What if Cobra had known from the beginning what Adder had planned? What if Cobra appearing at our table that night had been a ruse to distract me long enough for Becca and Adder to slip out unnoticed?

Hmm, I liked that idea. Then reality set in and I realized those were a lot of what ifs. I tossed the pen down, and propping my feet up on my desk, folded my hands in my lap. Looking around the room, I let my mind mull over the possibilities.

My eyes settled on Abby's picture staring down at me from one of the shelves. It was almost as if I saw reproach in the eyes gazing at me. A desire to stand and flip the picture over hit me.

That's silly, said the tiny voice in my head.

"She's being so stubborn," I muttered aloud. "And just when I need her advice."

Whoa, Jensen, arguing with yourself? Not a good sign. I looked away from the picture, and my gaze caught the telephone sitting on the corner of my desk.

Why don't you call her, lay the whole problem out, and ask for her help? said the voice again.

Brilliant, Jensen, brilliant.

Abby had been a little frosty on the telephone, but she did accept my invitation for supper at my house that night. It meant I would actually have to cook something, but I'd made a vow to provide better meals for Tink. Tonight was as good a time as any to start.

Spaghetti, garlic bread, and salad was the menu I'd decided on, so after work I found myself standing in the aisle of the grocery store, looking over various cans of sauce. As I was perusing the contents of one of the cans, a familiar face caught my attention.

Everything about her said "tired." Her faded hair hung limply around her shoulders. And her flip-flops slapped the floor slowly as she pushed her cart down the aisle toward me. It took me a moment to place the face, but after a second I remembered where I'd seen her.

Janet, the waitress from The Viper's Nest. I'd wanted to

talk to her, and now fate had placed her in my path. Talk about luck. With a quick glance over my shoulder for other shoppers, I moved my cart down the aisle.

She was busy studying the selection of canned vegetables on the shelf, so she didn't see me approach. Smoothly, I moved my cart at an angle, effectively blocking any escape. Janet's head whipped around in surprise.

"Hi, Janet, remember me?" I said in a pleasant voice. "I don't think I gave you my name—Ophelia Jensen." I held out my hand.

She ignored my hand and turned back to the cans of vegetables. "You were with the woman who killed Adder."

"She didn't do it," I replied to the back of her head, and dropped my hand.

"Police say she did," she said, still not looking at me.

"They're wrong." I lightly touched her arm to get her attention. "I'd really like to ask you some questions about that night."

Her head jerked toward me, and she gripped the handle of her cart tightly. "You're kidding, right?" She leaned in close. "Do you know what El Serpiente does to people who rat them out?" she hissed.

"I have an idea. Look, I don't care about the drugs and the prostitution—"

Her eyes opened wide as she cut me off. "How do you know about—" She slapped a hand over her mouth.

"Their illegal activities?"

She nodded.

"It's a small town, Janet, rumors fly constantly." I laid my hand over her knuckles, now white from grasping the shopping cart. As I did, I let my psychic shield down for an instant.

An image of Janet and two small children in a rundown trailer flashed across the screen in my head.

"Look," I said reassuringly, "I know you have children to protect, and I promise—"

"How do you know about my kids?" Her eyes narrowed in suspicion as she interrupted me. "A lucky guess?"

I looked from side to side, checking the aisle again before I answered. "Not exactly."

"What, you some kind of a psychic or something?" she asked in a voice ringing with disbelief.

"Shh." I cast a nervous look around the store. "Let's just say I have talents not everyone knows about."

She stepped back, her eyes hard. "I suppose you're working with the cops?"

"No, I'm on my own, trying to help a friend." I stepped back, too. Nothing would be gained by crowding her. "I understand about your children, and I'll keep your name out of this, Janet."

Her eyes were downcast, and I felt her defenses slowly collapse. "I'm just trying to get by, you know?" she said, lifting her head. "Thanks to my worthless ex, money's tight and the tips are good at The Viper. I can make more cash there in a week than in two weeks someplace else. I keep to myself, take my pay, and go home. I steer clear from what goes on after closing . . ." Her voice hitched. "The system can come down hard on women like me, and I don't want my kids taken away."

I felt a rush of sadness at Janet's plight. How many women were out there, just like her? No options, no choices without an education to make a better life for themselves and their families. No self-esteem.

"Janet, I'm sorry to put you in this position, but I'm trying to help an innocent woman, who in her own way has been kicked around, too."

She snorted derisively. "I saw her, saw how she looked. A woman like her has lots of chances."

"Maybe she did, but she didn't use them. And now she's a bitter woman, alone, who may spend the rest of her life in prison for a crime she didn't commit."

Her eyes narrowed with skepticism. "How do you know she didn't do it?" Her face cleared. "Oh yeah right, you're—"

"Shh." Putting a finger to my lips, I stopped her.

"All right," she said, giving in. "But don't come to The Viper."

I waved my hands in front of me. "Don't worry. I won't," I said emphatically. "What time do you get off work?"

"Two."

"As in two A.M.?"

"Yeah, it's a bar."

"Hmm . . ." I paused, thinking over possible places to meet. Suddenly one occurred to me. "There's an old church and cemetery on a gravel road about a mile from The Viper. We could meet there later tonight."

"An old cemetery?" She shuddered. "That's kind of creepy."

"I agree, but I can guarantee we won't be disturbed."

Her eyes slid away from mine. "Okay."

Quickly, I gave her simple directions to the old church, and as I watched Janet's tired steps carry her down the aisle, the thought struck me: Becca wasn't the only one in a jail.

All during supper with Abby there was an undercurrent of tension between us. Tink kept looking at us with questions in her eyes, but we said nothing. I was worried what Abby's reaction might be when we finally had time to talk alone. Would she cling to her anger, or would she listen to me with an open mind?

After Tink went upstairs to study, I poured two glasses of tea, let all three animals out in the backyard, and suggested to Abby that we sit outside.

We took our glasses out to the patio and silently watched the animals chase around the yard.

I looked up at the sky. The moon was waning, but there was still enough light to make out Lady and T.P. sniffing the ground, hot on the trail of some elusive squirrel. A short distance from them, Queenie, acting like a jungle cat, stalked something we couldn't see from where we sat.

"Nice night, isn't it?" I asked, breaking the silence. "And would you look at that moon?"

I was very, very careful not to point.

Abby caught my tone and gave me a sly look.

"Hey," I said with a cheeky grin. "I didn't point."

"Humph," she sniffed, and turned away, but not before I caught the glimmer of amusement in her eyes.

"Abby," I said leaning toward her, "I'm sorry if what I said or did insulted your beliefs. I didn't mean to, but there's a lot of things you were taught by the women of our family that I don't understand."

"I know you don't." She sniffed again. "And that's your mother's fault. She didn't want me to teach you."

"She didn't?"

"No, and we argued about it after you were born."

"Really?" I said in a shocked voice. "You argued with Mom?"

Man, I'd have liked to have seen that fight—it would've been one to sell tickets to. Two immovable forces clashing. Sparks would've lit the night. The concept boggled my mind.

I settled back in my chair. "I'm surprised you and Mom still speak."

"We didn't for a while, but your grandfather couldn't stand the rift. He insisted we make peace. Sat us both down and told us exactly what he thought of our childish behavior." A smile played at the corner of her mouth as she remembered. "He was right, of course."

"Wow."

The smile faded. "But we made up only after I agreed to respect Maggie's wishes and not cloud your mind with the old beliefs." Abby turned toward me. "At that time, we didn't know if you were one of the chosen." She sighed deeply. "I think that was really the root of the problem. Maggie had always resented that the family gift had passed her by, so she chose to live a life among that which can be proven. One heavy with rules and light on intuition."

"And as an English professor, she had her rules."

"Yes, and she raised you in an intellectual environment; an environment where the old ways didn't exist."

For the first time in my life I considered what it might have been like for Margaret Mary to have Abby as a mother, growing up in the huge shadow that Abby cast. Without the talent that flourished in the other women in our family, it would have been a struggle to find her own way, her own path, out of that shadow.

Abby reached over and touched my leg. "I can almost hear the wheels in your head spinning, dear." She sat back in her chair. "Don't be concerned. Your mother and I came to terms with our differences years ago. I recognize how difficult it's been for her, but after I was in the hospital last year, I think she finally realized she has her own gifts. Ones that are just as valuable as the ones we have."

Now that she mentioned it, Margaret Mary had been easier to talk with lately. When she and Dad had come to Iowa for Christmas, specifically to meet Tink, I had fun spending time with her. The conversations were no longer centered on what I did or didn't do.

I took a sip of tea and gauged how to bring up the subject we needed to discuss: what was bothering Abby.

Setting my glass down, I turned sideways in my seat and took in her profile. "Abby . . ." I began.

She looked over at me and smiled. "I know. I've spent many hours in thought recently." Turning away, she stared out at the night. "I see you coming into your own, my dear. You're a mother now yourself, and much to my shame, I acted out of a fear that there'd be a time when you wouldn't need me. I got pushy, and—"

"Abby!" My shocked voice drowned out her next words. "There will never—"

She held up a finger to stop me. "I've always felt such a bond with you, and I don't want to see it slowly slip away. Maybe I was trying to hold onto it a little too tight." She took a long breath. "I don't want to be one of those old ladies whose children and grandchildren only visit them out of guilt."

"I *cannot* believe you thought I'd ever feel that way about you," I said, almost insulted.

She shook her head sadly. "It happens all the time, dear. Look at some of my friends. Their children and grandchildren are busy with their own lives. They don't have time for Grandma." Her voice sounded weary. "And let's face it, our society doesn't have much room for the elderly. Not like when I was a girl in the mountains. We took care of our old back then."

I rolled my eyes in the darkness. "I don't see you as elderly."

Abby sat up stiffly in her chair. "I don't see myself that way, either, but the calendar says I am."

"Ah," I said with a toss of my hand, "who cares what an old calendar says? We'll ignore it. And as far as still needing you, I do. As a matter of fact, I want your opinion . . ."

And as the animals frolicked across the yard, I told Abby everything I'd learned.

Twenty-Two

Even though I'd told Abby everything, I was true to my word to Arthur and only alluded to the extortion racket that El Serpiente was trying to run.

"So you're meeting this waitress at the old Worthington church?" she asked.

The night had taken on a chill. Abby and I had moved from the patio into the living room. I sat on the couch with my legs tucked underneath me, while Abby faced me in a chair on the other side of the coffee table. The tension that had plagued our evening earlier disappeared after our talk, and I felt closer to her than ever.

"Is it safe? Do you trust her?" Abby asked, her voice full of concern.

I stifled a yawn and glanced at the wall clock hanging above the mantel. Almost ten o'clock, and with all the tossing and turning I'd done the night before, I hadn't slept well. It was catching up to me. Gosh, I hoped I stayed awake during my meeting with Janet.

Lowering my hand, I smiled at Abby. "Sorry. I'm a little tired tonight."

"I imagine you are—you've been a busy girl today," she

replied with a grin. "Are you sure you're up to meeting with this woman tonight?"

"I have to be." I plucked at my old afghan lying across the arm of the couch. "I need to learn as much as I can from her. She works at the bar and sees the gang members come in and out. She might tell me something she'd be reluctant to tell Bill."

"But will you be safe?"

"I think so," I said, folding my hands in my lap. "She just wants to be left alone and take care of her kids the best she can."

Abby passed a tired hand over her eyes. "I feel sorry for her."

"I do, too. I see her as someone who's trapped in a life that she doesn't want, but she doesn't see any way out for her and her children."

Leaning her head against the back of the chair, Abby sighed. "I was so sure you needed to stay out of this investigation, but I see now I was acting out of fear. Fear that you could handle the problem without me."

"I think you're being a little hard on yourself."

She raised her head and gave me a weak smile. "Thanks. It will take me a bit to figure out what lesson I was to learn, but I will."

"There's always a lesson, isn't there?" I asked, giving my shoulders a roll to loosen the tightness I felt building. My nervousness was worse than I was letting on, and I wasn't looking forward to facing Janet, in the middle of the night, in the middle of nowhere.

"Yes, there is," she said with a wink. "And one of the lessons I learned from raising your mother was that I didn't tell her often enough how proud I was of her." She leaned forward and clasped her knees. "I won't make the same mistake with you."

I felt Abby's love reach out and surround me. And it did more to settle my nerves than all the shoulder rolls in the world.

"I am proud of you, you know," she continued. "This time you made a choice to use your talents without any prodding on my part." She smiled broadly. "In fact, you stood up to me and did what you felt was right. That took courage, Ophelia."

I held up a hand "Wait a second, before you give me too many pats on the back. I *was* prodded. Darci wouldn't let me be." I tugged on my lip. "And speaking of Darci—how much of this do I tell her?"

With a look of total understanding, Abby nodded. "You're worried she'll tell Danny?"

"You got it. You should see them together, Abby, it's disgusting." I shuddered. "He pulls and yanks on her, tells her what to think. Yuck. I hardly recognize her." I plucked at the afghan again. "I'm worried she's going to let him move in with her, and if that happens, he's going to systematically take control of her life."

"I think Darci's smart enough to not let him do that. She may go along with it for a while, but she'll eventually get tired of it."

I puffed out my cheeks and blew out a slow breath. "I hope so." Straightening my legs, I scooted down on the couch. "If she tells Danny that I questioned Janet, he'll be all over me. And I don't need another lecture." I remembered Bill's warning at the hospital and turned my head to look at Abby. "'Course, if Bill gets wind of this, I won't have to worry about Danny's reaction. I'll be in the cell next to Becca, and I don't think I'd be much help to anyone from there."

A thoughtful expression crossed Abby's face. "Hmm,

I know of a more direct way that might give you your answers."

"What's that?" As if I needed to ask, I thought.

"Go through the murder scene as a psychic."

I was afraid she was going to say that. A glimpse of the images that I'd witnessed the night of the murder flickered before my eyes. Groaning, I turned my head away and stared at the ceiling.

I stood in the center of my living room with my hands on my hips, stewing with frustration. It was one-fifteen in the morning and I couldn't find my dang car keys. If I didn't find them soon, I'd be late for my meeting with Janet.

Crap. I tapped my foot in irritation. What a great psychic. I couldn't even find a set of blasted keys—how did I think I could track down a killer? I'd searched pockets, shelves, even T.P.'s crate to see if the little bugger had made off with them somehow. Where were they?

Abby slept in the guest room so Tink wouldn't be alone when I went to meet Janet. If it hadn't been so late, I would have woken her to see if she could find them.

I noticed the clock: one-twenty. I had to hurry. Stomping into the kitchen, I started searching the one place I hadn't looked yet—the kitchen drawers. How my keys would manage to get in there, I didn't know, but I was desperate to find them.

Yanking open drawer after drawer, I searched each one madly. Finally, I reached the last one, which contained my dish towels. Rummaging through the drawer, I hurled towels over my shoulders in my crazy search. I was almost at the bottom of the drawer when I spied the keys lying precisely in the center of one of the towels. It was as if someone had hidden them there.

If Tink thought this was a funny joke, she was mistaken. I was not amused.

I ran out the door and fifteen minutes later was parked at the old church, waiting for Janet.

I'd never noticed how dark it was without the comforting streetlights surrounding me. To my left lurked the shadows of headstones, the guardians of the dead. From the woods circling the old cemetery, I heard crickets and the lonely call of a whippoorwill.

It occurred to me that I probably should have picked a less spooky place to discuss murder. Oh well, it was too late now.

The sound of crunching gravel announced an approaching vehicle. Oh please, I thought, let it be Janet, and not a county deputy out on patrol. The last thing I needed was to explain what I was doing out there in the middle of the night. I slunk down in my seat as it got closer and waited to see what happened. Would it pull in next to me or drive by?

I held my breath as I glimpsed a car kill its lights and drive in. I craned up and glanced over. No light bar on top. I exhaled. Whew. For a second I saw Janet's face in the dim light of her dashboard before she turned off the ignition of her old car. Sitting up straight, I flashed the dome light on and off so she could see it was me.

She threw her door open and shut it quickly. Rushing over, she opened the passenger door and slid in. With a slam that echoed above the song of the crickets, she jerked it closed.

"Thanks for coming," I said, noticing that her eyes were round with fear.

"Yeah, sure." She wiped a shaky hand across her forehead. "But couldn't you have found someplace a little less creepy?" she asked with a nervous glance at the headstones.

"Sorry, but like I told you, we won't be disturbed."

She scooted around in her seat until she faced me. "Look, I need to make this quick. A neighbor girl watches my kids at night and I need to get home."

"Did Cobra leave The Viper after we did?" I asked, getting to the point.

"Yeah, but that's not unusual. He leaves early most nights. The guys tease him about having a woman in town."

"Do you know his real name?"

"No." In the dark, I could sense her puzzlement. "Why all the questions about Cobra? He was one of Adder's best buds."

"I've seen him in town more than any of the other bikers, that's all," I said, keeping my tone cool. "How long has he been with El Serpiente?"

She leaned against the door. "I don't know—a few months, I guess. He's kind of a legend in the gang, and all the guys give him space."

Her words aroused my curiosity. "Why is he a legend?"

"They have to prove themselves in order to join El Serpiente. You know, to be accepted," she explained.

From what I'd learned about outlaw bikers, I didn't think their rite of passage would resemble a fraternity prank. "Like kill someone?"

Janet shivered. "It wouldn't surprise me, but I haven't heard any stories of that. I was told they usually beat some rival half to death."

Oh, that's better, I thought. Not kill them, just make them wish they were dead.

"So how many guys did Cobra put in the hospital in order to earn the status of 'legend'?"

"Well, I did see him go after a guy with a broken beer bottle one night, after the guy insulted him. That's one of the reasons nobody messes with him." She shook her head.

"But that's not why he's a legend. I guess it's because he did something so crazy, no one could believe he did it."

"Like what?"

"He stole a police car right out from underneath the cops."

"I suppose it was parked at a doughnut shop," I commented sarcastically.

"Yeah," she said in surprise. "How did you know?"

I rolled my eyes. "That is so trite."

"Huh?"

"Never mind," I said with a wave. I didn't feel like explaining the old joke about cops and doughnuts. "Do you know where Cobra's from?"

She shook her head again. "They don't talk much about their lives before joining the gang, but I did hear him mention California a couple of times."

"Like he'd lived there?"

"I don't know."

"What about Adder, where did he live?"

"That's funny you should mention Adder. Adder and Cobra were the ones talking about California."

"Did it sound as if they'd known each other before they came to Iowa?"

"No, it was more like they were swapping stories." She shifted in her seat. "I don't know why you're asking these questions about Cobra. He isn't as bad as the rest of them."

"Really?" I tried to hide the doubt in my voice, but she picked up on it.

"He isn't," she said defensively. "He treats the waitresses decently when the other guys aren't around."

"And when they are?"

She hunched her shoulders. "He acts like the rest of them, but it's like he really doesn't mean it, you know."

No, I didn't know. I was convinced the guy was a killer.

"He's stuck up for me a couple of times when a trucker was bothering me," she continued. "Like I said, nobody messes with Cobra."

I had a feeling I'd be wise to drop the questions concerning Cobra. I didn't want Janet running back to him and telling him I was snooping around.

"Is there anything else you can tell me about Adder?"

"He likes—liked," she said, correcting herself, "women. He bragged about how many he'd had and what he'd done to them. Bad things. That's why I wasn't surprised when they said one of them killed him."

"Is there anything else you can remember about the night of the murder?"

Janet was silent for a moment. "Not really." She snapped her fingers. "Wait. The next day I went in early and Cobra was there. He looked like he'd been up all night and was still wearing the same clothes." She nodded her head at the memory. "And that's weird. Cobra's cleaner than the rest of them, and he doesn't wear the same thing day in and day out. His knuckles were all skinned up, too."

"Like he'd been in a fight?" I asked. Maybe he hadn't stabbed Adder in his sleep. Maybe he'd hit him first.

"That's what I asked him—if he'd been in a fight. He laughed and said I should see the other guy."

Right. The other guy was lying in a pool of blood.

"Then what happened?"

She lifted a shoulder. "Nothing. He got up and walked away. I noticed he had grease on his boots and the knees of his pants. Next time I saw him, he'd changed."

I touched her lightly. "Thanks, Janet. I appreciate what you've told me—"

"And you'll keep my name out of it? Right?" she asked anxiously.

I nodded. "Yes, I will."

She let out a sigh. "Thanks. Oh hey, I've got a question for you."

"Shoot."

"Would you do a reading for me sometime?"

Her voice sounded so hopeful, so desperate to know better times were ahead, that I didn't have the heart to explain I didn't do readings.

"Sure," I said, smiling.

Twenty-Three

I rolled over in bed and sniffed the air. Umm, frying bacon. I sniffed again. Pancakes. Gosh, did I love it when Abby spent the night. No cold cereal this morning. And coffee would be waiting for me when I made my way downstairs.

Stretching my arms high above my head, I looked over at the clock on my nightstand: 10:30 A.M. Since I had to work on a Saturday morning the next day, I had the luxury of going in late today. And after my covert operations last night, I was thankful.

I threw on a robe, ran a comb through my hair, and brushed my teeth. By the time I'd reached the kitchen, my stomach was rumbling and my mouth watering. I couldn't wait to tear into Abby's homemade pancakes and fresh cured bacon. A quick look around the room told me she had been up awhile. The mess I'd made hunting for my keys was gone. The counter was clean and all the drawers were shut. I bet if I looked at the dish towels, they'd be folded neat and tidy.

Abby stood at the stove, her long silver braid hanging down the center of her back as she flipped pancakes. She wore an old robe, left here for sudden overnighters. Sneaking up behind her, I gave her a quick hug while the smell of the baby powder she used every night enveloped me.

She spun around and gave me a tap on the arm with the spatula. "You shouldn't startle an old lady."

Giving her a cheeky grin, I snagged a piece of bacon off the platter and popped it in my mouth. "Remember, last night we agreed you weren't old?" I said, taking a step back.

She shook the spatula at me. "Don't talk with your mouth full."

Giving her another grin, I sauntered over to the refrigerator and grabbed the orange juice. I poured two glasses and set them on the table. "Tink get off to school okay?" I asked, walking back to the stove and picking up the platter of bacon.

Abby placed the last of the pancakes on a warm plate and shut off the stove. "Yes, she woke up with a headache, though, so I made her some willow bark tea."

When it came to herbal remedies, Abby was a walking drugstore. Her purse was full of little Baggies of this and that, all legal of course, and she always had a cure for any ailment that came up.

We both sat at the table and passed the food to each other, filling our plates. For the first time since entering the kitchen I really looked at her.

Her eyes were cloudy and her movements seemed slow. An air of tiredness hung about her.

Concerned, I laid my fork down. "Abby, are you okay?"

"I'm fine. I just didn't sleep well last night," she said, pouring syrup over her pancakes. "It was after you left, I heard the puppy whining, so I got up and let him out for a bit." She rubbed her arms as if she suddenly had a chill. "I've always been comfortable in your house, but last night I couldn't shake a feeling of unease." She gave her head a quick shake. "When I finally did get back to sleep I had strange dreams."

"How strange?"

"They weren't prophetic dreams, if that's what you're thinking. I've lived with this talent long enough to tell the difference between a normal dream and one that's trying to tell me something—"

"Wish I could," I interrupted.

"You will as you get older," she said in a comforting voice. "No, in this dream I thought I saw someone watching me from the corner of the bedroom. It startled me so much that I woke up." She gave me a small smile. "No one was there, of course, but it made it difficult to get back to sleep."

I took a sip of orange juice. "Probably all the talk about murder and mayhem triggered the dreams."

"How did you sleep?" she asked.

"Fine, no dreams, no nothing. Only odd thing that happened to me last night was that I couldn't find my car keys." I cocked my head. "Did Tink say anything about playing a trick by hiding the keys?"

"No. Why?"

"I found them buried in with the dish towels, like someone had hidden them there." I lifted a shoulder. "I figured Tink was joking around."

"No, she didn't say anything about your keys. She did ask me to remind you about eighth grade graduation next week—"

I slapped my forehead, cutting her off. "That's right! It's next Thursday, isn't it?"

"Yes, and she also wanted me to remind you that you agreed to be one of the chaperones at the dance after the ceremonies."

Peachy, eighth graders—can't wait to spend an evening watching them with an eagle eye.

Abby saw the look on my face and gave me a tired smile. "It will be good for you."

Putting down my fork again, I gave her a helpless stare. "Are you sure I'm doing okay at this motherhood thing?"

"'Course you are," she assured me.

I remembered the guilt that I'd felt at Pete's. "I'm not so sure. I feed Tink bad meals, I'm involved in a murder investigation—that's not exactly a normal life for a teenager."

She arched an eyebrow. "Hmmm, let's see . . ." She paused. "Your grandmother's a witch, you're a psychic and studying folk magick, and the teenager you're worried about is a medium." Abby chuckled. "In what world could that possibly be considered 'normal'?"

I laughed. "I see what you mean. We're not exactly a *Leave It to Beaver* kind of a family to begin with, are we?"

"No, but that's okay. It makes us unique," she said, her green eyes sparkling with amusement. She sobered. "Speaking of murder investigations, did you learn anything helpful last night?"

I gave her a short synopsis of what Janet had told me.

"And you're sure the killer is this Cobra?" she asked.

"Yup, I'd recognized his eyes in my dream."

"Ophelia, a lot of people have gray eyes."

"So what?" I said with a wry look. "I should run around checking out everyone's eyes?"

"No, but it sounds like this Cobra has some kindness in him. He's been nice to Janet."

"Ha," I snorted, "so was that guy who turned out to be the BTK killer. He was nice to some of his victims." I stopped for a second. "Right before he killed them with about as much emotion as someone squashing a bug."

Abby frowned. "But the man from your dream is in prison now, isn't he?"

She'd hit on one of the flaws in my theory.

"Yes, but maybe he escaped."

"I would imagine it's not that easy to run from a facility like that."

"I agree, but it has been done. I thought I'd research the murders of the two teens a little more. Maybe even call the newspaper that published the article I read." I picked up my now empty plate and carried it to the sink. Crossing back to Abby, I leaned down and hugged her shoulders. "Thanks for breakfast, but I've got to run. Still have to shower and change for work. Leave the mess, okay? I'll take care of it later."

She patted my hand and said nothing.

I was glad to be heading home after work. It had been, what? A week since Darci's birthday? And here I was, snooping around again in a murder investigation and worrying about outlaw biker gangs. I shook my head in dismay. I needed some down time. Too many things happening in too short a time. My brain felt as if it was ready to blow. Tink and I would have a quiet dinner and watch TV. I'd lay aside dreams, runes, and trying to track down a killer for one night. Tomorrow afternoon would be soon enough to research the teens' murders in California.

This weekend would also be soon enough to follow Abby's suggestion and go over the murder scene. It wasn't something I looked forward to doing. I'd already had violent deaths play out on the private movie screen in my mind, only the faces of the killers had always been hidden. Maybe this time it would be different.

I shuddered at the thought of what I knew it would feel like. The dreams and visions left me shaky and almost physically ill, but they had shed light on the crimes and helped bring killers to justice. . .

My ramblings came to a halt when I turned away from the door of the library and saw Cobra leaning against his bike, parked right behind my car.

Options ricocheted in my brain. I could run back inside and call the police. And tell them what? That I suspected a big bad biker was lying in wait for me? Then I'd have to explain why I thought he was loitering outside the building. Not something I wanted to share at that point. I could run to my car, but he struck me as the type who feeds on intimidation. A bully. And the only way to stop a bully is to confront him. I'd have to pretend a brashness I didn't feel.

I took a deep breath. Fear, the size of a peach pit, lodged in my throat. I swallowed twice and prayed my knees weren't shaking so hard that I'd fall down the steps. Hoisting my backpack higher on my shoulder, I began to descend the stairs.

As I did, Cobra's long legs ate up the distance between us. I watched him get closer and closer while I hung onto the stair railing with white-knuckled panic.

Get a grip, Jensen, I told myself. *It's still daylight and he's not going to strangle you on Main Street in front of witnesses.*

The thought gave me some relief. I took the last step and let go of the railing.

He stopped right in front of me. "I heard you were the librarian," he said with a sneer in his voice.

"Yeah, I am," I said pulling myself up straight. "Why? You want to check out a book?"

Good job, Jensen. Your voice only trembled once.

"Bet you think I don't know how to read," he said with a smirk.

I lifted an eyebrow in a silent question.

Taking my reaction as a challenge, his eyes narrowed and he moved forward into my personal space.

He was so close that I could almost smell the soap he used. Fighting the desire to take a step back, I refused to budge, and met his icy stare with one of my own.

The smirk dropped away and a nasty expression replaced it. His cold eyes, starting at the top of my head, traveled all the way down my body and back again.

I felt like a piece of meat, and it made my stomach twist.

Show no fear echoed in my brain.

Raising my head higher, I took step away. "I'd love to stand here and discuss your taste in reading," I said, and began to walk to my car, "but I must get home."

"That's right, you have a daughter, don't you?" he asked, stopping me in my tracks. "A teenage daughter."

I whirled around, my face a mask of anger, but he was already moving in the opposite direction, toward his bike.

"I suggest you go home, take care of your daughter," he called over his shoulder, "and mind your own business."

My anger fled, chased away by numbing fear. If I didn't mind my own business, would his next victim be Tink?

Twenty-Four

I ran to my car, my loafers slipping in the newly mowed grass. I jerked the door open with shaking hands and threw myself inside. Slamming it shut, I hauled my backpack onto my lap.

Cell phone, I needed my cell phone.

Frantically, I dug through the bag, looking for the phone. Keys, billfold, Kleenex, but no cell phone. I dumped the contents on the seat next to me, spilling half the stuff on the floor. Spying the phone, I grabbed it, flipped it open, and hit our home phone number on speed dial. As the phone rang in my ear, I stuck the keys in the ignition and started the car. Without a glance, I shifted into gear and peeled away from the curb, into the street.

Thank goodness no other cars were coming.

The phone rang and rang, but no one answered. *Where was Tink? She was supposed to go home right after school.* The answering machine clicked on and I heard Tink's voice asking the caller to leave a message.

Frustrated, I punched End and dialed Abby's number. It rang once, twice, three times, but no one picked up. After ten rings I shut the phone and tossed it on the seat next to me.

Coming to a rolling stop at the intersection, I argued with myself about calling the police. What could I tell them? Cobra had threatened Tink? He hadn't, not in so many words, but the meaning had been there nonetheless. Stay out of his business, or else.

Breaking several traffic laws, I sped down the quiet streets of Summerset. After what seemed like forever, my house came into sight. In the distance I saw two people sitting on the front porch step. Even from several blocks away I recognized Tink's fair hair. My heart slowed to a normal rhythm and my foot eased off the gas.

As I turned the corner, I tried to school my face into a normal expression. I didn't want to alarm Tink with my fears. I pulled into the driveway, took a long breath, and got out of the car.

"Hey kiddo, how's it going?" I said, walking up to Darci and Tink. "Hi, Darci."

Tink stood up and grinned, but I noticed a paleness on her cheeks.

"Still got a headache?" I asked, hugging her a little too tight.

"Yeah," she replied, returning my hug. She took a step back and a puzzled look crossed her face. "What's wrong?"

"Nothing," I said with a quick shake. "It's been a long day."

She accepted my answer and her expression shifted swiftly. "Did Abby remind you about graduation and the dance?"

"Yes, she did, and I've got it on the calendar."

"Cool." And for the next few minutes Darci and I heard all about the dance, what everyone planned to wear, what decorations would be used, and who the latest break-ups and hook-ups were.

I stood there watching her animated face as she talked. She was so excited about this dance. It would be her first. After living a reclusive life with her aunt and uncle, these normal teenage experiences thrilled her. And I knew I'd do whatever it took to make sure nothing spoiled this for her.

She glanced at Darci, then at me. "I'm going to go call Nell. I forgot to ask her what shoes she's wearing."

Smiling, I ruffled her hair. "That's right, got to make sure you have the right shoes."

"Yeah, the wrong ones can ruin an outfit," she said as if it were the most important thing in the world. She spun on her heel and headed for the door.

"Hey," I called out, "do you want some willow bark tea for your headache?"

"No, if it's okay, I'd rather have an aspirin."

"Fine, they're in my bathroom."

I watched her run in, letting the door slam behind her. When she was safely inside, the fear that I'd felt earlier came hurtling back and my knees buckled. Dropping all pretense of being okay, I sank to the step next to Darci.

"My gosh, what's wrong?" Darci asked with worry.

Quickly, before Tink reappeared, I told her about my run-in with Cobra.

Darci shot to her feet. "That's it. I want you out of this," she said, pacing back and forth in front of me.

"Take it easy, Darce," I told her, feeling calmer now, after sharing my experience. "When you stop and think about it, Cobra was only trying to intimidate me."

"Worked, too, didn't it?" she said with narrowed eyes.

"Yup," I replied, nodding swiftly.

She eased down next to me. "You have to tell Brett or Bill."

"Darci, I can't. Not without explaining why," I said in a

plaintive voice. "I know Cobra is the killer, but I don't have any proof."

"What if I talked to Danny?" she asked.

"No," I grabbed her arm. "You can't say anything to him. I promised Janet that I'd keep her name out of it." I gave her arm a slight shake. "She's got two little kids, Darce, and she's scared to death El Serpiente will come after them if they learn she talked to me."

"But it sounds like she's already told Cobra about you," she reasoned.

I pulled my fingers through my hair. In my fear, I hadn't thought about that. Clasping my hands in my lap, I stared out into the street. "I know Janet thinks Cobra's different, but I still don't think she'd tell him she talked to me."

"The articles?"

"Must be. He read them, so he knows I'm checking out gang activity on the Internet, specifically the killings in California."

"Suppose he's been following you?" Darci chewed on her lip. "Have you had the feeling someone's watching you?"

I remembered searching the house for Tink's elusive shadow and the night I thought I'd seen someone over my shoulder.

"A couple of times." I frowned. "But it's been when I'm at home, inside."

"Maybe he's a window peeper?"

The notion of Cobra, tall and lanky, sneaking around my house, peering in the windows, should have scared me. Instead a bubble of laughter formed in the pit of my stomach and I chuckled. A totally inappropriate reaction, considering the circumstances.

Darci looked at me in surprise. "I don't think this is funny," she said indignantly.

"You're right, it's not, but I think one of the neighbors would've noticed a guy dressed in leather, lurking about my shrubs." My smile faded. "I don't know. The most important thing is to protect Tink. I'm going to call Abby. I've already decided the best thing would be for Tink to stay there for the next couple of days." I sighed. "I wish I could send her out of town until this is all over, but with eighth grade graduation coming up and the dance, I can't."

"No, she'd never understand."

I took a deep breath and nodded. "So what else can I do?"

Darci gave me a hard look. "Since you're determined to see this through, nothing. Call Abby, send Tink out there, and make sure someone's with her at all times."

"Yeah, we can do that. I'll take her to school every day, and Abby can pick her up. I'll also inform the school that Tink isn't to leave with anyone but Abby or me."

She thought for a moment. "But what about at night? Will she be safe at Abby's?"

"Safer than here." I felt the heat creeping up my neck. "Ah, uh, well, sometimes Arthur stays over at Abby's, so they wouldn't be alone. But I'm, ah, sure that if Tink—"

"Arthur would stay in one of the spare bedrooms," Darci finished for me.

I turned a deeper red.

She giggled and nudged my arm. "Don't be embarrassed. Everyone in town knows about their romance."

"Easy for you to say," I said with a grimace. "It's not your grandmother. Abby's love life is not something I like to think about."

"Look at the bright side. Knowing Arthur, if anyone showed up unexpectedly at Abby's in the middle of the night, he'd shoot first and ask questions later."

Rubbing my legs, I nodded again. "I'm glad you decided to stop by tonight, Darce. I feel better after talking to you."

"Hey, what are friends for?" she said, nudging me with her shoulder. "Danny's on duty tonight, so I was feeling at loose ends." Her face brightened. "I brought pizza and beer, by the way. And a six pack of pop for Tink. Pizza's warming in the oven and the beer's on ice."

"You *are* a friend," I said, breaking into a grin.

At that point I didn't know if my stomach had calmed down enough to eat anything, but I'd never tell Darci that.

"Hey, do you remember the first time you brought pizza over?"

"Yeah, I do." She rolled her eyes. "We ate the whole pizza and finished the six pack."

I laughed. "Right. And the next morning I felt like I'd been pulled through a knothole."

"Things sure have changed for us since then, haven't they?" Darci gave me a big smile.

"Oh, I don't know. We're in the middle of a murder investigation again."

Her smile dropped. "True."

"I was so freaked about Cobra that I didn't ask you about Becca. How is she?"

"As well as can be expected. She has a good attorney, and I know he'll do his best for her. I guess he expects the district attorney to eventually offer a plea bargain."

"But she didn't do it," I said with conviction.

Darci lifted a shoulder. "I know, but if she doesn't take it and is found guilty, she'd spend more time in prison."

"That doesn't seem fair."

"I agree, but that's the way it is."

We sat in silence staring out at the growing twilight. A squirrel capered in the big elm tree across the street, while birds searched out a roosting place for the night. Watching the peaceful neighborhood, it was hard to imagine such drama was occurring beneath the surface of our quiet town. Ned had used the right analogy when he compared El Serpiente to a cancer invading Summerset. And the cancer was growing.

Darci clasped her hands around her knees and broke the silence. "I really wish you'd give up this investigation, Ophelia. I couldn't stand it if anything happened to you or Tink because you were trying to help Becca."

"Quit worrying about the danger. Between Arthur and Abby, they'll protect Tink."

"Yeah," she said, turning her head to look at me, "but who's going to protect you?"

Twenty-Five

While Darci removed the pizza warming in the oven, I called Abby. The conversation included many warnings on her part, and finally, after several guarantees on my part that I'd be safe, she agreed. She'd pick Tink up after supper.

My confrontation with Cobra seemed to have drained every ounce of energy I possessed. With weary steps I climbed the stairs to Tink's room. I gave the door a light rap and it opened a crack.

Half of Tink's face showed in the slit, and she held her cell phone to one ear. "Yeah? Are we ready to eat?" she asked, moving the phone away from her mouth.

"Yes, but I want to talk to you first. May I come in?"

"Sure." She opened the door wider. "Got to go. See you tomorrow at school." With a flip of the phone, she turned her attention to me.

Crossing over to her bed, I sat down and motioned for her to join me. Posters of her favorite rock bands covered the walls, yet her stuffed animals were littered around the room. A mix of both a child and a teen. Soon the plush toys would slowly disappear as she shifted fully into being a teenager. I grimaced. I hoped we were both ready for it.

Tink tossed her hair over her shoulder and took a place next to me. Propping a bended leg on the bed, she looked at me with a curious expression. "What's up?"

"Well . . ." I plucked at the comforter, stalling for time while I thought of the best way to explain what was happening to me. "I'm going to have you spend a few nights at Abby's."

Her brow puckered. "Why?"

"I had a run-in with one of the bikers today—"

"I'm not leaving you alone." She shifted away and her shoulders hunched.

"Tink," I said in a reassuring voice, "I can protect myself, but I'm worried about you. I think that you'd be safer at Abby's."

She scrunched her eyes, and her mouth settled into a mutinous line. "I don't want to go."

"Sorry, kiddo, you don't get to vote on this one," I said, a small smile playing at the corner of my mouth. "I'll be okay, but I've got a feeling someone's watching the house. Until I feel it's safe, you're staying at Abby's." I inhaled a deep breath before continuing. "I'll pick you up in the morning before school, and Abby will be waiting for you in the afternoon."

"What about hanging out at Nell's?"

"Nope." I rubbed her arm. "Not for the duration. Sorry. When you're not in class, you'll be with someone we trust at all times."

She made a raspberry with her mouth. "That sucks. You make it sound like I'm a prisoner."

I took Tink's hand in mine and squeezed it. "I know it doesn't sound like much fun, and I don't want to scare you, but I've got a feeling—"

"A feeling? Or a *feeling*?"

"Huh?"

"You know," she said, tapping the center of her forehead with a finger.

"Oh," I said with a grin, "I get it. A premonition."

"Yeah." Tink watched my face with interest.

"I've had a few dreams, and I'm certain Becca didn't kill Adder, but I don't know who did. I have my suspicions." I shook my head. "And I've been ill at ease here at the house. Like something is waiting or watching . . ." I hesitated. "Have you felt uncomfortable in any way?"

Tink's eyes shifted away and she stared at one of her rock and roll posters. "No."

"Are you sure?" I asked, narrowing my eyes.

Something about the way she had said no blipped across my internal radar. Tink was a medium. What if the ghosts of the two murdered girls in California were somehow reaching out to her? Would they know their killer had escaped justice? Surely after seventeen years their spirits had crossed over and they were beyond caring about what happened on this side of the veil. I made a mental note to ask Abby what she thought.

Tink twirled a strand of hair around a finger. "'Course I'm sure," she said, examining the tip of the strand.

"No shadows? No sense of a spirit trying to reach you?"

"I swear," she said, turning her head and giving me a bright smile. "No spooks in the corner."

"Hey," Darci called from the bottom of the stairs. "Pizza's getting cold."

I slapped my legs. "We'd better go eat. Abby will be here soon."

"You won't change your mind?" Tink's face settled into a disgruntled frown as she gave it one last shot.

"Nope," I said, standing.

I followed her out of the room, watching as she skipped down the steps, her unhappiness forgotten when faced with a hot pizza. With a smile at the mercurial moods of teens, I turned to shut the door to her room when my nose picked up a whiff of cigarette smoke.

Dang it—last thing I needed was Tink smoking.

After Abby picked up Tink, Darci seemed reluctant to leave, so we settled in the living room with a couple of beers and watched TV. One uninteresting show after another flicked across the screen. Bored, I thought about rehashing my favorite murder theory, but I was tired of discussing the whole thing. Darci seemed to want to ignore it, too. So we sat, sipping our beers, with an occasional comment here and there about what was happening on the show. Finally, I broached a subject I'd been dying to ask her about.

"I don't mean to pry, but when you were here with Danny, I got the idea he was moving in . . ."

A flush spread over her cheeks.

"He is, isn't he?" I continued.

"Yes. I hate staying in that house by myself." She took a slow drink from her glass. Setting it down, she watched me with uncertainty. "You don't approve."

"It's not up to me, Darce. It's your life. If he makes you happy . . ." I tried to hide the doubt in my voice.

"He does, he does, I feel safe when I'm with him," she said, leaning forward. "At times, what we have is almost perfect." She traced a finger down the side of her glass. "I know that's hard for you to believe, but it's the truth. When we're alone . . ." Her voice trailed away and she stared off into space for a moment. Returning her attention to me, she continued in a stronger tone, "And I know he seems kind of bossy at times, but his suggestions are for my own good, really."

I wondered if she was trying to convince me or herself.

"You don't have to explain—"

"I do," she broke in. "Your opinion matters to me, Ophelia."

Oh brother, what could I say? She wanted my blessing, and I saw the guy as a control freak, and most of the time being around him set my teeth on edge. How could I dig myself out of this?

"I'm sure Danny has many good qualities," I finally replied.

Jeez, Jensen, what a wimpy thing to say.

"Yes, he does," she said defensively. "He wants to do something with his life, be successful. Not like most men around here who are content with just getting by."

"By successful, does he mean make a lot of money?" I asked. "Because if that's what he wants, he's in the wrong line of work. I've seen in *The Courier* what Summerset pays its officers. Not much."

Darci picked up her glass and drained it. As she put it back on the coffee table she looked at me with a flash of annoyance. "He received a small inheritance a few years ago and invested the money in stocks. He's doing okay."

"Danny's finances are none of my business." Irritated myself, I crossed my arms on my chest. "And I wasn't insinuating that being a police officer isn't an achievement. It's an honorable thing to do with your life. All I meant was that a person doesn't get rich being a cop." Leaning forward, I looked at her intently. "Just don't pin who you are on who you're with, Darci. Whether Danny's successful or not doesn't change what kind of person you are. And I think you're pretty terrific, with or without him."

Her eyes slid away and I could see that the conversation wasn't going anywhere positive. I noticed her empty glass and pointed to it. "Do you want another beer?" I asked, to change the subject.

She eased back in her chair. "I suppose," she sniffed.

I had a choice. I could let Danny cause a rift between us or I could swallow my feelings and keep my opinions to myself. Darci was my friend, and I wasn't going to let Danny come between us. I chose the latter.

Tamping down my own aggravation, I smiled hopefully. "Hey, don't be mad. Anyway, what do I know when it comes to men and relationships? I don't even date anyone."

Darci's face softened. "You could if you wanted to." She eyed me with speculation. "I've been thinking of something different we could do with your hair."

I chuckled. "Hold that thought. I'll get your beer, and then you can explain your make-over plan, okay?"

"Okay." Darci wiggled in anticipation.

Standing, I picked up her glass and walked to the kitchen. "One thing, Darce," I called out. "No waxing the eyebrows. Last time, I thought I'd die from the pain."

Her laughter drifted in from the living room, but abruptly stopped. "Ophelia, get back in here." Her voice rang with excitement.

I rushed into the living room, the open beer can forgotten.

Darci bounced up and down in the chair as she stared at the TV. She held the remote channel changer in one hand and pointed to the screen with the other. "Look."

The show was *American Justice*. The words "Rogues" and "California" immediately caught my attention. The voice-over was telling the story of the two murdered hitchhikers.

Darci looked up at me with a puzzled expression as they

showed the girls being picked up by the bikers. "I thought you said Cobra was one of the killers? That guy isn't Cobra."

"Darci," I said with exasperation, "he's an actor. They're doing a reenactment."

"Well, they could've picked someone out who at least looked like him," she huffed.

"D— Oh never mind." I shook my head and ignored her. I wasn't going to argue with her about the show's casting choices.

My eyes never leaving the screen, I sank to the couch and watched as two mug shots flashed onto the TV.

" . . . Michael Cutter and Josiah Brown are currently serving life sentences in the California State Penitentiary for the murders of Becky Dawson and Tracy Matthews . . ." the announced intoned.

Another picture appeared on the screen.

" . . . However, Gregory Roberts is still at large, after escaping fifteen years ago."

The eyes of a predator, hooded and flat, looked out at Darci and me. A shiver ran up my arm. The photo may have been seventeen years old, but I could still feel the coldness of the man's soul. And it shone from his eyes, as dark and gray as a winter's day. They were as chilling in the picture as they'd been in my dream.

A person can change their face, but they can't change their eyes.

Darci turned to me, confusion written all over her. "Is that an actor, too?"

"No," I said, my voice short.

"Well, it's not Cobra, either."

"You're right. It's not."

In my head, I saw my favorite theory crash and burn.

* * *

After Darci left, I checked the windows and doors at least three times. Arthur had told me where to go to purchase my very own Louisville Slugger, and I intended to buy one tomorrow. Along with a new dog crate that I still hadn't gotten around to purchasing.

T.P. had been better. No more shoes were eaten—he settled on the one he'd already destroyed. In fact, it was his favorite chew toy, and now hardly recognizable as ever having been a shoe. He'd left the trash alone and accidents were down to a minimum, and usually in the hallway on the tile. Much better than on the carpet and rugs.

The only issue I still had with the dog was the toilet paper. He had a fondness for it that surpassed everything else. We'd taken to keeping the bathroom door shut at all times, but if we forgot, he'd make a beeline for that room. And I swear, he could rip all the paper off the roll faster than a squirrel darting across the road. Keeping up with the demand was killing me at the grocery store.

But now T.P. was safely in his crate, in my room, along with Lady and Queenie. I didn't have the heart to leave him alone in the kitchen tonight. With the doors shut to both my room and the bathroom, I hoped it would keep him from his heart's desire.

Snuggled in my bed with all the animals curled up in their respective spots, I thought about the demise of my main supposition.

Cobra wasn't involved in the two murders in California. That didn't mean he still wasn't responsible for Adder's murder, but now I had no motive for Cobra to kill him. And without a motive, I was back at the beginning. And why had I been so convinced the murderer was Cobra? Because I didn't like him? There were several people who were on my

Don't Like list. Mr. Carroll immediately sprang to mind, but I hadn't been rushing around trying to prove he was a killer.

Had I desperately twisted events to suit my premise?

If I wanted to help Becca and Darci, I needed to put personal issues aside, or I'd never learn the truth.

Cobra did threaten me. Why? Was he worried I'd stumble onto evidence of El Serpiente's illegal activities?

Okay, so now I have a reason for his warning. What else?

My thoughts returned to my dream. If the killings in California weren't related to Adder's death, why did I dream about them?

I punched my pillow a couple of times in frustration and curled up in a ball. I wished I had Abby's ability to tell the difference between a "real" dream and a psychic one. I rolled over and laid an arm across my eye as if to block out the way my mind was twisting and turning yet not reaching any conclusions.

I was wearing myself out with all this stewing. Reaching over, I shut off the lamp and tried to sleep.

The howl of two dogs had me bolting out of bed a few hours later. I looked at the clock: 6:00 A.M. What had set them off this early in the morning?

Suddenly, over their yowling, I heard the shrieking of sirens. I ran to the window and looked out. In the distance I saw orange flames shooting high in the sky, and great billows of black smoke blocked the rising sun. The acrid smell of smoke leaked through the windows of my old house. Somewhere on Main Street, a building burned.

The library!

After pulling on sweatpants, I grabbed a flannel shirt and shoved my feet into tennis shoes as I buttoned the shirt over my pj's. I knew I looked a fright, but I didn't have time to worry about style when the library was burning.

Without bothering to tie my shoes, I bounded down the stairs and out the door. Seconds later I was in my car tearing down the street for the second time in less than twenty-four hours.

Twenty-Six

I parked my car as close to the scene of the fire as possible. Thanks to numerous police scanners owned by the ordinary citizens of our small town, the streets were already crowded with gawkers. Some had even brought lawn chairs, so they could be comfortable as they watched the town burn. I pushed my way through the throng.

A police cruiser with its light bar flashing sat at one end of the street, and a county sheriff's department vehicle was parked at the other end. Fire trucks from neighboring towns barreled down the already water-soaked pavement from the opposite end of the block, to be waved past by the county deputy. Other vehicles that tried to slip in behind the fire trucks were halted and motioned to move along.

Downtown was as bright as day from the flames of the fire, and I craned my neck to see over the people in front of me. At what I saw, my legs grew weak with relief and I exhaled a long breath.

It wasn't the library burning so brilliantly, but *The Courier*.

Immediately, I felt guilty. How selfish was I to be thankful it wasn't the library now crumbling into a pile of cinders?

What about poor Ned? Somewhere in this crowd he watched his business go up in flames.

Another idea jumped into my head. There were apartments upstairs, above *The Courier*. Had the tenants managed to escape the inferno? I knew of at least one young family with a baby who rented from Ned, and there might have been others.

A sickness crept into the pit of my stomach as my eyes roved the crowd, trying to find the young family.

I finally spotted them standing huddled together under a blanket, with their baby clutched tightly in their arms. Their faces had a shell-shocked look.

A woman stood beside them with her back toward me. A long silver braid snaked down her spine, and a flannel shirt hung down past her hips, covering most of her nightgown. On her feet she wore bright yellow galoshes. The ones she wore when watering the plants in the greenhouse.

Abby.

I shoved and pressed my way through all the people, toward where Abby stood with the young couple.

"Abby," I said when I was next to her, laying a hand on her arm.

She turned and smiled. "Don't worry. Tink's at the bar with Arthur." She held up a thermos. "He's making coffee for the firemen." Her eyes moved back to the young couple. "Is there anything else I can do for you?"

The young mother rocked her baby on her hip and kissed the top of his head. "No, my mother's coming from Aiken." She hugged the sleeping child closer to her. "We'll stay with her until we find someplace to live."

"Did you manage to save anything?" I asked.

"No." The woman's voice broke. "We lost everything. Our wedding pictures, all the baby's clothes." She tilted her head toward her husband, resting against him. "I don't even have diapers for the baby."

I gave her a weak smile. "Well, I don't have diapers, but I do have clothes that will fit you. I'll make sure I get them to your mother when she arrives from Aiken."

"Thanks," she mumbled, fighting back the tears.

Abby gave the couple a smile and stepped away, drawing me with her.

"What about Ned?" I asked.

"No one was in *The Courier* office," she said quickly. "And they were able to evacuate the apartments in time." She glanced over her shoulder at the flames. "It's too late to save the building, so now they're trying to stop the fire from spreading."

A real estate office was in one of the limestone buildings flanking *The Courier,* and there was a beauty shop in the other. There were apartments above both businesses. I watched the flames lick closer to each building. If the firemen weren't able to contain the flames, the whole of Main Street could be torched. Even now the smoke and water damage alone would cause financial hardship for many of the businesses.

I shook my head at the waste.

"I'm going to see if I can find Ned," I said, glancing over at Abby.

"That's fine, dear," she replied, and shook her thermos. "I need to fetch more coffee."

I watched her stride down the street toward Stumpy's, her bright galoshes slapping her legs as she walked. Later I would join her to check on Tink.

Turning on my heel, I scanned the faces, looking for Ned. I spied him on the corner, taking pictures of his burning building. I walked up to him and lightly touched his arm.

He lowered his camera and a tight smile stretched his lips. "Hey, Slugger."

"Ned, I'm so sorry about *The Courier*. Are you okay?" I asked.

He raised his eyebrows and grimaced with a soot-stained face. "Yeah. I'm thankful no one was hurt." His eyes traveled to what was left of his office. "Great story, isn't it? Too bad I don't have a place to print it, or a paper to run it in."

"Is there a temporary office you can use?"

"Sure. I'll work out of my house and take the paper up to Aiken if I have to. Ed will let me use his press." He eyed the burning building. "If those bastards thought this would stop me, they're wrong."

I didn't have to ask what "bastards" he was referring to.

"You think El Serpiente set the fire?"

Before he could answer, a small explosion sent everyone ducking for cover.

Danny, in his cop uniform, walked the perimeter of the crowd, telling everyone to move back.

Ned took my arm and guided me toward the big elm tree on the corner.

Narrowing my eyes, I studied him. "You didn't answer my question."

Indecision flitted across his face. "Brett asked me to keep my mouth shut."

"About what?" I asked.

Ned looked away as he shifted his weight from one foot to the other. "The note."

"What note?" When he didn't answer, I tugged on his shirt. "Come on, don't hold out on me now."

With a sigh, he explained, "Last week a note was shoved under the door."

I slapped my head. "The piece of paper lying on the corner of your desk," I said in a firm voice. "I noticed you kept glancing at it as we talked."

"Yeah." His lips formed a wry grin. "I was afraid you'd pick it up and read it. Guess I wouldn't make a very good poker player, would I?"

Ignoring his remark, I shook his arm. "Quit stalling and tell me what the note said."

"Shoot." He kicked at a stone lying at the base of the tree. "Promise me you won't allow this to fuel any of your theories?"

"Okay," I answered reluctantly.

"The note warned me to back off on the editorials—"

"But that's what you said you were going to do," I cut him off.

"You're right. I guess I didn't back off soon enough. Or they wanted to make sure I got the point."

A crash drowned out my words as we watched the roof fall in, sending cinders flying into the air.

Main Street was thick with smoke from the smoldering building. It looked like the worst of the fire was out and the rest of the businesses would be saved. The street was littered with plastic coffee cups, wet paper, and charred pieces of wood. Thick hoses snaked from the hydrants down the middle of the street. Even though the fire was under control, it still required the presence of firemen to guard against flare-ups. One truck remained on duty.

From the look of things, there'd be no customers today on Main Street. Even if the cars could negotiate around the hoses and the truck, the thick smoke would be enough to keep businesses closed. After a quick call to Claire, the decision was made to close the library, too. Hopefully, by Monday morning the mess would be gone and it would be a normal day.

Feeling useless, I wandered down the street looking for Abby. My steps led me to Stumpy's Bar and Billiards. Cupping my hands against the glass, I peered in the front window. No Abby, or Tink, but Arthur stood behind the bar. Tapping on the window, I waved.

Seeing my nose pressed up to the glass, he smiled and motioned me in.

"Abby just left with Tink. Goin' home to open the greenhouse," he said as I strolled across the room and took a seat at the bar.

I took a quick look at the clock hanging by the aged mirror. Past eight already. "I didn't think about the time. Sorry. I suppose you're on your way home?"

Arthur cackled. "Well, soon. These old bones can't take late nights and early mornin's anymore."

"Oh," I said, moving off the stool, "I'll get out of your hair."

Maybe that was a wrong choice of words since Arthur was as bald as a cue ball.

"Sit down for a spell. I got some cleanin' up to do first." He held up a pot. "Want some coffee? There's enough left for one cup."

I shook my head. "No thanks, I've had too much as it is."

Turning his back to me, he dumped the coffee down the bar's drain. "Shame about *The Courier*," he said as he wiped out the pot. "S'pose them bikers were behind it?" He threw me a look over his shoulder.

"Probably," I said with a frown. "The problem is going to be proving it."

He turned to face me across the bar, laying his liver-spotted hands on the shining surface. "Damn nuisance." His voice echoed in the empty room. "That's what they are."

Right, and drug dealers, and pimps, and several other nasty things we couldn't imagine.

Arthur straightened and rocked back and forth on his heels. "Well now, Abby's been tellin' me about your troubles with those yay-hoos—"

I stretched a hand out, stopping him. "Thanks for helping with Tink, by the way."

He tossed away my thanks with a shake of his head and smiled. "Don't mind at all. That little girl's a real charmer. Goin' to be a beauty when she grows up."

"She is, isn't she?" I replied with pride.

Arthur's face sobered. "Abby's mighty worried about you."

I nodded. "I'll be okay. I can take care of myself."

"I got a little somethin' that might help you." He reached down and hid something behind his back. "Before I give it to you, you gotta promise me you won't let on to Abby that I gave it to you," he said, trying to make his face stern. "Don't want her thinkin' I'm encouragin' you."

"Okay," I answered in a voice tight with anticipation.

He held out a package, crudely wrapped, with bits of paper sticking out, an old-fashioned bow balanced precariously on top. When my eyes widened with delight, he beamed.

"Picked it up for you myself, yesterday."

"Ohh, thank you, Arthur," I exclaimed, ripping off the paper.

"You're welcome," he said and wagged a finger at me. "Don't go tellin' her where you got it."

"I won't," I promised, my eyes never leaving the polished wood.

I traced a finger around the letters, burned deep into the beautiful grain. Arthur had even had OPHELIA engraved on my very own Louisville Slugger.

Twenty-Seven

It was sweet of Arthur to buy me the bat, I thought as I walked back to my car. I couldn't imagine using it on someone, but it made me feel safer. The weight felt good in my hand, and I took a little practice swing, smiling at how stupid I probably looked.

I placed the bat in the seat next to me and started the car. The fire at *The Courier* was another tragedy in town that could be blamed on El Serpiente. How much longer would they be able to get away with their intimidation and dirty deeds? I wondered if I should drop the whole thing. There'd been some serious stuff going down, and the best people to handle it were the authorities. My blundering around could make the situation worse.

At the four-way stop I saw two bikers out of the corner of my eye. They were parked along the side of the street, leaning against their bikes as they looked toward the burned-out shell of *The Courier*.

Admiring their handiwork?

Turning my head, I squinted to see them better. I couldn't make out their faces, but I recognized the lean, easy posture of Cobra.

My anger sparked. They were watching the once beautiful building smolder, a building that had stood for a hundred years and now was nothing more than rubble. And a young family might have died in that blaze. Their disregard for human life caused my temper to flare as hot as the fire that had destroyed the newspaper office. They had to be stopped, and I felt my resolve strengthen.

Maybe my psychic radar would pick up something at Darci's? Maybe not who killed Adder, but a clue about his life. A tip I could pass on to Bill and Brett that might help bring El Serpiente to their knees.

The thought made my lip curl with pleasure as I eased through the intersection. I'd like nothing better than to see them *all* led off in handcuffs.

Pulling into my driveway a few minutes later, I noticed my front door open a crack. Dang, I'd been in such a hurry that I'd forgotten to lock it. The same thing I'd accused Tink of doing, I thought sheepishly. Not trusting T.P. to stay in the yard, I hoped he was still safely inside.

The minute I crossed the threshold, my senses went on alert. The air around me crackled with a foreign energy. *Someone had been in my house.* Alarmed, I ran to the car for the bat.

Were they still in my home? Or was it just another elusive shadow? A trick of my imagination? No, the energy that I'd sensed was real. I had to find the animals.

Back in the house, I stood in the hallway and called for them. All three appeared at the top of the stairs. Patting my leg, I tried to coax them down, but only Lady left her perch.

She tripped down the stairs and glued herself to my side.

"Someone was here, weren't they, girl?" I asked, and, not for the first time, I wished she could answer me.

Slowly we made our way to the back porch, where I checked the door. It was still locked, with the dead bolt Danny had recommended.

Whoever had been in the house had gone out the same way they came in. At least, I hoped they'd left.

Lady and I checked the kitchen, the living room, the dining room. And as we did, the energy that I'd felt earlier began to slowly slip away. That left two rooms downstairs—the guest bedroom and my office. We'd check my office next.

The door was slightly opened, and I tightened my grip on the bat. Lifting it to my shoulder, I was ready to clobber anyone standing on the other side of that door.

But just as I was about to swing the door wide, I stopped. Should I call the police instead of marching in? What would I tell them? A biker had it in for me because I was snooping around in his business? I felt the presence of someone in my house because I was psychic? Nope, not a good idea. I didn't want to talk to Bill or Brett until I had to.

Wiping a sweaty palm on my pants and gripping the bat again, I pushed the door open with the toe of my shoe.

I gasped.

My crystals lay scattered on the rug. My favorite lamp was tipped on its side. Chair cushions had been tossed across the room. My desk looked like someone had wiped it clean with an arm. But my pictures and beloved books suffered the worst. The pictures had been smashed, fragments of glass sparkling everywhere, and the bookcases were empty, the books lying every which way on the floor. Some of them with their pages crinkled.

My runes!

I rushed to my desk and jerked the drawer open. It was completely empty except for the worn pouch holding my great-grandmother's stones. With a shaky hand I reached down and grasped the bag. The vibration of the runes shot up my fingers.

The stones were singing to me, and it wasn't a happy song.

With the bat still in one hand, I clutched the pouch to my chest and scanned my office, shocked at the wanton destruction of my private space, my place of magick. Unshed tears gathered in the back of my throat and I felt violated beyond my imagination.

How could someone do this? Invade my home like this and destroy my special things?

A white hot spot of anger began to burn in the pit of my stomach.

How dare they? *They?* How dare he? I had no doubt in my mind who was responsible. Cobra had seen me at the fire, and he'd seized the opportunity to send me another little warning. First he made veiled threats against Tink, and now this. He was trying to strip away my sense of home, my sense of security.

I had no intention of letting him get away with it.

Once, out of anger, I'd called the elements—Earth, Air, Fire, and Water—to punish a killer. At the last minute I'd stopped because of Abby's teachings.

This time I wouldn't have to call on the fury of nature—I had plenty of my own. And my fingers tingled with the pent-up power of it.

I still believed in Abby's teachings, that it was wrong to hex someone. I might not hex him, but it didn't mean I sure as hell couldn't scare the crap out of him.

I drove to the corner where I'd last seen Cobra. Just my luck, he was gone. I didn't want to confront him at The Viper's Nest. I was angry, but I wasn't stupid. Even armed with my

Louisville Slugger and a head full of spells, I'd be no match for a bunch of bikers. I'd be outgunned and outmaneuvered.

Did they carry guns? That was illegal, wasn't it? Like they'd care, Jensen.

Gripping the wheel tighter, my eyes darted back and forth, hoping to find a lone biker, and hoping it would be Cobra. Finally I was rewarded with the sight of a biker ahead. Was it Cobra? I sped up until I was right behind him.

I caught the biker's profile when he turned his head. Yes, it was Cobra, just driving along enjoying the morning, checking out the scenery.

He pulled slowly into the parking lot of the sale barn, without signaling, of course. I whipped in behind him and headed him off as he made his U-turn. His bike skidded on the loose gravel and he almost lost it. He recovered swiftly, and I saw his mouth move as he swore at the idiot who'd cut in front of him.

I slammed the car into Park and with bat in hand jumped out.

"Are you nuts? You almost made me dump my bike," he said, getting off and taking a step toward me.

I closed the distance between us and pointed my bat at his chest. "I don't give a damn if you wreck." I shoved the bat at him. "You stay away from my house. You stay away from me. And most of all," I said waving it in front him, "you stay away from my kid."

A look of disbelief crossed his face as he eyed the bat. "Are you crazy?"

My eyes narrowed. "You don't know the half of it, slick. You'd be wise to take my warning seriously."

Standing that close to him, I could see dark flecks of color in his gray eyes.

He took one step back. "You know I could yank that bat

right out of your hands, don't you?" he asked with a smug expression.

I eyed him up and down, as he'd eyed me in front of the library. "Sure you could. You're bigger and stronger, but I suggest you don't."

"Oooh, I'm scared." He pretended to shiver. "What will you do to me?"

His attitude only fueled my rage. "Know anything about curses?" I asked in a cold voice.

"Curses?" He shifted back a step. "You are *crazy*."

"No, not crazy, just a witch."

Crossing his arms over his chest, he threw back his head and laughed.

As I watched him laugh at me, I thought about the family journals going back over a hundred years. One said that in order to banish, you had to understand conjuring. That diary had listed all sorts of horrible things that could befall a person. How they were caused and how they were cured. My family had always been more interested in the cure than the cause, but with this guy, I might make an exception.

"So what are you going to do?" he asked when he finished laughing. "Shoot a fireball at me? Twitch your nose and make me disappear?" He smiled at his cleverness.

"Nope, can't do that." I grinned maliciously. "But how would you like to have boils all over your body?"

His smile slipped a bit "You can't do that."

"Oh yes, I can," I said, nodding emphatically. "I'm also a psychic, and I can read you like an open book, buster." I stepped closer. "I can know your biggest fears and your darkest secrets."

"I don't believe you."

My hand shot out and I grabbed his upper arm right on top of the snake tattoo. Staring into his eyes, I opened my mind, and images flashed in my head so rapidly I could barely make them out. Words poured out of my mouth.

"False, not real. You're protected by the eagle, not the snake. Stars surround you. Many lives, you've lived many—"

He jerked away, breaking the connection, and the images stopped as suddenly as they'd begun.

"You *are* freakin' weird, lady," he said, turning on his heel. He marched back to his bike, threw a leg over the seat and, with a swift kick, caused the engine to howl to life. Without a glance, he peeled out of the lot, throwing gravel.

I cupped my hand to my mouth and called after him. "Hey, don't forget about the boils."

Twenty-Eight

I stood in the middle of my wrecked office trying not to let the tears fall. My anger had faded after my confrontation with Cobra, leaving me feeling hurt and upset, but crying would serve no purpose.

Suck it in, Jensen, and get this mess cleaned up.

I walked over to my favorite picture of Tink and picked it up. It had been taken right after she came to live with me. In the photograph, Tink knelt in the backyard with her arms around Lady's neck, and they were both looking straight at the camera. Smiling, her violet eyes shone with happiness.

Tracing a finger down the deep gouge in the photo, a tear slid down my cheek. That moment in time would never come again. I couldn't go back and retake the picture. I couldn't even make copies. The photo had been taken with my digital camera and had long since been erased from the memory card.

Sniffing, I wiped my eyes with the heel of my hand and put the picture in its destroyed frame down. Squatting, I began to pick up shards of glass when the doorbell rang.

I stood and brushed away the tears that had continued to fall, even though I'd promised myself not to cry.

When I reached the front door, I saw Darci standing on the porch. I took a deep breath and opened it.

"Hi," she said with a smile that fell away when she saw my expression. "What's wrong?"

Without speaking, I motioned for her to follow me.

At the threshold of my office, Darci gasped. "Who did this?" she asked.

"Cobra."

"Are you sure?"

"Who else?"

She shook her head sadly. "I should've listened to Danny and not asked for your help."

"It's not your fault—"

"Yes, it is," she said, not letting me finish. "I pulled you into this mess. First, he makes veiled threats concerning Tink." She swept her arm in a wide arc. "And now this."

"I don't think Cobra will bother me again," I said, crossing my fingers behind my back.

A surprised look crossed her face. "Why?"

When I'd finished relating my conversation with Cobra, Darci's mouth hung open and her eyes were wide.

"That was foolish. Why didn't you call Bill or Brett?"

"It wouldn't have done any good. I was the one stupid enough not to lock the front door." My eyes scanned the shambles. "And do you think whoever did this left any evidence behind?"

"No."

"See. A call would've been pointless."

"But to track Cobra down? He could've killed you."

I waved away her concerns. "It was Saturday morning in Summerset, for Pete's sake. No one would commit murder in broad daylight, along one of the busiest streets in town."

Darci cocked her hip and stared at me. "But what about later?"

I laid a hand on her arm. "Look, for some reason the idea of having boils all over his body—"

"You wouldn't really do that, would you?" she cut in.

"Are you kidding? If Abby found out I'd done something like that, she'd kill me." I paused. "Even if it was to a rat like Cobra."

Darci looked at me skeptically.

"Well, I wouldn't," I said defensively. Shaking my head, I recalled Cobra's reaction during our confrontation. "It wasn't the curse that got him, it was something I said when I did my reading."

She tapped her chin, thinking. "Eagles, snakes, stars. I don't get it."

"Neither do I," I said with a shrug. "Eagles eat snakes, don't they?"

"I don't know." She shuddered.

"Maybe, since I saw stars, the whole thing is related to his zodiac sign."

"When was he born?"

Rolling my eyes, I tilted my head and glanced up at the ceiling. "How would I know, Darce? His birthday didn't exactly come up in the conversation."

"Right. Did you see anything to do with Adder?"

"Nope, and nothing I felt had anything to do with the killings in California seventeen years ago."

"We already know he isn't one of the three Rogues 'cause of the show last night."

"Yeah, but it doesn't mean he isn't a brother or a friend of one." I chewed my lip and thought for a moment. "I think we need to forget about those murders for now. I'm still convinced they're somehow tied in, but I don't see how. If we're going to help Becca, we need to concentrate on Adder's murder." I nodded, making a decision. "I need to know more about Adder. For example, what was his real name?"

"Steven Romano," Darci said calmly.

"How do you know?" I asked, my tone suspicious.

"Georgia," she said with a toss of her head.

"I suppose Alan told her?"

"No, Adder's sister."

My mouth dropped. "Adder's sister? How does Georgia know his sister?"

"The sister is staying there, waiting for the medical examiner to release the body."

I slapped my forehead in frustration, then grabbed Darci's arm, pulling her out of the office. "Come on."

She stumbled behind me with a perplexed look. "Where are we going?"

"To talk to Adder's sister."

A dark-haired woman dressed in a prim white blouse and long skirt sat on Georgia's front porch. Her legs were crossed demurely at the ankles and she held an open book in her hands.

I flashed a look at Darci. "Adder's sister?"

"It must be," she said, nodding. "She's the only guest Georgia has right now."

I studied the woman. "I think it would be better if you let me handle this alone."

"But—" she began to argue.

"If she knows you're the cousin of the woman accused of killing her brother," I explained, "she might not agree to talk to me." I observed Adder's sister. Her head remained down. "She's not paying any attention. Slip around to the back, see what you can find out about her from Georgia. I'll come get you when I'm finished."

Darci pouted. "Okay."

As I approached the porch, I got a better look at the woman. Her dark hair, shot with gray, was twisted into a tight bun, and curly strands had escaped. Heavy eyebrows, thick as woolly worms, made an almost straight line across her brow.

An insane thought jumped into my mind. *Man, would Darci like to take her tweezers to those.*

"Hi," I said in a friendly voice as I crossed the porch to where she sat. "I'm Ophelia Jensen."

Raising her head, she watched me, a hint of suspicion lurking in the depths of her brown eyes. A gold cross glinted against the white material of her blouse.

"Deloris Romano," she said, and extended a pale, slim hand.

I shook her hand, and without waiting for an invitation, sat in the wicker chair next to hers.

"Ah, *Capote: A Biography*," I said, pointing to her book. "I've read that. It's very good."

She glanced down at the open pages. "Yes, I prefer biographies."

"It's been very popular at the library." I gave her an ingratiating smile. "I'm the local librarian, by the way."

"Really?" she replied, lifting her heavy eyebrows and sizing up my blue jeans, my baggy University of Iowa sweatshirt, and my tennis shoes with their flopping laces.

I bent down and tied my shoes. Straightening, I settled back in the chair and tried to look relaxed. "Yes, we have a very nice library. Of course, it's closed today because of the fire. Too much smoke, you see, but normally—"

Shut up, Jensen. You're rambling.

I pressed my lips tightly together to stop the inane flow of words. And as the silence lengthened, I decided my oblique approach was *not* working. Subtlety had never been my strong suit. I'd get right to the point.

"I'm sorry for your loss," I said quietly.

Her eyes flew wide. "You know about Stevie?"

"It's a small town and, umm, well . . ." My voice trailed off as I tried to think of a way to explain. There wasn't one. "Ahh, I'm kind of looking into your brother's murder—"

"I thought you said you were a librarian?"

"I am. Without going into details, let's just say I'm convinced the wrong person has been accused."

She snapped her book shut and her face hardened. "I only want to take my brother home." Her eyes watched a swallow dip and weave in the late afternoon sky. "Stevie never knew peace in life; I can only pray he does now in death, but I doubt it."

"You don't care if his killer is brought to justice?"

Gathering her things, she stood and made a move to leave. "Not really. Stevie's fate was sealed when he joined that gang, and his life has brought nothing but pain to my mother."

I threw out my hand to stop her. "Wait."

She paused.

"Please, wouldn't it bring comfort to your mother to know her son's killer was punished?"

I watched while emotions flitted across her face. Anger, resistance, and finally resignation. With a sigh, she lowered herself back onto the chair.

"What do you want to know?" she said softly.

Scooting forward in my chair, questions bounced around in my brain. Where to start?

"Did Add—ah, Stevie hook up with El Serpiente in California, or somewhere else?"

"California. It's where we live. Los Angeles." She stared off into space, remembering. "He was the baby and the only son. My parents spoiled him from the day he was born. He could do no wrong in their eyes." Her eyes drifted down to her hands clutched tightly in her lap. "Stevie was sixteen when Papa died, and he started running the streets. I tried to tell Mama that he was up to no good, but she wouldn't listen."

"Is that when he joined El Serpiente?"

"Pah, those bums," she replied, her tone derisive. "Motorcycles, drinking, and God only knows what else." She fingered the gold cross at her neck. "By the time he was eighteen, his feet were firmly set on a bad road."

"How long has it been since you've seen him?"

"Years, and it's broken my mother's heart." Her face tightened in bitterness. "Last time he came home, it was because he had no place else to go. He'd been beaten, stomped by men wearing boots with metal studs in the soles—"

"Another motorcycle gang?" I said, breaking in.

"Yes, The Rogues. Stevie said it was a turf war." She brushed the stray curls away from her face. "It's too bad they all didn't wipe each other out. Maybe those girls who were murdered wouldn't have died."

"You know about the young hitchhikers who were killed?"

She turned her head slowly and looked at me. "Of course. It was all over the news."

"Did Stevie know the three men charged with the killings?" I asked, trying to hide my excitement.

"I think so. It happened about the same time as his beating." She shook her head. "We pleaded with him not to go back to the gang, but he ignored us. Said they were his brothers, his family. And what were we to him?" she asked, her eyes filling with tears.

I didn't know what to say, and I couldn't watch the pain fill the poor woman's face.

"Ahh," she said with an angry swipe at her tears. "It's over. Now Mama and I can remember Stevie as he was as a child and forget the man he became."

We sat in silence—alone with our thoughts. I glanced at Deloris and watched as her face softened with memories. I felt sorry for her. She'd loved the little boy, but hated the man.

Maybe now her family could find peace, too.

Twenty-Nine

"At least I have a tie in with the murders in California now,"
I said to Darci as we drove back to my house.

She gave me a dubious look. "A pretty weak one."

"Yeah, but it means Adder was involved in the turf wars
with The Rogues." I thought for a moment. "I wonder if
they've moved into the Midwest, too?"

"I could ask Danny."

"Oh, right." I snorted. "As if he won't know why you're
asking him about it."

"You don't think I can worm the information out of him?"
she asked with an arched eyebrow.

"Yeah, you probably could," I replied with a chuckle.

"What do we do now?"

"Is Danny on duty tonight?"

"Yes."

"Good, I'll meet you at your house in a couple of
hours."

"Why?"

My shoulders shuddered. "I'm going to go over the murder scene."

* * *

Once home, I made my preparations. I couldn't use my office to center myself until I'd cleared the room of negative energy, so after my bath in sea salt, I meditated in my bedroom. I found it hard to concentrate. I don't know if it was dread at what I might see that was making it so hard or something else. Whatever the reason, I had difficulty emptying my mind. Finally, I gave up and left for Darci's.

Standing on her porch, I fidgeted, shifting my weight back and forth, glancing nervously right and left. When she opened the door, I stepped inside, expecting waves of discomfort to hit me. Nothing.

Maybe this wouldn't be so bad after all.

Out of the corner of my eye, I saw boxes piled in the living room. A fancy stereo system with huge speakers sat in the corner, next to a big screen TV. Danny's.

Darci's eyes followed mine, and she struck a defensive pose. "Boys and their toys," she said with a sweep of her arm.

Pretty nice toys, I thought, but didn't reply.

"I told you Danny's done well with his investments."

"I didn't say anything," I replied in an injured voice.

"You didn't have to—it's written on your face."

"Darci," I said firmly, "this is going to be tough enough. We don't need to have a discussion about Danny right now."

Her face crumpled. "I'm sorry."

I took a deep breath. "It's okay. Let's just get this over with."

She nodded, and I followed her to the bedroom with steps as heavy as someone on their way to their execution. I stepped around Darci and paused in the doorway. Closing my eyes, I let the energy flow through me and connected with my sixth sense, then opened my eyes and wandered around the room.

By the bed, sexual tension filled the air. In my head, I tried to fast forward past it and was rewarded when I felt it slowly fade away.

My eyelids drifted shut again, and I opened my mind.

Anger and then hatred crept with stealth into the room. And fear, but not Becca's, not Adder's. Someone else's.

With my eyes still closed, I turned toward the door and tried to see who felt the fear. In my mind I saw two figures, their faces hidden in the dim light of the room. One of them moved hesitantly into the room, while the other remained at the door. Dark spots across the carpet marked his steps. He paused at the bed, and I witnessed Adder through the eyes of the killer. I felt his rage, and hiding below the rage, absolute fear. A raised arm came into my line of vision, and I watched it make a swift arc down.

Suddenly, the image shifted to a dark night and a stretch of highway, and I heard the sound of a motorcycle roar.

My eyes popped open and my knees buckled. With a whish of air from my lungs, I sat down hard on the bed. Realizing where I was, I jumped to my feet and whirled around with a horrified look. Staring at the bed, images tumbled through my head, then I felt a hand on my arm, shaking me.

"Ophelia, snap out of it." It was Darci's terrified voice.

I shook my head as if to clear what I'd seen. "What?" I croaked, finally turning to her.

"This is too spooky," she said through lips pinched so tight they were white. "We're getting out of here."

She pulled me out of the bedroom, through the house, to the kitchen. Dragging a chair away from the table, she firmly shoved me down.

"What happened?" I asked with a shaky voice.

She rubbed her arms. "You didn't look like you," she exclaimed. "You snarled and raised your arm as if you were stabbing someone." She shuddered. "I thought you were possessed or something. Are you okay now?"

"A glass of water," I mumbled. "My head hurts."

Darci flew to the sink, grabbed a glass and turned on the faucet. When the glass was full, she rushed to the table and placed it in front of me. "Do you want an aspirin?"

"No," I said with a shake that made my head throb. "I'd better not."

A flicker of the images and the emotions I'd felt in that room still whispered in my brain. I fought to silence them. Taking a deep breath, I imagined a clear bath of white light pouring over me, drowning the murmuring.

Darci left the kitchen and was back a moment later, carrying an afghan. She wrapped it around me, tucking it tightly around my legs.

With a trembling hand, I picked up the glass and took a sip of water while she hovered over me.

"Well, that was fun," I said sarcastically, in an attempt to ease the tension ricocheting around the room.

"I don't think so," she said in an irritated voice. "You scared me."

"Scared me, too." I took a deep breath and felt a trickle of calm beginning to flow through me.

"Can you tell me what you saw?" she asked as she pulled out a chair next to me.

"Two men. Didn't see their faces," I replied in a jerky voice as I rubbed my temples. "One came in the room, while the other stood in the doorway . . . I felt the emotions of the killer. He was angry and afraid."

"Of getting caught?"

"No." I pursed my lips, thinking about it. "Something else. Something about Adder was causing the fear."

"Was the murder out of fear or anger?"

"Fear," I said confidently.

"Why did he fear Adder?"

"I don't know. I didn't pick up on the reason."

"Could it be blackmail?"

"I suppose. It's all kind of a jumble right now. Maybe after I think about it for a while, it will become clearer."

Then I remembered something I'd seen, and touched her hand. "The killer tracked something across the floor. I saw the marks—"

Before I could finish, Darci jumped up and ran from the room. A few minutes later she was back. She crossed the room and sat.

"No marks now, but the carpet's lighter in spots. Like somebody scrubbed it. I never noticed."

Great. Tidy killers who cleaned up after themselves.

Driving home, I was so tired that my eyelids kept wandering down. I'd jerk and they flew open. Lucky for me Darci's house wasn't that far from mine.

In spite of my exhaustion, I realized I hadn't talked to Tink all day, so, with almost numb fingers, I dialed Abby's house. Tink was having a great time, and no, she really didn't have time to talk right now. Abby had given permission for Nell to spend the night. They were going to watch movies, eat popcorn, and stay up until dawn. No, she wasn't having headaches. Everything was fine and I needed to quit worrying. Before she hung up, though, I did get a quick, "Miss you."

Smiling, I put the receiver down and went to do my nightly security check. All was as it should be, but the dogs decided they needed a run around the backyard. Reluctantly, I followed them out the back door. Sinking into a chair on the patio, I propped my feet up and laid my head back.

When I woke up, the moon was higher in the sky.

"Okay guys, that's it. I'm not sleeping out here tonight."

I called them and they chased across the yard as T.P.'s short legs tried to keep up with Lady's longer stride. Laughing, I bent down to pick him up but was rewarded with a yip.

"Fine," I said, putting him down, "have it your way."

The dogs ran through the house and up the stairs, with me bringing up the rear. T.P. turned at the top, saw me, and beat it back down the steps.

"Oh no, you don't." I made a grab at him as he hurtled past, headed for the bathroom. Spinning around on the narrow step, I moved to follow him. I'd forgotten about my floppy laces, and before I could catch myself, I tumbled down two steps and landed ungracefully on my bottom. One foot had curled underneath me as I fell.

Wincing at the pain shooting up my leg, I tried to stand, but my right foot wouldn't support my weight. I felt the pressure build inside my shoe as my foot began to swell. Grabbing the banister, I hauled myself to my feet and hobbled down the rest of the stairs.

Dang shoelaces! They never stayed tied, I thought as I half limped, half hopped into the kitchen for the phone.

It looked like I'd be taking a trip to the emergency room that night instead of curling up in my nice soft bed. At least I had clean socks on.

As I waited for Abby to answer the phone, I glanced down at my throbbing foot.

The laces were tied.

Thirty

Only a week before, I'd sat in this hospital with Darci, waiting for doctors to examine Becca in the emergency room. Now I was the one in the E.R. They took X rays and prodded and poked my foot until it hurt like a son of a gun. And to top it all off, the doctor had given me a choice between splitting my favorite blue jeans at the outside seam or wearing a hospital gown. Not wanting to flash patients and doctors on my way out, I'd chosen ripped jeans. I think the nurse took perverse pleasure in slicing them up to the knee.

As I stared at the ceiling, the smell of rubbing alcohol and antiseptic made me want to sneeze, and more than a little self-pity knotted in the back of my throat.

Why this and why now? Didn't I have enough *issues*? I still felt freaked out over what had happened at Darci's. Whatever the explanation was for my experience, I didn't like the idea of a killer crawling around in my brain. The thought scared me. And just *how* was I supposed to ferret out a killer—make that two killers—if I were laid up with a broken foot?

I snorted in disgust.

"Quit your stewing, Ophelia," Abby said, her voice breaking the silence in the tiny cubicle.

I rolled my head toward where she sat in one of the ugly green plastic chairs. "I can't have a broken foot," I whined. "I don't have time for this."

Abby bowed her head, but not before I saw a smile tug at the corner of her mouth. When she raised her head, her face was serious. "It doesn't make any difference if you have the time. It is what it is—"

"Ha," I said, not letting her finish. "You always say that."

"If I do, it's because it's true. You can't control everything, my dear."

"I don't want to control everything. I want to find the killers and end this mess. Let my life get back to normal." I shifted my foot, and pain raced up my leg.

Abby chuckled. "Normal?"

"Okay, bad choice of words." I turned my head and resumed staring at the ceiling. "Peaceful? Is peaceful too much to ask?" I looked over at her.

"No, but you were the one who made the choice to get mixed up in this murder investigation. You're going to have to see it through."

"How can I, if I'm laid up with a broken foot?"

"I'm sure you'll think of a way." Abby studied me for a moment. "How did you say you tripped?"

"I guess I spun around too fast on the step when I made a grab for T.P." Crossing my arms over my chest, I tried to remember the exact sequence of events. "I thought I tripped on my shoelaces, but I couldn't have. They were tied and—"

Before I could finish, the doctor buzzed into the room carrying an X ray. He flipped the light box on and shoved the exposure into the holder.

"Yes, as I thought," he said, pointing with a pen to a spot

on the picture. "The tip of the fifth metatarsal is broken off."

"Excuse me?" I said.

"Right here." He drew an invisible circle around a portion of the X ray. "Your little toe. The bone ends in a tip on the side of your foot. You broke the end off," he said, turning and smiling at me.

Right, easy for you to smile, I thought. It's not your foot that's broken.

I didn't voice my opinion. "What are you going to do? Put my foot in a cast?"

"Yes. For now we'll do a temporary one, and in a couple of days, after the swelling is down, we'll put on a walking cast."

"Just around my foot, right?"

I could live with that.

He shook his head. "No, the cast will be to the knee."

"What? For that little thing?" I said, waving toward the light box.

"'Fraid so. In order for it to heal properly, we need to keep the entire foot immobile. That means going up to the knee with the cast." He crossed the cubicle and stood looking down at me. "It won't be so bad. Once the walking cast is on, you'll be able to have more mobility. Until then you'll use crutches. *But*," he said stressing the word, "I want you off that foot for the next couple of days. If you're not, the swelling won't go down."

I groaned and rolled my eyes.

"Be right back with the plaster," he said with a reassuring pat to my shoulder.

"I'll take you to the farm and you can stay with me," Abby said, her mind made up.

"No."

"Why not?"

"I can't get up your stairs on crutches."

"I can make up the couch."

"Listen, Memorial Day is next weekend, and you have enough to do at the greenhouse, making up the flower boxes for the cemeteries—"

"Tink can help," she said, sitting straighter in her chair.

"Yes, she can, but the whole point was to keep her safe. She might not be safe if I'm at the farm." I felt my stubbornness settle in. "If you're worried about me, maybe Darci can stay a couple of nights, until I get the walking cast." I tugged on my bottom lip. "I really don't think Cobra's going to bother me again, but I can't be sure," I said more to myself than Abby.

She rose from her chair and came to stand by the examination table.

"I heard that." She eyed me suspiciously. "Why do you think he won't harass you anymore?"

"Ah, well," I muttered, my eyes shifting away from Abby. "I kind of threatened him."

"With what?" Her voice was deceivingly mild.

"A curse," I blurted.

"Ophelia Mette Marie Jensen, you can't do that," she scolded, waving a finger at me. "It's unethical, it's against—"

"I wasn't really going to *do it,*" I defended myself. "I just wanted to scare him. And it worked, I might add." I wiggled with satisfaction and ignored the ache in my foot. "He turned tail and ran."

"What kind of curse?"

"Boils," I whispered.

"What?" she said, cupping her hand to her ear, "I didn't hear you."

"Boils." My voice echoed in the cubicle.

"And where did you find this curse?"

"In one of the journals," I said, feeling like a child being chastised. "You're always telling me I should read them. I'd think you'd be happy I'm finally paying attention to our heritage," I replied with an indignant sniff.

"That particular journal was written so we could understand the cause—"

"I know that."

"—not," she shook her finger at me again, "as an instruction manual for hexes."

I squirmed on the table. "I get it, okay. I didn't do it, even though he's got it coming for what he did to my office and for threatening Tink."

Abby crossed her arms and tapped her foot. "No, you *don't* get it. Whether someone has it coming or not is not for you to decide. There is justice in karma. People pay for their misdeeds."

"Yeah, well . . ." I sounded skeptical, but held up my hand to stop the arguing. "Let's talk about something else. I have a question I need to ask you."

From the look on her face, I could see Abby wasn't finished with this topic, but she nodded in agreement. "What is it?"

"Darci said I acted like I was possessed when I was at the murder scene." I rubbed my chin nervously. "Was I?"

"No. I would guess the violent energy was affecting you—" She broke off, lost in thought. "I'll warn you. You've opened up to what happened in that room. It might cause flashbacks."

"What?" My voice was full of horror as I jerked my head off the pillow. "I might go after someone with a knife?"

Abby gave me a tolerant look. "No, of course not. But you're plugged into it now, and you might experience more dreams about the murder."

Lovely.

"What about these pain pills?" I asked, handing the bottle to Abby.

We were back at my house. She had helped me navigate the porch stairs with my crutches and then to totter back to the guest bedroom. It had been a struggle getting my jeans off, but finally I was sitting on the bed clad in my underwear and sweatshirt.

"Humm," she said, taking the bottle from me and reading the label. "I know your foot hurts," she went on when she finished, "but it might not be a good idea to take these. It's hard to tell how the medication would work on you in your weakened state."

"You mean because I let my psychic shield down earlier?"

"Yes, you need to recharge your batteries so you have some control. If you can manage without them, I would."

I looked longingly at the pills and thought about the relief they'd bring to my aching foot.

"I have some herbs that might help," she said, watching me hopefully.

"Probably tastes like ditch water," I muttered to myself.

Choosing between drinking one of Abby's nasty potions or taking medication that might trigger severe dreams didn't seem like much of a choice at all. I opted for a third selection. I'd tough it out without herbs or pills.

She handed me my pj's, which she'd fetched from my bedroom. "Do you need help getting undressed?"

"No," I replied in a glum voice. "I can do it myself."

She turned and left the bedroom to give me a little privacy.

Privacy? Ha! There'd be people running in and out of

there for the next few days until I convinced everyone I could manage by myself. The self-pity I'd been feeling earlier came welling up. My foot hurt, my office had been trashed, my kid wasn't safe in our home. I was worn down to my last nerve.

A knock at the door pulled me out of my pity party.

"Are you dressed?"

"Yeah," I replied, hoisting my heavy foot onto the bed.

Abby walked in, looking concerned. "I'm staying here for the rest of the night."

I gave a long sigh and shoved myself up in the bed. "You don't need to."

"I want to." Her tone brooked no opposition. "I'll sleep on the couch."

"Abby, you'll be uncomfortable."

"No, I won't. I want to be near in case you need me."

"Thanks for the offer, but I'm not going to want anything." I yawned deeply. "I'm so tired that I'll be asleep in seconds."

"Nonetheless, I'm staying."

I couldn't argue anymore. "Okay."

Abby hesitated. "I went in your office."

"It's a mess, isn't it?" I slipped lower in the bed. "That dang Cobra—"

"He didn't do it."

My tired eyes popped open. "How do you know?"

She cocked her head and said nothing.

"Right." I nodded slowly. "Who did?"

"Someone with a lot of negativity and frustration." She studied my face with puzzled green eyes. "It was strange. I heard knocking when I walked around the room."

"Knocking?"

"Yes, knocking on a door as if someone wanted in."

"You didn't feel any anger?" I asked, making an effort to

keep my eyes open.

"Oh, whoever trashed your office is mad at you, but it's because you're not paying attention to them."

"That's crazy." My eyelids dropped. "Okay, so Cobra didn't wreck my office," I muttered as I felt sleep about to claim me. "Good thing I didn't hex him with boils after all."

Thirty-One

"Did you sleep well?" Abby asked, buzzing into the room carrying a tray.

I pushed up in bed and reached for the crutches. "Yeah, but right now I've got other concerns."

She put the tray down on the dresser and steadied me as I rose to my feet, er, foot.

"Do you need assistance?" she asked.

I felt the blood rise to my face at the idea of being escorted to the bathroom. I hadn't had someone take me to the potty since I was three years old. "No," I replied in a curt tone.

When I returned, Abby had straightened the bed, and to my surprise, Tink sat on a corner.

"Tink," I cried, happy to see her.

Her lips curled up in a big smile. She jumped off the bed and ran over to help me. A slim hand grasped my upper arm while she took baby steps beside me.

I grinned to myself. Tink was so petite that if I went down I'd pull her right with me. Situating my body, cast and all, back under the covers, I eyed the tray Abby placed on my lap. It held a steaming cup. "What's that?" I asked in a dubious voice, pointing to it.

"Solomon's seal. It helps bones knit, among other things. Drink it, it won't kill you," she said, tilting her head. "I added plenty of honey."

I took a cautious sip. It wasn't bad. Then, taking a large swallow, the warm, sweet tea ran down the back of my throat and seemed to fill me with a sense of well-being. Suspicion immediately reared its head.

"What *other* things does Solomon's seal do, Abby?"

"Lots of things," she prevaricated.

Thinking I wouldn't like her answer, I hid my feelings behind a sweet smile. "Like what?"

"All right, not that I think you're possessed," she said, holding up a hand, "but Solomon's seal can also be used to banish ghosts and other psychic nasties. It protects."

"It's okay." I drained the remaining tea. "I'll drink a gallon of the stuff if Solomon's seal helps me not relive yesterday in my dreams."

Looking down, I picked up my fork and moved the scrambled eggs around on my plate. "You must've raided your fridge. Mine was empty," I said, and took a bite.

"It isn't now. I loaded it up with simple meals that I'd made and frozen. Vegetable soup, spaghetti, things you can warm up in the microwave." She picked up my sweatshirt and laid it over the arm of the chair. "The meals will tide you over until your walking cast is on."

"Thanks." I laid down my fork and looked at Tink, who'd been sitting quietly on the corner of the bed. "So what have you been up to?"

"Not much," she said, her eyes downcast. "Helping Abby with the Memorial Day flower boxes. We had a lot of customers yesterday." She raised her head, her violet eyes were filled with worry. "Are you going to be okay?"

"Sure, I am. It's a teensy bone, this big." I held up my

thumb and index finger to show her. "And I have to wear this big, heavy thing." I waved at my cast, propped on the bed. "Can you believe it?"

Tink didn't answer, but she made an attempt to smile.

Then it hit me. *You're a dunce, Jensen. Tink's mother died from a tumble down the stairs. No wonder she's worried.*

I moved the tray and held out my arms for a hug. "I'm okay, truly," I said, wrapping my arms around her.

My eyes met Abby's over Tink's shoulder and, with a quick nod of approval, she left the room.

Tink returned my hug, then sat back. "You're sure?"

"Yes."

"And you tripped?"

"I think so."

"Really, it didn't feel like you were pushed?"

Tink's mother had been shoved, causing her to fall.

I grunted. "'Course no one pushed me. I was here alone."

Her face cleared a little. "Are you going to back out of chaperoning the dance on Thursday?"

"No. I should have the walking cast on by then. As long as I don't have to chase some kid, I should be okay."

"We're too grown up to play any silly games," she said with a roll of her eyes.

"What? No 'pin the tail on the donkey'?" I asked, pretending to be amazed.

"Aaah!" The sound came from deep in her throat. "This is a dance—"

"Gosh, don't think I can dance," I cut in, teasing her.

"You wouldn't—" She stopped and thought for a moment. "Would you?"

Her face registered her horror at the idea of me on the dance floor, in front of all her friends.

"Don't worry. Even if I didn't have this cast, I've never been much of a dancer. Anyway, all the guys there will be too young and too short." I shook my head and chuckled. "None of those kids would have the nerve to dance with an adult."

She grinned with mischief. "Mickey Dahl would. He has a crush on you."

"Get real," I said in a shocked voice.

"No, really, he does." She nodded. "The kids were talking about it at school once. He's liked you ever since you helped him with his science fair project in elementary school."

I had an image of red-haired Mickey, who came about to my shoulder, waltzing me around the floor while I dragged my heavy cast. My laughter shook the bed.

While I was laughing, Abby bustled into the room. "You haven't finished eating," she said with a glance at my half-full plate.

Talking seemed to wear me out, and I yawned. "I'm sorry. I don't think I can finish," I replied, leaning back against the pillows.

"Don't you want me to stay with you?" Tink asked.

"Oh, sweetie, I'd love for you to stay, but I'd worry." I stroked her hand. "All I'm going to do is sleep. And Abby needs you at the greenhouse." Covering my mouth, I yawned again.

Abby laid a hand on Tink's shoulder. "Come along, dear, and let's let Ophelia sleep."

Tink rose reluctantly, leaned over and gave me a quick peck. "I'll be back tomorrow."

Abby picked up the tray and planted a kiss on the top of my head. She turned and, with the remains of my uneaten food in one hand and her other resting on Tink, the two of them crossed to the door.

I was almost asleep when I heard Abby speak to Tink.

"Don't worry, dear, I've a feeling this will be over soon."

By the time I woke up, it was early evening. I couldn't remember ever sleeping that much. Abby had said I needed to recharge; maybe she'd slipped a little something in with the Solomon's seal?

I thumped down the hall with my crutches and into the living room. Darci sat curled up on the couch reading a copy of *In Style* magazine.

Great, a new babysitter.

Raising her head, seeing me, she threw down the magazine and jumped up. "What are you doing out of bed?" she asked, rushing over and taking my arm.

"If I spend any more time in that bed," I said with a jerk of my arm, "I'll get bedsores."

"Are you hungry?"

"What is it with you and Abby?" I grumbled. "All you want to do is fatten me up and make me sleep."

"Tsk tsk," Darci clicked. "Wake up on the wrong side of the bed, did we?"

With a glare in her direction, I tottered over to a chair and plunked down.

Nurse Darci grabbed a throw pillow and placed it on the coffee table. Gently lifting my leg, she slipped the pillow under my cast, elevating my foot.

Dusting her hands in front of her, she gave me a pleased look. "There. Better?"

Before I could answer, she ran off to the kitchen. I heard her banging around and using the microwave. Minutes later she returned carrying a steaming cup.

"Here," she said, setting the cup on a coaster. "Abby said for you to drink this when you woke up."

I'd been kidding about drinking a gallon, but it appeared Abby had taken me seriously.

Darci slid the coaster to a different spot on the table. "Is that close enough? Can you reach it?" She moved it again. "How's that?"

I grasped her wrist before she could slide the cup one more time. "Would you knock it off? I'm not an invalid. It's one tiny bone."

Suddenly, it felt like ants were crawling up my leg underneath the cast. "If you want to do something for me, find me something to scratch my leg. It's bugging me," I said, trying to wedge my fingers down the cast.

"You can't. If you break the skin under the cast, you could get an infection."

"Please?" I gave her my most pitiful look.

"Nope, Abby left me in charge."

I shoved myself back against the chair in a pout. "Fine."

"Abby cleaned your office," she said, changing the subject.

"She did?" I asked, sitting forward.

"It smells really good, like herbs."

"Ah." The light of realization dawned. "Abby felt uncomfortable in there earlier. She smudged the room."

Darci sat down on the edge of the coffee table. "What's that?"

"First she opens all the windows, then she burns sage leaves in an abalone shell. Walking through the room, she wafts the smoke around the windows, doors, and into all the corners. As she does, she pictures the room filling with white light and peace."

"Sounds lovely." A thoughtful look crossed Darci's face as she handed me my crutches.

Together we walked back to my office, where I paused in

the doorway. Except for the ruined pictures, everything was as it had been before it was ransacked. My crystals glowed around the room, my books returned to the shelves and in their proper order, and the old lamp had been righted. But most important, the air felt and smelled different. The slight tang of sage carried with it a sense of renewal.

I limped into the center of the room and stood propped up with my crutches. Closing my eyes, I let the atmosphere seep into me. Sending my energy out into the room, I made it mine once again.

With a deep breath, I opened my eyes and smiled at Darci. "This is—"

Her chirping cell phone, hanging from her waist, interrupted me. A flash of irritation crossed her face as she read the number. She flipped the phone open. "Hello?" she answered, leaning against the door frame.

Crossing to my desk, I sat on the chair, booted up my computer, and tried not to eavesdrop. Hard to do when someone's standing four feet away.

"No." Darci's voice was clipped. "No . . ." She paused. "I told you I'd be spending the night at Ophelia's," she answered in a firm tone. "No, I don't think that would be a good idea."

She stood straight as she listened to the voice on the other end. "Ophelia is very tired, and I don't think a lot of company would be good for her."

Her eyes narrowed in frustration. "More stuff? I don't know where we'll put it." She hesitated as she lowered her head. "Of course I want you to feel like it's your home, too."

Darci raised her head and rolled her eyes. "Look, I've got to go. I'll talk to you later."

She paused and listened to the voice at the other end.

"Yes," she answered into the phone, hesitating. "Yes." She moved the phone away from her ear and spoke louder. "What? What? I can't hear you. I think you're breaking up." Grabbing a piece of paper from the desk, she held it next to the phone and crumpled it loudly into the receiver for a few seconds, then snapped the phone shut with finality and tossed the crumpled page into the wastepaper basket.

Looking down, Darci covered her eyes momentarily and shook her head. Then she turned, gave me a false smile, and shoved the footstool over for my leg.

"Thanks," I said, and laid my leg across the stool before returning my attention to the computer screen. "New phone?" I asked, not looking at her.

"Yes."

I turned and watched her flop down in one of the wing chairs.

"Danny bought it for me." She looked at the cell phone in her hand as if it would bite her. "He calls me all the time to check in."

The words "check in or check on" came to mind, but I said nothing, looking back at the computer screen.

"It's not that I don't want to talk to him, but does it have to be this much?"

I grasped the tip of my tongue with my teeth. No way was I going to answer *that* question.

Thirty-Two

A moment later Darci popped out of the chair and spun around. "It really feels great in here."

Relieved she'd dropped Danny as a topic, I smiled. "It's the smudging."

"Hmm?" She stopped her spin and stroked her chin. "I know you can't do it now, but do you think you could smudge the room in my house?"

She didn't have to say what room she meant. I shuddered at the thought of going back there.

I leaned back in my chair and crossed my arms. "I think that's a good idea, Darci. I also think it wouldn't hurt for Abby to do some of her magick. Kind of add some extra oomph to the smudging."

Darci put a hand on her chest and blew out a long breath. "Thanks. I feel so uncomfortable in my house right now. I need something that'll wipe out the bad vibes."

"If anyone can do that, it would be Abby."

After pulling the extra footstool next to the desk, she sat. "Whatcha looking for?" She leaned to the side and peered at the computer screen.

"I'm looking for more articles about the murders in

California," I said, twirling the mouse around on the pad.

"The hitchhikers?"

I pointed the arrow to one of the stories listed and clicked the mouse. "Yup."

"You're really convinced Adder's murder is tied to those killings, aren't you?"

I nodded slowly as my eyes scanned the open Web page. "It has to be. They keep popping up in my visions. Adder grew up in California and was involved in the turf war between El Serpiente and The Rogues." I winced at the ridiculousness of two motorcycle gangs in Summerset. "Sounds crazy, doesn't it?"

"A little." She raised her eyebrows and shrugged. "When the right opportunity comes along, I'll see what Danny knows. If The Rogues are somewhere in Iowa, it's not such a stretch to think they know that El Serpiente is operating in Summerset. Maybe they want a piece of the action."

I elbowed her. "Just be careful when you talk to Danny. I don't want him running to Bill and ratting on me . . ." Hesitating, I thought about Bill's warnings. "Since my foot's broken, do you think he would really arrest me?"

Darci laughed. "I think if he knew you were playing detective again, you could be in a body cast and he'd still throw you in jail."

For the next half hour Darci and I cruised Web site after Web site, looking for information about the killings in California. I'd printed off what looked like a ream of paper containing stories about The Rogues, El Serpiente, and the two young teens. If I'd known exactly what I was looking for, it would've helped, but I didn't. I only hoped when I reviewed these articles, something would pop out at me.

After I'd moved on to the next site, Darci jabbed me in the arm. "No, go back."

My face wrinkled in a frown. "Back to where?"

I was getting tired again, and my eyes were beginning to blur from staring at the computer screen.

"Back to that last site with the pictures at the bottom."

"I didn't see them," I grouched.

"That's because you were in too big a hurry and didn't let them load."

"There," I said, hitting the Back button. "Happy?"

"Yes, thank you," she replied with a smirk.

Drumming my fingers on the desk, I waited for the page to appear. It was taking forever, but I quelled my desire to move to the next site. Finally, the page finished and I scrolled down.

Darci had been right. At the bottom of the article were pictures, a couple of which I'd already seen—Gregory Roberts's mug shot from *American Justice* and the three Rogues in handcuffs. The third photo was of Gregory and his girlfriend.

They were posed leaning against a motorcycle and smiling into the camera. Well, the young woman was smiling. Gregory glowered at the camera with a disgruntled expression, as if he didn't want his picture taken. Wearing shorts and a skimpy top, the girlfriend had both arms around his waist, and her legs, looking tanned and shapely, stretched out in front of her. She was a real babe, except for one feature.

"My gosh, would you look at those ears?" Darci gasped, and grabbed my arm. She leaned forward and took a closer look at the screen. "I can't believe she wouldn't have had them fixed. And she should *never* wear her hair in a ponytail."

"Otoplasty, ear surgery is called otoplasty. A kid I went to school with had it done," I said, looking at the young woman's ears, which seemed to jut straight out from her head, with the tips cupped forward. "Unfortunately for him, his ears started to stick out again a year later."

Darci's eyes narrowed as she studied the young woman. "I don't mean to be unkind," she waved at the screen, and her eyes widened, "but she looks like Dumbo."

While she continued to stare at the screen, her hands drifted up and touched her ears, as if checking out her ear size.

Chuckling, I pulled her hand down. "Forget the girlfriend and look at Gregory. Ever see anyone who remotely resembles him around here?"

"The picture's, what? Seventeen years old?" Crossing her arms, she squirmed forward on the footstool. "But those eyes? Ugh, they're creepy. I think I'd remember eyes like that." She turned to me with hopelessness written on her face. "What are we going to do? We're not any closer now than we were a week ago."

"Maybe not." I rubbed my outstretched leg distractedly.

Suddenly the lights surged, then flickered and died. A second later they flashed back on and there was a soft whir as my computer rebooted.

"Great," I said in disgust. "I hope that didn't fry my hard drive."

After the screen came on, it looked like all was well. I glanced at Darci.

She sat hunched over, her whole body a picture of dejection. "I don't understand how any of this is going to help Becca."

"We know there were two men now—"

She perked up and snapped her fingers. "The second man? What did he look like? Can you describe him?" she asked, the words rushing out.

"No, his face was in the shadows."

"How tall was he?"

"I don't know." I tried to recall the fleeting glimpse of the man in the shadows. "Taller than Arthur, but not as tall as Ned."

"Cobra's height?"

"No, Cobra's taller than Ned."

I could see her going through a list of men in her head, searching for someone to compare to the man in the shadows. "Danny? Was he Danny's height?"

"I don't know," I said, rolling my eyes. "Maybe. I'm rotten when it comes to judging height."

"Eyes? Hair?"

"Darci," I said in a tired voice, "I only saw him in my mind for a second. I don't remember how he was dressed, didn't see his face, don't know the color of his eyes or his hair. All I know is that the killer wasn't alone."

Rubbing the small of my back, I stretched. "Man, I cannot believe how tired I am. Who would've thought breaking a tiny bone would take this much out of me?"

Standing, Darci picked up my crutches and helped me to my feet. "You'd better get back to bed."

I thumped into the bedroom with Darci following me.

"Do you need anything?"

"No, just more sleep, I guess." I wiggled in the bed, trying to find the right spot for my cast. Giving up, I scrunched down until I was on my back staring at the ceiling. "Don't forget to check the windows and doors, and make sure to keep the bathroom door shut. T.P. is still getting out of his crate." Turning on one side, my eyelids closed. "And the bat's in the kitchen," I mumbled.

"Got it." I heard the laughter in Darci's voice.

The room went dark, and Darci's soft steps whispered across it, accompanied by the sound of her chirping cell phone.

* * *

Days passed by in a blur. The more sleep I had, the more I needed. I spent dreamless hours in bed, only to wake up still exhausted. Abby came and went, checking up on me daily. Even in my stupor I saw her expression grow more and more concerned. She tried to persuade me to see a doctor, but all I wanted to do was sleep.

When the morning of my doctor's appointment finally arrived, Abby bustled into the house, threw my covers off, and insisted I get up and bathe. After wrapping the temporary cast in plastic, she hurried me off to the bathroom and hovered outside the door the whole time. When I'd finished and was bundled in my robe, she helped me to the kitchen and washed my hair in the sink.

Getting dressed took forever. Lethargy slowed my movements, making it an effort to perform the simplest of tasks. At long last I was ready, wearing no makeup, my hair hanging about my shoulders, and dressed in sweatpants and a T-shirt.

Abby escorted me out the door. My spirits lifted the minute the sun warmed my skin; it seemed to energize me. I took a slow step, pausing to inhale the fragrance of my neighbor's lilac bushes. I paused and inhaled again. How many days since I'd been outside? Sunday? Monday? I couldn't remember.

Although the sky was clear, the air around me felt heavy, and not only with the scent of lilacs. Hobbling down the step, I glanced at Abby, holding my arm. "Is it going to rain?" I asked her.

She lifted her head and seemed to sniff the air. "Yes. This afternoon. A storm's coming in."

I had always been somewhat sensitive to the changes in the weather, but Abby was unerring in her predictions. She could've had a great career as a weatherman, and wouldn't have needed Doppler. I pictured her standing in front of a huge weather map while predicting storm fronts and tornadoes, her face beamed into thousands of homes via television. The thought made me smile.

Abby caught my grin. "What's so amusing?" she asked, opening the car door and helping me in.

"The idea of you as a weatherman. You would've been a legend."

"Oh you and your funny ideas." She tried to fix a stern expression on her face but failed. "It's good to see you smile," she said softly, and shut the door.

It felt good to smile. I couldn't remember the last time I'd done that, either.

At the doctor's, Abby insisted I also be given a checkup in addition to my new cast. I tried to explain that I was feeling better, less tired, but she wouldn't listen. When the doctor pronounced nothing wrong, I gave her an "I told you so" look, but she ignored that, too.

We were pulling out of the parking lot when my stomach rumbled loudly.

"Hungry?" Abby asked with an amused glance.

I nodded.

"How about one of Arthur's hot sausage sandwiches?"

My mouth watered and I licked my lips. I loved his sausage sandwiches. "French fries, too?" I asked, wiggling my eyebrows at her.

"Of course," Abby answered with a chuckle.

When we walked into Stumpy's, Arthur waved at us from behind the bar. The crowd was light for a Wednesday. A couple of businessmen sat at a corner table with the remains of their lunch in front of them. Pete Polaski was seated near the windows, alone. He acknowledged us with a tight-lipped nod.

Sliding into a booth, I was relieved I no longer had to drag those hated crutches with me everywhere, but my relief was short-lived when the crack of a cue stick hitting a pool ball caught my attention. Looking over a shoulder, I saw Cobra playing pool with—what was Mr. Roly-Poly's name?—oh yeah, Rattles.

When I turned, I saw Abby looking past me with a frown.

"Do you want to leave?"

"No," I replied, adjusting my leg under the table. "I'm fine."

Arthur hurried over to take our orders, clucking over my misfortune as he did.

A few minutes later a shadow fell across our table. I looked up to see Cobra watching me with a speculative grin.

"How'd you break your leg? Fall off your broom?"

"No, trying to catch a toad to do my spell for boils," I whispered archly. I patted the bench. "Sit down and I'll give you another reading."

Without a word, he turned on his heel and stomped out of the bar.

"Ophelia, it isn't wise to taunt him," Abby hissed at me. "What if he spreads it around town you're a witch?"

"Oh, pooh. Who's going to believe a lowlife like him?"

Thirty-Three

"Do you want me to help you into the house?" Abby asked as we pulled into my driveway.

"I'm not an invalid," I said indignantly.

"Humph," she snorted, "the past couple of days you've been acting like one."

I narrowed my eye and stared at my house. Next to Abby's, it had always been my refuge. Why did the idea of walking up my steps and into my home suddenly fill me with trepidation?

Hiding my feelings from Abby, I plastered a smile on my face. "I know, I think it was from being cooped up. I'm not used to being so inactive. It was good to get out today."

She patted my hand. "I was worried."

"Don't be. I'll be fine. I have to be. Tink's eighth grade graduation program is tomorrow, and then there's the dance."

"I'm glad to hear you're going. She's been worried, too."

Opening the door and lifting my leg out, I used the door frame to pull myself out of the car. "See," I leaned down and said triumphantly, "I can manage."

"Tink and I will be over later."

"Okay, and Abby, tell Tink to bring her stuff. I think it's safe for her to come home."

"I agree."

I waved at Abby, pulling out of the drive, before walking up to my house with a gait that reminded me of a peglegged pirate. As I unlocked the door, I hesitated. Looking over my shoulder at the dark clouds rolling in from the west, I couldn't understand why I was so uneasy to enter my own house.

Stop it. You're letting your imagination get the best of you again. You have nothing to fear in your own home.

With a resolute nod, I opened the door and walked in. Glancing around the hallway, I didn't see any of the pets.

That was odd. They usually met me at the door.

I called their names, and the three of them appeared at the top of the stairs.

"No way," I said, eyeing the stairs. "I'm not coming up to get you."

Determined not to go to bed again, I decided to watch a movie—one of my favorites: *Return of the Thin Man*. Popcorn and a movie. What better way to spend a stormy afternoon?

While I was in the kitchen making my microwave popcorn, I heard a car pull in the driveway and thought that Abby must've come back. I went to the dining room window, looked out and saw no car. As I turned away from the window, I heard a crash in the kitchen.

Hurrying back, I found the bowl upside down on the floor with the popcorn scattered across the tile. T.P., smelling food, had come downstairs and was now scarfing up my popcorn.

"Stop it. You'll get sick," I said, shooing the puppy away from the mess.

T.P. gazed up at me with nervous eyes and then quickly skittered back into his crate.

"Honestly," I muttered to the dog, grabbing the broom and dust pan. "You've been so nervous lately."

T.P. whimpered at the scolding but didn't make a move.

I cleaned up the popcorn and made another bowl. And as I thumped into the living room, a slow roll of thunder sounded in the distance. The storm was going to hit before long. I hoped the electricity wouldn't go off.

After inserting the DVD, I curled up on the couch and grabbed the remote. I hit Play and settled back to enjoy the movie. Fifteen minutes into it, the DVD skipped. I pushed Rewind and started it over again. Ten minutes later it froze just as William Powell lifted the martini glass to his lips. Hitting Rewind, I tried to start the movie a second time, but then the TV screen went black. Disgusted, I hit the On button and the TV blared to life, the sound ten times louder than it had been.

Quickly muting the volume, I stared at the remote. Did I hit the volume button when I tried turning it back on?

That's great, Jensen, you can't even work a remote control.

As I studied the remote again, the screen went black.

"Oh, I give up," I said aloud, and tossed it on the couch.

Sitting there munching my popcorn, I listened to the wind pick up. From my nice, safe place on the couch, I could hear the branches on the trees outside the living room window groan. The thunder and lightning was getting closer. I played the game I had as a child, counting the seconds between the flash of lightning and the sound of thunder. Five seconds. That meant the storm was only five miles away. It would be on top of my house soon.

The front door opening and closing stopped my game.

"Abby?" I called out.

Did I hear a whisper?

I looked over my shoulder and called again. "Abby?"

Still no answer.

Over the sound of the thunder, I thought I heard footsteps cross the hall and walk into the kitchen.

"Tink!" I yelled, my voice tight with fear.

Silence.

"Is someone there?" I asked, pulling the afghan close to my chin.

With a pounce, Queenie landed on my lap.

"My God, you scared me to death!" I exclaimed, rubbing her ears.

Then I heard footsteps again and my hand froze on Queenie's fur. Paralyzed, I listened to them come out of the kitchen and climb the stairs. If it was Tink, why hadn't she answered me? I heard the floorboards above my head creak as footfalls walked down the upstairs hallway, headed for Tink's room. Seconds later the door to her room slammed.

Maybe the sudden change in atmospheric pressure caused the door to slam? Okay, I'd heard of that. Maybe it had been Lady in the kitchen? But how did the front door open?

I wasn't alone.

My adrenaline surged. Pushing Queenie off my lap, I struggled to my feet and hobbled as fast as I could to the kitchen.

Where had Darci put the bat? I had to find the bat.

The storm broke and torrents of rain lashed the windows while I madly scurried around looking for the bat. A bolt of lightning cracked, and instantly, thunder, as loud as a freight train, rattled the plates on the wall.

The noise was followed by a moment of total stillness, and once again I heard footsteps above me. They were walking down the upstairs hall.

I grabbed the phone and spied the bat at the same time. Punching in Abby's number with trembling fingers, I clutched the bat to my chest and stared wild-eyed at the kitchen door.

The steps were coming down the stairs.

"Answer, Abby, answer," I prayed aloud.

Another crack of thunder startled me, and I almost dropped the ringing phone.

Rain continued to pound the windows as the storm resumed its intensity. I held the phone so tightly my hand ached. Another flash of lightning lit the kitchen as bright as a thousand candles. A branch rapped at the window like bony fingers. I clomped over to the sink and stared out while my breath caught in my throat and I waited for someone to answer the phone.

I heard steps in the hallway coming toward the kitchen.

"Hello?" Abby's voice sounded in my ear.

"Thank goodness!" I cried, and lowered my head.

In my sink lay a bloody knife.

Voices murmured around me as I slowly opened my eyes. Abby's and Tink's faces hovered above mine. I'd fainted.

I pushed away the cool hands stroking my face and struggled to sit up. With Abby on one side and Tink on the other, they lifted my shoulders. Once upright, dizziness spun my head and little black dots floated in my vision. I swallowed twice to fight back the nausea.

Still clutching the bat in one hand, I pointed a shaky finger at the sink. "Kn-Kn-Knife," I stuttered.

"What knife?" Abby asked.

"There's a bloody knife in the sink," I said, dropping my hand, which had suddenly become too heavy to hold up.

Abby shook her head. "There isn't a knife, Ophelia," she said gently.

Tink, her face white, sat back and burst into tears.

Abby flashed her a stern look and made no attempt to comfort her.

I eyed both of them in confusion. What was going on?

"We need to get you off this floor," Abby said, taking my upper arm in a firm grip. "Tink, help."

With both of them lifting at the same time, I managed to get on my feet, still clutching the bat.

Abby reached out and began to pry my nerveless fingers from the smooth wood. "Let go."

"No." I resisted. "Someone was here. I heard footsteps, first in the hallway, then upstairs. They might still be here, hiding."

"Oh, I'm sure he is here, but a bat's not going to help you against a ghost," she replied in an even voice.

The bat clattered to the floor. Picking it up, Tink continued to cry.

"I don't get it," I said, my eyes darting back and forth between the sobbing Tink and Abby's severe face.

"You will after Tink explains." Abby took my arm and began to escort me from the kitchen. "Won't she, Tink?"

Tink's sobs were her only answer.

Abby maneuvered me onto the couch and tucked my old afghan around my lap. She took a seat next to me.

Tink sat on the coffee table across from me. Her head was bowed as if she couldn't look me in the eye. Guilt was in every line of her body.

"Tink, what's going on?"

Her head dropped lower.

"Tell her," Abby commanded in a curt voice.

Tink sniffed twice and wiped her nose on her sleeve. "I used Melinda's Ouija board," she muttered under her breath.

"Huh? When?"

"When I spent the night with Nell." Her voice cracked. "The night after the murder."

My eyes flew around the room as I tried to absorb what she was saying. Lady and Queenie wandered out and took up spots near us to watch the excitement.

"Oh Tink," I said with disappointment. "What were you trying to prove?"

She wiped her nose again. "I was tired of all the teasing and I thought if I scared Melinda, she'd leave me alone."

Hmm, same thing I attempted with Cobra. Guess I wasn't setting a very good example.

"I called Melinda from Nell's," Tink continued. "She'd fished her board out of the garbage when her dad threw it away. The three M's met us at Darci's—"

"Where?" My voice rang in the living room.

Lady lifted her head at my outburst and tilted it to stare at me in confusion.

"Darci's."

"How did you get in?"

"We snuck around back and climbed in through the window on the porch."

"Wasn't it locked?"

"No, the lock doesn't work."

I frowned. "How do you know?"

"Darci showed me. We'd been shopping and went back to her house, only we were locked out and Danny won't let her keep a key outside. We climbed in the window."

I wondered how many other people in town knew Darci's little secret. Kind of put the "locked door" issue in a different perspective. Anyone who knew about the defective window could have had access to Darci's house the night of the murder. And why in the devil hadn't she said something about it to Bill?

Tink watched me apprehensively. "Go ahead," I encouraged her. "What happened next?"

Her gaze shifted away. "We went into the bedroom and used the Ouija board."

"I suspect there's more to it than that."

"The other girls sat back and watched while Melinda and I asked questions." Tink rubbed her face, still not looking at me. "At first the spirit said he was a little boy, but when we asked what year he was born, the thingy—"

"Planchette?" I filled in for her.

"Yeah, that's it." She nodded. "It started spinning like crazy. I thought Melinda was doing it, but she looked as scared as I felt."

"It was moving on its own?"

"Yeah. Then I asked if there were other spirits in the room, and all of a sudden we smelled cigarette smoke. Mindy and Mandy looked so afraid, I thought they were going to wet their pants."

Nice image.

"Come on, let's hear the rest of it."

Tink lifted her head and looked at me with huge eyes. "He tried to choke Melinda," she said in a hushed voice. "And I saw him."

Thirty-Four

I threw my head back on the couch and stared at the ceiling. "Calling forth spirits in a room where a murder had occurred twenty-four hours before? Of all the—"

"They jumped up and ran," Abby said, taking up Tink's tale. "They did think to grab the board, but they didn't close the session and didn't go into this with any type of protection. Nothing."

I raised my head to see Tink's drop in shame.

"The ghost attached itself to Tink and followed her home," Abby concluded in disgust.

"Why didn't I sense him?"

"You're not a medium." Her eyes were focused on Tink.

"Why didn't he contact Tink?"

"I'm sure he tried, but Tink's finally learned a great deal of control, and he couldn't get through. So he tried other means."

"My office? You said someone was angry because I wasn't paying attention."

"Your office, T.P. escaping from his crate whenever your back was turned, the missing keys, the shadows Tink thought she saw, the feeling you had that someone was watching you—"

"I thought it was Cobra," I muttered.

"Well, it wasn't," she said in a firm voice. "It was Tink's ghost."

"T.P.'s unease around Tink?"

"Probably. He sensed the spirit around Tink, and it scared him."

My brow wrinkled. "But why not Lady and Queenie?"

"My dear, they've lived with you all of their lives, by now they're familiar with odd occurrences. T.P. is young, and just like humans, young animals are more sensitive."

We sat in silence while my head tried to process all this information. Bottom line? I had a ghost in my house who threw temper tantrums. Peachy.

Abby's voice broke into my thoughts. "I suspect, after your experience at Darci's, you were too wide open. The ghost was able to plug into you, so to speak, and draw off your energy. That's why you were so tired, but felt revived once you were out of the house."

Not only temperamental, but an energy vampire, too.

"The ghost isn't some six-year-old, is it? It's Adder?"

Abby's head bobbed in agreement.

Tink gazed at me in misery. "This is my fault." The water works started again. "I just wanted them to leave me alone. I'm so sorry—"

"Tink . . ." I leaned forward to comfort her, but Abby put out a hand, stopping me.

"Tink needs to learn that her talents aren't a toy to be played with. Her actions have repercussions."

Jeez, Abby wasn't cutting the kid any slack at all, and it surprised me. Tink was hardly more than a child, and children—heck adults, too—make mistakes. I studied Tink. On the other hand, when working with talents like ours, mistakes could be costly in insidious ways. Maybe it was good that she felt some pain over her carelessness.

"What do we do now?" I asked, glancing from Tink's unhappy face to Abby's unsmiling one.

"Unless you want the ghost of a dead biker as a permanent houseguest, I suggest we figure out a way to banish him."

"And how do we do that?" I asked, dreading her answer.

"We have a séance."

A séance made perfect sense, but was Tink ready to undertake one? Or would her lack of experience only make things worse?

"Do you think a séance is wise?" I asked.

"I see no other options. From what I learned as a child watching Aunt Mary, spirits either need help crossing over, or they have unfinished business to attend to, or they want something."

Duh! Adder probably expected us to bring his killer to justice.

A sudden idea made Abby's suggestion more appealing. "Do you think Adder might tell Tink who killed him?"

"I wouldn't count on it," she replied, bursting my bubble.

"If he did, then my only problem would be finding a way to point Bill and the other investigators in the right direction."

"I sense there might be other issues in relation to the killing that must be resolved," Abby said. "And the only way it will happen is for you to continue on the path you're taking now."

My eyes traveled to Tink. "Are you okay with this?"

"Yes," she answered in a soft voice and sniffed. "It's my fault Adder's here. I won't be so scared this time if you and Abby are with me."

"Do you think she's ready?" I asked, my attention sliding back to Abby. "Can she get rid of him?"

"I believe so. We'll add our energy to hers." She slapped her legs and stood. "I think your office would be the best place to hold the séance. I have a few things with me, so I'll go prepare the room."

Abby picked up a paper sack lying on the floor next to the couch and left the room.

After she did, Tink and I sat in silence for long moments, each of us lost in thoughts of what was about to happen.

Tink broke the silence first. "Ophelia, I am so sorry—"

I leaned forward and took her hand in mine. "I know you are, sweetie, but you're going to have to set aside your guilt for the time being. I don't know what it's like to be a medium, but I do know magick works better with positive energy rather than negative." Lifting her chin, I made her look at me. "Have you learned anything from this?"

"Yes," she said, her eyes darting away.

"Tink, I've made several mistakes myself over the years, and our talents aren't always easy to live with—"

"I know," she said before I could finish, "but what if the spirit would've harmed you?"

"He didn't."

"I think he pushed you on the stairs."

"All righty, then." I tried to keep my voice light, but Tink's suspicion hadn't occurred to me. "One more reason to get rid of him, isn't it?"

"Yes," she said, still not looking at me. "Are you going to ground me?"

Ah-ha, she was worried about the dance. She was such a kid. I didn't doubt she truly regretted the role she'd played in all of this, but in the end her own self-interests came to the forefront.

"Not this time," I shook my finger under her nose, "but don't be bringing any more ghosts home, okay?"

Her eyes met mine and she smiled weakly. "Okay."

Looking over her shoulder, I saw Abby in the hallway, motioning us to come ahead.

I paused at the doorway. Abby had lit every candle, and with the rain now beating a gentle patter on the roof, the muted candlelight created a warm and welcoming atmosphere. It seemed in contrast to what we intended to do, but maybe that was Abby's purpose—using the tranquility to coax an angry ghost into crossing over to the other side.

In the center of the room, she'd made a circle of salt and herbs. The middle of the circle held incense, a bowl of water, several of my crystals, and a black candle. The crystals were placed to the north and represented the element Earth. To the east, tiny threads of scented smoke wafted up from the burning incense. The element of Air. Straight to the south, the black candle's flame danced. It symbolized the element of Fire, and black was the color for banishing. And finally, to the west, a clear bowl of water sparkled in dim light. The element of Water. By honoring the four elements, Abby wasn't taking any chances.

With a kind smile on her face, she stroked Tink's hair. "Are you ready, dear?" she asked gently.

Tink's head bobbed once, and holding hands, our incongruous trio stepped into the circle. With much difficulty, I made it to a seated position. Hands tightly clasped around the candle, bowl, incense, and crystals, we were ready to begin.

Suddenly the dream of Tink and the circle of stones flitted through my brain. "Wait," I said, releasing Abby's hand and pointing toward my desk. "Would you bring my runes into the circle?"

Abby rose and picked up the pouch from the corner of my desk. Stepping over the circle, she again sat down next to me.

I opened the bag and fished around until I found the stone I sought. Algiz—the rune of sanctuary. I held my left hand out with the rune nestled in my open palm. "This is the sign of protection. It will help defend you from attack, Tink."

She closed her hand over mine, and I felt the stone grow warm while its energy tickled my palm.

Violet eyes tinged with fear turned to Abby. "What do I do?"

"Take a cleansing breath and let your mind float free. You're protected within the circle, and no matter what happens around us, it can't cross the boundary I've made."

"You're sure?" Skepticism echoed in her voice. "He tried to choke Melinda."

"I'm sure. He can't touch you."

After a worried look at Tink, I closed my eyes and concentrated on what I needed to do. I emptied myself of all thoughts save the force I felt throbbing in the air around me. In my mind, I gathered that power to me and let it flow through my hand into Tink. Opening my eyes, I saw a pale lavender light spread around her as she sat there focusing her intent. Her aura. A quick look at Abby told me she saw it, too. The aura grew and changed to a darker purple, while gold flecks seemed to twinkle in its depths. Tink's concentration increased.

A hollow rapping, almost as if it came from inside the wall, suddenly reverberated in the room. The temperature dropped. Tink opened her eyes and became fixed on a spot just over my left shoulder.

The hair on the back of my neck stood straight up, but I resisted the need to look around. I glanced at Abby.

Her eyes shone with intensity as she focused on Tink, lending all her strength and talent to Tink's. Her hand lightly squeezed mine to let me know so far all was well.

My eyes slid back to Tink and I watched as she cocked her head as if listening to voices only she could hear. A frown marred her face and she shook her head no.

A book flew from the shelf and landed just next to the circle.

Tink's face tightened with determination and her mouth settled into a firm line. As she did, the purple light around her swirled and tiny beads of sweat broke out on her forehead.

Behind me, I heard something rattle, shaken by the force of invisible hands. Peripherally, I noticed the candles outside the circle go out one by one, darkening the room.

Tink's attention never wavered, and in a voice filled with assertiveness, she said one word: "Yes."

Quick, cold winds blew through the room, making the flame of the black candle sputter and almost die. Papers on my desk scattered into the air, as if caught by a whirlwind.

Tink's eyes narrowed to violet slits and her body trembled. The aura surrounding her reached out and encompassed both Abby and me. My ears popped.

And with that pop, the séance was over. Tink's shoulders slumped forward and the purple light died. Silent moment after silent moment ticked by until finally I spoke in a shaky voice.

"Well?"

Eyes drained of their spark gazed at me. "He's not leaving."

Thirty-Five

"What do you mean he's not leaving?" I exclaimed.

Tink sighed deeply. "He's not leaving until his killer is found."

"Great," I said in an acerbic voice. "I don't suppose he told you who that might be?"

"No. I—" She broke off and rubbed her forehead.

Abby squeezed my hand in warning. "Go back to the living room while I clean up," she said, rising along with Tink. "I think it would be a good idea for you both to stay at my house tonight." She placed both hands on Tink's shoulders. "If all else fails, I'll call Aunt Mary. She's been working with spirits longer than both you and I have been alive. She'll have a solution."

A couple of hours later, after packing a couple of bags for Tink and me and loading up all the animals, Abby and I were sitting in her parlor, drinking tea, her all around remedy for any crisis.

Tink had gone upstairs to bed as soon as we'd reached Abby's.

"Is she going to be okay? She's not going to fall into a stupor like I did, is she?"

"No, but she might if she stayed in your house—"

I cut her off. "We've got to end this, Abby."

"Find the killer," she said succinctly.

"I'm trying," I said, and ran my favorite ideas by her.

Abby stretched, holding both arms wide. "I think for now the best thing is to let it lay. Tink's graduation is tomorrow, followed by the dance. Waiting another twenty-four hours won't change anything."

She stood and headed to the doorway. "Stay with me," she said over her shoulder, "until we decide what to do."

She didn't have to tell me twice.

Silver and blue helium balloons tied to weighted bags with shiny ribbon floated above a refreshment table loaded with sandwiches, brownies, cookies, and punch. On the far wall, more balloons and bags had been arranged at both ends of a banner announcing CONGRATULATIONS. Several of Tink's classmates posed in front of the sign as their proud parents snapped their picture.

I'd already embarrassed her by taking numerous pictures of her standing by the banner. Some with just her, some with her and Nell, and some with her and a group of her other friends. They'd laughed and made silly faces as they reveled in the school year concluding and summer vacation starting.

Eighth grade graduation—a tradition dying out in many schools—but dating back to a time where many children, especially those living in rural areas, would go no further with their education. Back then the ceremony marked their passage into the adult world and meant they would begin working full-time on the family farms.

Now it seemed to symbolize that these young adults were no longer children. They'd made it through middle school and were headed to high school and their teenage years. Dating, driving a car, working at their first part-time job, were just around the corner for them, and they all seemed excited at the prospect.

The ceremony this afternoon had been a long one, as each kid was recognized for his or her activities during the school year. I couldn't help notice that Melinda Polaski crossed the stage numerous times to receive certificates for sports, choir, and cheerleading. Pete and his wife were there clicking away with their camera each time she took the stage. He would have lots of pictures to add to his wall.

I crossed the floor with my unbalanced walk and took one of the chairs lined up against the wall. Spying Tink standing with Nell, I beamed with pride. She might not have walked across the stage as many times as Melinda, but on the inside, where it counted, she was developing qualities that would take her far in life. Thinking back on yesterday, my smile widened. Her talent had amazed me, and she had handled herself far better than I would have at the same age.

The hours she and Nell spent primping and preening at Abby's had paid off. Tink looked lovely in the dress Darci had helped her pick out. Sleeveless and just skimming her knees, it was red with a bold pattern and fitted her slim frame perfectly. The "just right" shoes she'd spent hours discussing on the phone with Nell were gold sandals with thin straps and a slight heel. She'd arranged her long blond hair up in a loose twist on top of her head. Stiff little strands of hair stuck out from it, giving her a funky look.

As my eyes drifted away from Tink, I noticed the three M's across the room from Nell and Tink. They were gathered into a little circle around Melinda. Only fourteen, and already she had her own entourage.

Whispering to each other and looking pointedly across

the room, I could tell they were talking about Tink and Nell. Dressed almost identically in white dresses, they'd applied their makeup with a heavy hand, in what I'm sure was an attempt to look grown-up. Instead, they just looked cheap, I thought uncharitably.

I was still watching the three M's and wondering what they were up to when Darci slipped in next to me.

"Hey," she said, giving me the once-over. "You look nice."

Glancing down at my flowing skirt and light shell, I grinned. "Yeah? Well, I didn't think sweatpants would be appropriate." I stuck my cast out in front of my chair. "This thing kind of ruins the effect I was going for, but . . ." I gave a shrug.

Darci nudged me playfully. "You still look nice."

"Thank you. What are you doing here, by the way? I thought you were going home after the graduation."

"I did, but Danny's on duty again tonight, so I thought I'd hang out with you and help chaperone." Darci stopped for a moment. "I asked Danny about The Rogues, and he said—"

"Not now, Darci," I said. "This is Tink's night, and I don't want to talk about murder. We'll go over everything tomorrow."

I chose not to tell her about my new houseguest.

"I see the Polaskis are here," she said with a jerk of her head. "Why does he always wear those long-sleeve shirts?"

"Haven't you seen the scars on his forearms?" I glanced over at her. "According to Danny, Pete had an accident while welding. Sparks from a welder caught his shirt on fire."

"Really?" She whipped her head toward me in surprise. "My brothers always wore leather gloves with gauntlets whenever they used a welder. You'd think a mechanic would, too."

Any response from me was drowned out by the sound of music coming from the speakers. Lights dimmed, the mirrored ball in the center of the ceiling spun, and the dance began.

Immediately, a group of girls took to the middle of the floor, forming in a tight little knot similar to cattle bunching together before a thunderstorm. They bopped and gyrated while the music blared. Some had rhythm, some didn't, but it looked like they were having fun. The boys sat in the chairs lined up along the wall. A couple of them had cabbaged on to the helium balloons and were batting them playfully back and forth.

I narrowed my eyes and watched them thoughtfully. I hoped nobody got the bright idea to suck the helium out of the balloons. It might be hilarious to sound like Mickey Mouse, but inhaling helium could damage their vocal cords.

For now, the boys appeared to be satisfied just to knock each other in the head with the balloons, so I turned my attention to the other side of the room.

I spied Mickey Dahl sitting with a group of friends. It was easy to spot him with all that red hair. He sat forward, his bony wrists resting on his knees. His pants were too short, and I saw white socks peeking out from beneath the cuffs. Smart, with a bright future, he had a tough road ahead of him. His parents were a couple of the biggest drunks in town, and Mickey usually wound up taking care of them instead of the other way around. Poor kid, I hoped his high school years were better than his grade school years had been.

While Mickey sat watching the girls, his friends were doing the same. Clip-on ties lay discarded at their feet, and they were elbowing each other and pointing at the girls. Of course, if one of those objects of affection actually ap-

proached them to dance, it would be a different story. I knew
they'd all fall silent and suddenly find something fascinating
about the tiled ceiling above them.

A slow song began to play, and the group of girls left the
dance floor. A few of the braver kids came out in couples.
The girls had their arms draped over the boys' shoulders as
they shuffled back and forth, doing more swaying than danc-
ing. The boys had their hands on the girls' waists.

I took a closer look. Didn't want any of those hands drifting lower. While I watched, one couple did become a little
too friendly. I jabbed Darci in the side to ask her opinion
about whether I should march out on dance floor and separate them.

She didn't respond, so I nudged her again. Not taking my
eyes off the couple, I leaned sideways. "Darci, do you see the
couple off to the right?"

She grabbed my arm and tugged. "Forget the couple.
Look over by the punch bowl."

Turning my head, I saw Tink and Nell squaring off with
the three M's. I couldn't hear them, but I could see they were
arguing. Or at least Melinda was. Tink just stood there with
a superior look on her face. Melinda took a step toward her,
but Tink held her ground.

I scrambled to my feet, my eyes darting around the room,
looking for the Polaskis. Spotting Mrs. Polaski on the far
side, I hurried as fast as my uneven steps would allow. Placing a hand on Mrs. Polaski's arm, I waved in the direction
of the punch bowl and tried to make myself heard over the
loud music.

She didn't hear me, but her eyes followed my gesture. We
turned in unison, in time to see Melinda splash red punch all
over Tink's new dress.

It wasn't an accident.

Mindy and Mandy slunk back, leaving Tink and Melinda alone by the table.

My head whipped around and I glared at Mrs. Polaski. Uncomfortable, she nervously tucked her mousy brown hair behind her large ears.

Outraged, I hobbled away from her and headed toward Tink. As I crossed the room, a hundred threats, a hundred hexes, to rain down on Melinda sprang to mind. But no matter how angry or upset I was, I knew I couldn't do it. Melinda was a kid; I was an adult. Or supposed to be, even though I didn't feel very adultlike at the moment.

I reached the girls first and placed a hand on Tink's shoulder as the punch dripped off her dress. Melinda had a nasty, satisfied look, until her eyes met mine. Then the sneer disappeared and she whirled around, looking for her two friends, but they'd faded into the crowd of kids gathering a few feet away.

Tink lifted her chin and looked at Melinda with cool, violet eyes while a derisive smile played around her lips. "Polaski, you are such a *bitch*," she said in a voice dripping ice.

My eyes flew wide at Tink's language, but how could I scold her when I agreed with her assessment? "Tink," I said, making a halfhearted attempt. "You shouldn't—"

"I know," she said, giving me a nod and turning on her heel. Head held high, she walked toward the bathroom. A gaggle of girls followed close behind.

I gave Melinda one last glare and eased into the group myself.

Melinda was left standing alone, an empty cup in her hand, while her classmates stared at her like she'd crawled out from underneath a rock. She made a move to step away from the table, but before she could, her mother came up beside her, grabbed her arm and spun her around. Dragging her over to me, she shook her arm.

"You apologize to Ms. Jensen right now for what you did to her daughter."

From behind me, I felt the kids melt away, tired of watching the drama, while Melinda looked at me with rebellion in her eyes.

Her mother gave her arm another shake.

Melinda's eyes dropped. "Sorry," she muttered.

"Say it like you mean it," her mother hissed in her ear.

With a sigh, Melinda squared her shoulders and raised her head. "I'm sorry for spilling punch on Tink. Someone hit my arm. I hope her dress isn't ruined." She tossed her mother a defiant look before returning her eyes to mine.

Crossing my arms, I looked at her with an icy stare of my own, letting her know I thought her excuse was a load of bull.

Mrs. Polaski brushed her hair forward over her ears and opened her mouth to speak, but before she could, Pete appeared at his wife's side.

"What's going on?" he asked, removing his glasses and wiping them on his shirt.

"Your daughter dumped punch on Tink Harrison—"

"Melinda!" Pete said in a shocked voice.

Melinda's eyes filled with tears. "It was an accident, Daddy," she pleaded. "I didn't mean to, but Mom doesn't believe me."

Pete turned to his wife. "Well?"

Mrs. Polaski pushed strands of hair behind her ears, and again I noticed how large they were. And they curled forward like Dumbo's.

Dumbo!

I ignored the argument between Melinda's parents and studied Mrs. Polaski intently, searching for a resemblance to the picture of Gregory Roberts's girlfriend. Since I'd slept the last couple of days away, my mind seemed cloudy as I tried to recall the picture. The only thing I remembered about the girlfriend was her ears, and a lot of people had big ears. I needed to take another look at the photo.

Mrs. Polaski grabbed Melinda's arm and with a yank pulled the girl away. "You're going home," she said to her. "We'll be waiting in the car, Pete."

My eyes darted to Pete, and I shifted to take a better look at his face. What about him? Were his eyes gray? Nope, hazel.

Suddenly, one of the balloons came out of nowhere, hitting Pete on the side of his head. He clamped a hand over his eye and peered down at the floor.

"What's wrong?"

"I lost a contact," he said, crouching down and patting the floor.

"You wear contacts, too?" I asked in surprise while I watched him feel around for them.

"Yeah," he said, not looking up. "Terrible vision."

I spotted something glinting on the floor and bent to pick it up. "Here it is." I dropped the lens into his outstretched hand, and as I did, Pete looked up at me.

One brown eye and one gray eye stared into mine.

Thirty-Six

After pulling Darci to her feet, I gave her a slight shove toward the door. "Come on, we've got to get out of here *now.*"

"What on earth's gotten into you?" she asked over her shoulder.

"Not now. I'll explain on the way to my house."

I wanted to hurry, but I tried to keep my pace normal. I made my apologies to the parent watching the door, muttering something about a family emergency, and on the way out stopped in the restroom to find Tink.

She stood with a cluster of girls gathered around her. Nell dabbed at the stain with a wet paper towel.

"Melinda's so mean," one of the girls said.

Tink laughed. "At least my dress is the same color as the punch."

The girls giggled.

Pushing past them, I drew Tink out into the hallway.

"Are you okay?" I asked.

"Sure, Melinda's the one who looked like an idiot. Ahh, sorry I swore." Noticing my expression, she frowned. "Something's wrong."

"Yeah, and I've got to go. We'll talk about your language

later. I'm calling Abby to take my place. You stay with Nell until she gets here. Do not, I repeat *do not*, leave this building for any reason."

Her eyes widened. "Ophelia, you're scaring me."

I patted her face. "It'll be okay. I'll explain later. Just do what I'm telling you, okay?"

"Okay."

After quickly kissing her cheek, I turned and rushed out of the building and into Darci's waiting car. Pulling out my cell, I called Abby and, without launching into a big explanation, asked her and Arthur to take my place with Tink.

"Oh, and Abby," I said before snapping the phone shut. "Have Arthur bring his bat."

Darci's eyes slid toward me. "What is going on?"

"I don't know for sure," I answered, drumming my fingers on the door. "And I know this is going to sound crazy, but I think Pete Polaski might really be Gregory Roberts."

"What?" The car swerved toward the curb.

"Watch it. We don't need a wreck right now." My fingers drummed faster as the pieces jelled in my mind. "Adder recognized Pete as Gregory either the day they stopped at the garage or the night of your party. I don't know which."

"Are you sure?" Darci sounded skeptical.

"Pretty sure, but I need to look at those pictures we printed out. The ones of Gregory and his girlfriend."

"The girlfriend is Mrs. Polaski, I suppose."

"Yeah."

The car swerved again. "Really?"

"Yes, did you see her ears? They're just like the girl's in the picture."

"Wow . . ." Darci paused. "What do we do now?"

"Get those pictures to Bill and turn the whole mess over to him." I glanced out the window. "Right now, I don't care if he does throw me in the cell next to Becca's. At least the jail's not haunted."

"What?"

I fanned my hand at her. "Never mind. I'll explain that later, too, after we look at the pictures."

"But who's the second man?" Darci asked as she pulled into my driveway.

"I don't know," I said rushing out of the car. "Let Bill figure it out."

Darci clutched her purse and hurried to catch up with me. Once inside, we ran back to my office and each grabbed a handful of pages.

"Dang," I said aloud as I went through them, "they got all out of order when the ghost threw them on the floor."

Darci's pages slid from her fingers. "G-Ghost?"

"I told you, I'll explain later."

"No," she said, cocking her hip, "you'll explain now."

I sighed. "Long story—short version—Adder's spirit has taken up residence here thanks to Tink, and he's not leaving until his killer's caught."

Her head whipped around as her eyes darted from corner to corner. "You mean he's here now?"

"I don't know—I don't know where ghosts hang out when they're not haunting someone." I gave her an exasperated look. "If you want to know so bad, go ask Abby. I'm sure—"

A crash from the back porch interrupted me.

Darci's face lost all color. "The ghost?" she whispered.

Without warning, the mirror near Darci shattered into a hundred pieces, sending glass flying. The sound of the mirror breaking was followed immediately by another noise coming from the porch.

I pointed to Darci's upper arm. "You're bleeding."

Picking a piece of glass from her arm, she stared in disbelief as blood trickled down her arm.

Another sound from the porch had me scurrying around the corner of my desk. "I don't think the ghost's on the porch. Someone's breaking in." Grabbing my bat from the desk, I took Darci's arm and hustled her out of the room.

We'd made it to the bottom of the stairs when we heard the sound of the kitchen window breaking. Frozen, we searched for a way out.

"Come on." Darci grasped my waist with her good arm and half dragged me up the stairs and into the closest room.

The bathroom.

I turned the flimsy lock on the bathroom door and then hobbled over to the chair sitting in the corner, next to the tub. Dragging it to the door, I shoved it beneath the doorknob. One good kick from the other side would no doubt bust the door open and send the chair airborne, but at least it might slow the intruders down long enough for us to escape out the bathroom window.

I looked down at the cast on my leg. Who was I kidding? I wasn't going anywhere. Noticing Darci's purse still hooked over her shoulder, I pointed at the bag.

"Your cell phone," I said in a hushed voice.

With an excited look, she tore it open and pulled out the phone. Her face fell. "The battery's dead."

"Can you climb out the window?"

She looked at the gash on her arm caused by a flying shard of glass hitting her arm when the mirror shattered. "Yeah, I think so. The bleeding's stopped," she whispered while dabbing the cut with a washcloth. "But you can't get out the window with your broken foot." Her voice rose in desperation. "I can't leave you here."

Limping over, I gripped her other arm. "You have to," I said in a hushed tone. "Climb out the window, onto the porch roof. From there it's an easy drop to the ground."

In the faint light, I saw Darci's eyes narrow with stubbornness.

"I'm not going without you. We don't even know how many are in the house."

"I think two. We heard one come through the back porch, and one came in the kitchen window."

A loud crash from the living room below made us both jump.

I gave her a small shove toward the window. "We don't have time to argue. Get out that window and go for help."

With a sigh of resignation, she hurried to the window and slowly slid it open. She flipped the strap of her purse over her head and across her chest, then threw a leg over the sill. With one last look, she disappeared into the night.

I searched the bathroom, looking for a place to hide. The shower? No, it would be the first place they looked. Maybe the bathroom had been a bad choice. Better to hide in my bedroom.

And duh, Jensen, the bedroom has a phone in it. You could've called for help.

I heard another sound from downstairs. It sounded like they were opening doors and slamming them shut. Holding the bat tightly to my chest, I thought about how this was too much like my experience with Adder's ghost for comfort. Only now it wasn't a ghost, but real men who would not only scare me, but kill me. I preferred the ghost.

One of the men had to be Pete. Had he noticed my surprise when I saw that his eyes were actually gray? Who was the second man? Cobra? I hadn't seen him around town after our run-in at Stumpy's. He knew I'd been snooping around.

But how could he be connected to Pete? Pete had been a Rogue, and Cobra belonged to El Serpiente. I huddled in the corner of the bathroom, clutching the bat. The Louisville Slugger wouldn't make a difference. If Darci didn't hurry back, I'd be dead by the time she got here.

The house was quiet now, and the silence was more nerve-wracking than the noise. At any minute the bathroom door could fly open and I'd be found.

Did I have anything in my little bag of magick tricks? Nope. The threat of a hex wouldn't stop two killers. I didn't even have a crystal to toss at them if they crashed through the door. All I had was the bat.

I scooted across the floor on my bottom. When I reached the wall behind the door, I stood slowly. Cocking the bat on my shoulder, I was ready to bash the first one through the door. Wait a second—I could nail the first one, but what about the second one? My Louisville Slugger wouldn't be much of a match against two men. I needed to get to the bedroom.

I moved the chair away from the door as quietly as possible. Carefully, I turned the lock. The click seemed to echo in the tiny room. My breath caught. Could they have heard me? I pressed an ear to the door. Nothing. Opening the door a crack, I peered out with one eye. The hall was empty.

I eased open the door and slid into the hall. With my back pressed to the wall, I crept, as best I could with a cast on my leg, inch by inch toward the top of the stairs. Somehow I'd have to cross the open space at the top without being seen.

As I carefully made my way down the hall, I felt cold air gather around my feet and drift up my legs. I knew I wasn't alone—Adder's ghost lurked in the hall with me. I dismissed the knowledge from my mind. I didn't have time to fear a spirit.

Almost at the top of the stairs, the air around me fizzed with energy. But I didn't know if it came from me or from Adder's restless ghost.

Taking a deep breath, I prepared to make a mad dash across the open space. One, two, three—I pushed away from the wall and limped as fast as I could toward the bedroom.

"Ophelia," a voice called, stopping me cold.

Spinning around, I saw Danny on the stairs below me.

"Thank goodness," I said, my voice weak with relief. "Where's Darci?"

Danny didn't answer, but cast an anxious glance over his shoulder at a figure who stepped out from the doorway to the kitchen.

The cold gray eyes of a predator on a hunt stared at me across the distance. "Isn't she with you?" Pete asked.

I turned to run.

"Stop or I'll shoot you right now," Pete called out.

I froze and turned back toward them.

Edging past Danny on the stairs, it seemed that Pete sloughed off his mild-mannered demeanor like a snake shedding skin.

"Hold it," I said, threatening him with my bat.

He paused on the step. "So where is Darci? Her car's in the driveway."

"Hiding," I blustered.

Where was Darci? If her car was still in the driveway, did it mean she'd fallen off the porch? Was that the crash I'd heard? Was she lying in the bushes unconscious?

Pete took another step, wiping thoughts of where Darci might be from my head.

"Put down the bat."

"No. And if you shoot me, the neighbors will hear the shot and call the police."

Pete chuckled. "Maybe, but you'll be dead, won't you?"

Good point.

"Adder's here," I said, grasping at straws.

Another chuckle drifted up the stairwell as Pete took another step. "Adder's dead. He recognized me from California. I should have killed him that night years ago instead of just beating him up."

"That was grease on Darci's carpet. You tracked it in when you killed Adder," I said, another piece falling into place.

"How did you know?" Pete asked in surprise. "Danny did a good job cleaning it up." He took another step.

Maybe I could reason with him? "What about Melinda, Pete? Bill will figure out you killed me, you know. What will it do to her to learn her father's a murderer?"

Pete stopped. "She'll never know. And it won't be Bill investigating your murder. It will be Danny here," he said with a jerk of his head.

"And I bet he'll find a way to pin it on El Serpiente."

Pete's eyes leered at me. "Yeah, I'm thinking Cobra would make a good patsy. Everyone in town knows you've had trouble with him." His eyes dropped to the gun he held in his hand. "Danny's going to find this at The Viper's Nest." He looked quickly up at me. "Aren't you, Danny?"

"Ah, yeah, Pete," Danny stammered from below.

"Is that your job, Danny, cleaning up after Pete, hiding evidence for him?" I shifted so I could see Danny standing behind Pete. "Is it also your job to kill your girlfriend for him?"

"Danny doesn't like to kill, do you, Danny?" Pete said over his shoulder. "But he likes the money, don't you, Danny?

All the money we've been making running drugs to Canada in those cars."

I remembered the out-of-state plates. "You're hiding drugs in the cars in your shop," I said, more to myself than to Pete.

"Clever woman. I've still got my connections. My old 'friends' bring the cars to me, I fix them up," he said with a wink. "And they're off to Canada."

"And Danny's been covering up for you with the police."

"Yup, a sweet deal until El Serpiente decided to come to town and spoil it for me."

Pete took another step; four more and I wouldn't have a chance. If he weren't afraid of alerting the neighbors, he would've shot me by now. Even if I managed to knock the gun out of his hand with the bat, I'd still have to deal with Danny. Resignation settled over me. I'd run out of time.

The cold I'd felt before glided around me, stronger now, and my teeth chattered. I didn't know if it was from fear or the icy fingers that seemed to push me out of the way. Frigid air sucked the strength from me, weakening my limbs until I could hardly move. I slumped against the wall and my fingers loosened on the bat.

The atmosphere around me crackled, lifting my hair straight out from my shoulders, and I felt something brush past me.

"Hey!" Pete yelled.

Raising my head, I saw him stumble backward, as if pushed by an invisible force. His arms flayed as he tried to regain his balance. The gun went off, and the air whooshed as the bullet flew by my ear, the air redolent with the acrid smell of gunpowder.

Pete tumbled and began to roll down the stairs.

As he fell, Danny plastered his body against the wall. He

watched in horror as his buddy tumbled past him and landed in a heap at the foot of the stairs.

With a terrified look at me, Danny turned and fled. He'd made it to the door and was reaching for the knob when it flew open.

Darci.

Danny skidded to a stop in front of her. Her eyes narrowed as she took in the scene in an instant. Before Danny could push her out of his way, she clutched the strap of her purse and, with a mighty swing, cold-cocked Danny right on his handsome chin. His head snapped to the side from the impact, and his knees crumpled. With a satisfying thud, he pitched face forward onto the floor.

Stepping over him and Pete, Darci ran up the stairs to where I sat on the top step.

Throwing herself down next to me, she leaned close and scanned my face. "Are you okay?"

"Yeah," I said with a sigh. "Sorry about Danny."

Her face clouded. "I was beginning to suspect he was a jerk, but I didn't know he was a crook . . ." She paused. " . . . and an accomplice to murder." Her eyes traveled to first one, then the other of the two men lying in a heap. "I'm more disappointed in myself than anything else. The warning signs were there, and I ignored them."

"Danny was a pretty smooth operator. You weren't the only one he fooled, so give yourself a break."

"I suppose," she said with a sigh. "I guess as long as I learn from this, right?"

"That's what Abby always says," I agreed.

Her face cleared and she pointed to the two men. "Suppose we should tie them up until Bill gets here?"

I heard the sirens in the distance. Bill. She had to call Bill. Boy, was I going to have some explaining to do.

"Nah, sounds like they're almost here." I eyed Darci's purse, lifting it. "What's in there?"

A smile spread across her face as she reached into the bag. "This," she said, holding the object up proudly.

It was the adventurine crystal I'd given her for her birthday.

Thirty-Seven

A hand shaking my shoulder rousted me from a sound sleep.

"Go away," I said, batting at it. "I'm tired."

Bill had kept me up until all hours, grilling me about my involvement with Adder's murder investigation. Personally, I thought he should be paying more attention to Danny and Pete, but I wisely didn't share my opinion with him. I had agreed with everything he'd said while he paced back and forth in the tiny room, pausing only long enough to mop his bald head with a handkerchief. Finally, he ran out of steam and let me go.

Now, I opened one eye to see Darci's animated face level with mine as she crouched by my bed at Abby's.

"Come on, wake up, you're going to miss all the excitement." She shook my shoulder again.

I rolled over on my back and threw an arm over my face. "Like I need any more excitement. I've still got a ghost in my house that needs to be dealt with, remember?" I moved my arm and gave her a withering stare.

"Poohey," she said, waving a hand at me and standing. She crossed the room, picked up my sweatpants and tossed them at me. "Between you, Tink, and Abby, you'll figure out a way to get rid of him. Get dressed."

A sweatshirt landed on top of the pants.

"Don't you have to pick up Becca? They're releasing her, aren't they?"

"Already did. She's at Georgia's. She went before the magistrate this morning, and he released her on her own recognizance. She has to appear before a judge in order for the charges to be dropped," she said, bending over and grabbing my shoe.

"How's she doing?"

Darci picked at the laces of the shoe. "Okay. Better. After what happened, I think Becca's going to take a long hard look at her life." She shrugged. "She even mentioned moving back to Iowa." Darci looked over at me and smiled. "She wants to thank you in person."

"I know you're excited about Becca's release, but do we have to celebrate it right now?" I whined.

"We're not going to Georgia's to celebrate, silly."

I groaned as I sat up in bed. "If you're not trying to haul me over there, then what's going on?"

Darci's eyes widened. "I heard it over the police scanner. They're busting The Viper's Nest," she said, the words rushing out.

"So?" I plopped back down in bed.

She waltzed over to me, though how she managed to move so easily in those tight jeans, I didn't know.

Hey, tight jeans, tank top, sandals with two-inch heels. Looks like the old Darci is back.

She caught my expression and gave her clothes a quick look. "I just threw these on," she replied with a grin.

Right.

Crossing her arms over her chest, she pouted. "Come on,

even though Cobra wasn't our killer, wouldn't you like to see him led out in handcuffs?"

Hmm, after the way he tried to intimidate me, the image had a certain appeal.

"Okay," I said, throwing back the covers. "Let's go."

Darci and I stood at the fringe of the crowd, watching as one by one the members of El Serpiente were led from The Viper's Nest by officers in SWAT gear. They wore bulletproof vests over jackets that showed the emblem of whatever department they belonged to. So far Darci and I had picked out men from sheriff's departments in two counties and the U.S. Marshals. From around their waist hung, I think, every weapon known to man. On their heads, they wore helmets with visors down. Next to them, the big, bad bikers didn't look so big and bad.

I craned my neck as I watched the bikers being loaded into the waiting vans. "I haven't seen them bring Cobra out yet, have you?" I asked Darci.

"No, and from the looks of it, they're almost done," she replied, her eyes never leaving The Viper's entrance.

I watched in disappointment as the last biker was led out of the building.

Dang, Cobra had given them the slip.

I turned to leave when a deputy I recognized handed me a note.

"What's this?" I asked, confused.

"It's a note from that officer over there," he answered, and pointed to the man who'd hauled the last biker out.

I looked at the note in my hand, and then at the officer standing by the white van. His visor was down, but I had the feeling he was watching me. He was dressed in the same gear as everyone else and his jacket carried the insignia of the DEA. An eagle over a star.

An eagle? A star? I thought, finally getting it. False—not real? My hand had been on top of the snake tattoo that no doubt was fake. Many lives? In his line of work, he'd have a lot of different personas. What did Darci always say? Oh, yeah, for a psychic I could be really dense.

My groan had her turning around to stare at me.

Feeling like an absolute fool, I watched as the officer slowly lifted his visor. His gray eyes—eyes that I knew so well—danced with laughter. With a grin, the DEA agent saluted me, turned, and climbed into the van. As he did, I saw a ponytail peeking out from beneath his helmet.

A second later the white van pulled out of the parking lot and drove down the road in a cloud of dust.

"What? What is it?" Darci's voice sounded in my ear.

Holding the unread note tightly in my hand, I stared after the van.

Cobra—I'd threatened a federal agent with boils!